PLAYTHINGS OF THE PRIVATE HOUSE

'Breathtaking,' Madame whispered. 'Olena, you are even more desirable than I had been told. Do you enjoy showing your body like this?'

There was no point in denying it. Madame la Patronne clearly knew the methods of the Private House, and she would find out for herself that Olena was aroused. 'Yes, Madame,' Olena breathed. She had never found it easy to confess her sins. 'I know it's wrong. I just can't help it. I deserve to be punished.'

'You're very popular at the House,' Madame commented. 'I'd better have a closer look at you. Kneel on the seat of the sofa, my dear, and present your bottom.'

By the same author:

ONE WEEK IN THE PRIVATE HOUSE
AMANDA IN THE PRIVATE HOUSE
DISCIPLINE OF THE PRIVATE HOUSE
AN EDUCATION IN THE PRIVATE HOUSE
CAPTIVES OF THE PRIVATE HOUSE
PET TRAINING IN THE PRIVATE HOUSE

You can write to Esme Ombreux at:
esmeo@postmaster.co.uk

PLAYTHINGS OF THE PRIVATE HOUSE

Esme Ombreux

This book is a work of fiction.
In real life, make sure you practise safe sex.

First published in 2002 by
Nexus
Thames Wharf Studios
Rainville Road
London W6 9HA

www.nexus-books.co.uk

Typeset by TW Typesetting, Plymouth, Devon

Printed and bound by
Clays Ltd, St Ives PLC

ISBN 0 352 33761 3

Author's Note

As usual, in this new story you'll find characters who have appeared in previous Private House books. For the completists among you, here they are, together with the books in which they've appeared.

Jem Darke, the Supreme Mistress of the Private House, was introduced in the first story in the series, *One Week in the Private House*, and she has had at least a mention in every succeeding book. Julia, now chief of the guards, was also in *One Week in the Private House*, and, like her mistress, has had at least a bit part in most of the other books.

Madame la Patronne was the wicked dominatrix in *Amanda in the Private House*.

Olena and Barat, the former hardly less innocent than the latter, were taught how to be good in *Discipline of the Private House*.

Talia is the resourceful leader – with submissive tendencies – of the forest people who caused Jem and Julia so much bother in *Captives of the Private House*.

Anne, Talia's young lover, who appears briefly in this story, was introduced in *An Education in the Private House* and was also in *Captives of the Private House*. And, for no reason other than that I didn't need more characters, you'll find none from *Pet Training in the Private House*.

Esme Ombreux
May 2002

One

The robe was heavy, hot, and rough against Kym's skin as she waited under the portico before the tall, ancient doors. The rose that rambled up the limestone pillars was sprouting new blooms in celebration of the late-summer sunshine, but Kym wasn't enjoying the unseasonal weather: she merely wished that she could throw back the woollen hood that was almost smothering her. She felt a drop of sweat slide stickily down her spine.

Suddenly Kym felt alone and nervous. She looked over her shoulder. The limousine was still parked on the gravel drive, in the shade cast by the surrounding trees. The black coachwork shimmered in the heat. The driver, in a robe identical to Kym's, was sitting motionless at the wheel. The blinds had been pulled down all round the passenger compartment, but Kym saw one of them twitch. Her employer was watching her.

At last the door opened. A snooty-looking woman with a starched uniform and a professional smile welcomed Kym in. It was cool in the hallway. Kym was so relieved that for a few moments she said nothing. And then, as she turned her gaze from side to side, she found herself unable to speak.

The place was huge. It was ancient and littered with old-fashioned furniture, but above all it was enormous. The ceiling was as high as a house, and you could walk six abreast up the staircase. And this, according to Kym's employer, wasn't even the main house: this was just a

1

minor mansion, occupying only a tiny corner of the vast estate that surrounded the Private House. This was merely the part of the organisation that was accessible to the public.

The uniformed woman was waiting, one eyebrow quizzically raised. Kym gathered her thoughts. She remembered to modulate her voice, so that it sounded something like the driver's strange accent. From the pocket of her robe she tugged the leather purse which contained the emblem of age-smoothed wood.

'I have a message for one of the residents,' she said. 'It's urgent.'

Talia kept her gaze fixed on Anne's face and her fingers wrapped around Anne's hand. She wanted to imprint on her memory the bright blueness of her young lover's eyes, the moist pinkness of her lips, the softness of her skin. She saw Anne glance again at her wristwatch, and felt the now-familiar clenching of her insides as she was reminded how little time they had left together.

'The car's definitely late,' Anne said, and turned to Talia with a smile of such sweet sadness that Talia almost sobbed aloud. 'This waiting must be torture for you,' she added. 'Perhaps we should have said our goodbyes in my room.'

Talia stroked Anne's face, and then pulled her closer so that their lips were almost touching. 'We had better things to do in your room,' she whispered. 'I don't want to miss a second of being able to kiss you. I'm glad the car's late.'

Their open mouths met. Blindly Talia folded apart the unbuttoned front of Anne's frock and grasped her left breast, making her gasp. Talia was dimly aware of Anne's fingers sliding along her thigh, reaching under the hem of her leather skirt, and closing gently on the spring-clip that held a lock of Anne's blonde hair tightly against one of Talia's sex-lips.

'I do love you, Talia,' Anne breathed, and tugged on the keepsake until Talia started to moan.

The two women were so absorbed in each other that they hardly cared who saw them but, even though they were outside the front entrance of the public façade of the Private House, there was little danger of being seen. They were on an island of green surrounded by the circular sweep of the gravel drive, sitting side by side on a bench that was concealed by shrubs and banks of tall blooms. Through the flowers and branches, Talia could see small patches of the drive; she could keep an eye on the pile of Anne's suitcases and hatboxes; she could see the gateway through which, inevitably and all too soon, the car would arrive to take Anne away. But she and Anne, she was sure, were invisible.

This was the second time that Talia had had to say farewell to her young friend at the end of a summer. Repetition made the occasion no easier to bear. Anne had spent most of the summer vacation being trained at the Private House – although this year her Mentors had been obliged to admit that there was little more they could teach her. Talia had been allowed to arrange her own stay at the House so it coincided with the later part of Anne's course of tuition. For the past four weeks they had been apart only when they had separate classes. They had eaten, bathed and slept together. There was hardly a moment when they had not been touching each other, and kissing, and tickling, and spanking, and pinching, and squeezing, and caressing.

Anne had packed her cases the previous night, so that she and Talia could have the whole morning to themselves. They had simply remained in bed, as naked as when they had awoken together. As usual, they had given each other a spanking, and playfully they had continued to slap each other's bottom while their faces were pressed into each other's sex. Then, after they had licked each other to an orgasm, and cuddled, and played with each other's breasts, they agreed murmuringly that they both deserved particularly severe punishments, so that they couldn't possibly forget the day of their parting.

Talia's slim bottom, flattened against the hard surface of the bench, still smarted from the smacks that Anne had administered with strap and cane. Talia had been egged on by Anne, who had said that she deserved to be whipped hard for leaving, so she had given more smacks, and harder ones, than she had received.

'Stop touching me there,' Talia said. 'You'll make me come again. Stand up. I want to see your poor, sore bottom.'

'It is very sore,' Anne said, standing with her back to Talia and the skirt of her frock pulled up to her waist. 'But you know how irritable I am if I haven't had a spanking. I'll be sore all day, I should think.'

Talia's fingertips stroked the raised red lines that crisscrossed her friend's round, reddened buttocks. Talia hoped that Anne realised that each stripe had been applied with love and longing, and represented the pain of the couple's imminent separation.

'I wish I could have whipped you harder,' she whispered. 'I'd like these stripes to last until I see you again. You will wear this, won't you?' she added, pressing her fingers against the base of the plug that protruded shyly from between Anne's buttocks. Talia knew that Anne liked to be penetrated anally, and she had had the dildo made by one of the forest craftsmen as a going-away present: above the waisted base the wood, before being smoothed and varnished, had been carved into an exact copy of Talia's first two fingers.

'Don't worry, Talia,' Anne said, and glanced over her shoulder. 'I can't possibly forget you. And I promise I'll put your fingers in my bottom at least once a day, and make myself come while I think about you. If you keep pressing it, my dear, I'll start to come now. Oh, that feels so nice. Keep stroking my bottom, too.'

For a while there was silence. Anne leant forwards, and Talia manipulated the base of the plug and kissed and caressed Anne's heated buttocks.

'Stop,' Anne said at last. She looked over her shoulder and smiled. 'That's lovely, but it isn't fair. I want to do something to you.' She peered over the surrounding branches. 'That funny old car is still parked under the trees,' she remarked. 'It ought to be in a museum. It's been here ages. You don't suppose it could be my taxi, do you?'

Talia stood up, and continued to stroke her friend's bottom as she looked over her shoulder. Talia knew plenty about horses, but next to nothing about cars. She thought the vehicle sitting on the drive looked rather like a stagecoach to which had been added an engine and rubber tyres. But it was certainly big, and the black bodywork shone like polished jet.

'It can't be your car,' she said. Then she pulled aside the curtain of Anne's blonde hair and began to nibble her ear while she ground the palm of her hand against the base of the anal plug. 'We saw that robed woman come out of it, and go into the reception hall. Then a little while later she came out. But that was a long time ago.'

Anne was sighing with pleasure. 'Oh, Talia,' she whispered. 'Touch me. I'm nearly there.'

'Touch you where?' Talia asked with feigned innocence. Anne felt such shivers of delight whenever she was aroused that she often started to plead and beg. 'Anyway, I thought you were interested in that vehicle. I wonder why it's still here?'

'Please, Talia,' Anne moaned. 'Please make me come again before the car arrives to take me away.'

'You don't deserve any treats,' Talia replied. 'You're going away, and I know that you'll have fun with all those students.' She kept moving her hand against the base of the plug as she extended her other arm in front. Then she began to pat Anne's breasts until they bounced and jiggled.

Anne gasped a deep breath and turned to press her body into Talia's embrace. When she pulled back from the kiss her eyes were bright with mischief. 'Oh, yes, Talia,' she said. 'Please spank my titties. And I'll do yours. Use the belt from your skirt. But please let me come while you're smacking me.'

'The car could arrive at any moment,' Talia said, but she was already pulling the leather strap from the loops of her waistband. 'You'd better sit on the bench again. Hold the front of your dress open. That's right, and push your breasts forward.'

Talia didn't use the belt immediately, even though there was little time in which to punish Anne again for leaving her. She gazed lovingly at her young friend, who was waiting with her eyes closed, her lips slightly parted, her face uplifted, and her breasts bared and thrust out. She couldn't keep still, no doubt because the hard seat hurt her sore bottom and pushed the anal dildo deep into her.

'Can you feel my fingers inside you, my angel?' Talia asked. She touched the edge of the belt against the tips of Anne's breasts, and shared in the stab of pleasure that made the haloes of skin crinkle and harden.

'Yes,' Anne gasped. She opened her eyes and looked up at her lover. 'It's going to be months before you spank me again,' she said. 'This will be the last time for ages. Do it really hard, please, Talia.'

'Of course I will,' Talia said. 'I just hope there'll be time for you to do mine afterwards.' She pulled her short skirt up to her waist and placed her left foot on the bench. She tried a leisurely, experimental swing with the belt, so that its tail caught the underside of Anne's left breast.

Anne sighed. 'That's lovely,' she said. Her gaze dropped from Talia's face and rested on the junction of her thighs. Her eyes were shining with excitement: it was a continual source of pleasure and embarrassment to Talia that her young friend found Talia's private parts fascinating and arousing. Both of the lovers enjoyed shaving and plucking each other's pubes and labia, but Anne was obsessive about depilating Talia with tender thoroughness. 'May I touch you?' Anne asked. 'While you're whipping me? You're open and very wet.'

'Of course,' Talia said, and shivered as she felt Anne's fingers glide along the split of her sex.

'So pretty,' Anne murmured. 'You smell wonderful. Can I lick you, Talia?'

'In a little while,' Talia said teasingly. She began to swing the belt to and fro, making Anne's breasts blush and dance. She felt Anne's fingers pushing into her vagina.

Anne's breasts were bright red when Talia stopped to rest her arm. Anne looked up at her with eyes that were hooded, barely focused, and cloudy with desire. She smiled and sighed, and moved her fingers inside Talia. 'You haven't finished?'

6

'Just resting,' Talia reassured her. Then as Talia happened to look over the shrubs, towards the portico of the mansion, she saw the doors open. A figure, in robes identical to those worn by the woman and the driver from the big, black car, emerged hurriedly from the mansion and stopped, looking from right to left.

That must be Olena, Talia said to herself. The heavy robe would have been shapeless enough to disguise almost any physique, but it couldn't conceal Olena's generous curves. Talia had heard that the exotic, dusky-skinned beauty had come from a remote community whose people wore thick, all-covering robes.

Anne murmured impatiently, and tried to use her fingers to tug Talia towards her. 'Wait,' Talia told her. 'I'll start again in a moment. I think Olena's leaving in that old car.'

Olena was walking hesitantly towards the gleaming vehicle. One of its doors opened as she approached. The interior was dark; Talia imagined that it was cool, and mysterious, and smelt of leather upholstery.

It was only when Olena was about to step on the running-board of the car that she hesitated. It seemed to Talia that Olena peered inside and, after exchanging a few words with the passengers, recoiled and backed away.

Talia heard a shout, then the engine started. The roaring noise drowned Olena's voice as she struggled to make herself heard. The car moved forward with the door open. Suddenly, arms emerged from within the car, and pulled Olena into the dark interior. Talia saw her struggling. The door slammed shut, and the car almost collided with another vehicle at the gates before speeding away.

'What's the matter?' Anne asked. 'Please carry on smacking me. You can't stop now.'

Talia sighed. 'I have to, my angel. Your car's here. And we must make ourselves look respectable. We're not in the House now.'

'Oh, bother,' Anne said. She pulled her fingers from Talia's vagina and grinned cheekily as she licked them. She jumped to her feet. 'One more big, long kiss,' she said, 'and then I have to go to college, and you have to return to the

7

forest.' She pressed herself against Talia, who felt her own conical breasts being enveloped by Anne's larger, hot globes. 'At least I've got a few things to remind me of you,' Anne giggled.

'It's not for ever,' Talia whispered when they ended their kiss, but she knew that she was reassuring herself as much as her young lover. 'I'll write to you.'

She couldn't stop the tears rolling steadily down her cheeks as she watched the taxi driver load Anne's cases into the car. She managed to smile when she waved at the car, as it receded in a cloud of dust. Then she was alone, standing on the gravel drive in the late summer sunlight. Her vulva was cool and sticky under her skirt, and already she was so used to the clip gripping her labium that she could hardly feel it.

She had to think of something other than Anne's departure. That business with Olena, for instance. It had looked as though Olena was being kidnapped. It had all happened so quickly that Talia wondered whether she had imagined it. But the expression of alarm on Olena's face had been unmistakable. Talia would have to report the incident. It would take her mind off losing Anne.

Olena had the vehicle's width of sumptuous leather seating to herself, but she remained huddled in one corner. She was still suspicious of the two women sitting opposite her, in spite of everything the older one had said to try to reassure her.

The younger woman – hardly more than a girl, Olena realised – was dressed in a robe like Olena's. But she was not, as she had claimed, one of Olena's people. The community was small, and Olena would have recognised anyone from it. The girl had said her name was Kym, which was not a name that was used among Olena's people. And, once concealed behind the blinds, she had cursed the heat and the robe with words that Olena found shocking. The girl had shrugged the heavy garment from her shoulders so that her bosom was almost exposed and it was clear that she was wearing no undergarments. Olena

8

pulled her own robe more tightly about her body. She knew that no woman from her community could speak and act as shamelessly as Kym.

The older woman made no attempt to pretend to be one of Olena's people. She made Olena uneasy. She was short, slight and pretty; she had a wide, ready smile, and her words to Olena had been entirely friendly. There should have been nothing daunting about her. But Olena had spent two years in the Private House, and she had learnt to notice the subtle hints in a person's appearance that indicated a tendency to perverse pleasures.

The woman's clothing, for instance, was black: a short, tailored jacket over a dress that clung to curves so shapely that the woman's waist must have been constricted by a corset. Her hair, too, was dark, and cut in a short bob with wings that hung alongside her jaw in points that were as sharp as the heels and toes of her little boots. She was wearing gloves of black lace. Even her eyes were large and black. She had introduced herself as Madame la Patronne, and had said that she liked everyone to call her Madame. Like her clothing, this form of address reminded Olena of the formality of the Private House.

Above all, though, Olena found that she couldn't help responding in intimate, embarrassing ways to Madame's dark appearance and quietly confident manner. Olena had been brought up to know that certain parts of her body were shameful, and that certain feelings, such as pride in her appearance, and desire, and carnal pleasure, were sinful. As she had grown from a girl into a woman Olena had discovered that, like her breasts and her bottom, her wicked feelings had blossomed. Sinful thoughts had filled her head just as the ever-growing new curves of her young body had felt increasingly uncomfortable under her constricting robe.

She had become so voluptuous that even the most voluminous robe failed to conceal her shape. She had noticed that the men and boys of her community stared at her. When they stared, she had felt embarrassed, of course, and ashamed – but also a little pleased, though she knew that even to be aware of their attention was a sin. Far worse, and far more wicked, were the little tickling shivers of pleasure that she had begun to feel when she thought about the boys staring at her, or when, while washing, she touched the parts of her body that the boys seemed most to look at, and that she knew were the most forbidden.

By the time Olena had left the security of the community, to attend college in the city, she had become convinced that no one could be as wicked as she was. The women in the city wore clothes that left exposed their arms, their calves, and sometimes their shoulders. They laughed and flirted with the young men. Olena had found herself comparing her body to theirs – she realised with a stab of sinful pride that she was more curvaceous than any of them – and wishing that she too could wear bright, light clothes.

Olena's guardian in the city, a young man named Barat who was a friend of her family, had allowed her to dress like the women with whom she attended college. But when he had discovered that she had sinful thoughts and feelings, he had determined to punish her. The mere thought of being spanked had been enough to make Olena's lewd, wicked thoughts more urgent and pleasurable than ever. Before he had had the time to carry out his threat, however, he and Olena had been drawn into the strange world of the Private House.

In the Private House Olena had been encouraged to plumb the depths of her lewdness and to request as many punishments as she wanted. But no matter how often she surrendered to her lustful yearnings, and no matter how often she bared and lifted the perfect spheres of her buttocks towards the lash, the perverse thoughts continued to breed in her imagination. In fact she had soon learnt that the chastisements seemed only to encourage her lickerishness.

Almost immediately Olena had become the centre of attention. The denizens of the House flocked to see her. Her voluptuous beauty alone would have been enough to draw crowds. But the way that she blushed, and squirmed, and sobbed, every time that she was ordered merely to undress, was endlessly fascinating. Furthermore, her sexual arousal was always as immediate and obvious as her embarrassment. No matter how often she was made to exhibit herself, and give and receive pleasure, and suffer under the whip, she remained as ashamed and contrite as she had been on the day she had arrived in the House.

Although her sense of shame was still as overwhelming as the elders of her community could have wished, she had soon learnt not to feel guilty. If she misbehaved – and she did so, every day – then she would submit to discipline. If she enjoyed the punishments – and she found that she always did, no matter how hard she tried to resist the feelings – then she had to endure the additional humiliation of being exposed as a wanton. And if being humiliated only fanned the flames of her pleasure – and she soon found out that nothing aroused her as much as being punished and put on display at the same time – then everything combined to confirm her belief that her sense of shame was justified.

Olena had learnt that no matter what she did, she remained sinful and wicked. But thanks to the tuition she had received in the Private House, she now knew that she could enjoy finding out just how sinful and wicked she could be.

Most of the people Olena had met in the last two years were of two sorts. Olena was one of those who found pleasure in submitting to the control and discipline of others. Madame la Patronne, Olena was sure, was of the opposite persuasion.

Olena couldn't help feeling tremors of excitement whenever she found Madame's dark eyes lingering on her. The fact that she was, despite all of Madame's assurances, a prisoner, in a vehicle taking her to an unknown destination, only increased her nervous arousal. She was grateful for the thick cloth of her robe, which concealed the physical evidence: her nipples felt taut, and she knew that had they been visible Madame and Kym could not have failed to notice that they were erect. As the vehicle trundled quietly over the road the slight vibration made the delicate tips of Olena's breasts rub against the coarse material.

'Where are you taking me?' Olena asked yet again. 'I know that the message from my community was a trick.'

Madame looked hurt, and then smiled. 'Not a trick, Olena, my dear. You're entirely safe with us. We don't mean you any harm.'

Did Madame think that bland assurances would be enough to placate her? Olena refused to be charmed, even though it would have been easy and pleasurable to defer to Madame. She turned to Kym. 'But my mother isn't ill, is she? You told a lie, just to lure me from the House.'

Kym shrugged. 'I say what I'm told to say.' She nodded sideways towards Madame. 'She's the boss.'

Madame cast an annoyed glance towards Kym and then turned to face Olena. 'I admit that I instructed Kym to exaggerate a little,' she said. 'But I had to be sure that you would leave. I've heard so much about you, and I wanted to meet you in person.' She leant forwards and gazed at Olena with eyes that appeared incapable of guile. 'You look almost smothered in those heavy robes. Don't you feel a little warm?'

'No,' Olena said. 'Not at all.' She crossed her arms, turned her face away, and tried to think of anything but revealing her body for Madame's inspection.

Olena could hear, outside the carriage, the sounds of other vehicles. Increasingly often the progress of Madame's car was impeded. Occasionally, and more frequently, Olena heard shouts, and bursts of music.

We're entering the city, she thought.

Talia stood a pace behind the black-uniformed guard who had escorted her into the Supreme Mistress's chamber. She could feel that her face had reddened, and she was angry with herself for being discomfited.

Even though Talia was the elected leader of the foresters, and even though she and her people had enthusiastically embraced the pleasures and discipline of the Private House, she still felt awkward when in the presence of other people engaged in intimate acts. Particularly when it was obvious that she had interrupted their mutual pleasure. And more particularly when the people concerned were Jem, the Supreme Mistress of the Private House, and Julia, Jem's favourite lover and leader of her guards.

Even Julia, who could usually be relied on to be a paragon of austere self-control, appeared slightly irritated by the presence of Talia and the guard. She was, after all, Talia thought, in an especially vulnerable position: she was lying, naked, across a large, velvet-covered footstool, with her wrists tied to her ankles and her face, obscured by her long, dark hair, almost touching the floor. Her prominent, muscular buttocks, which were glowing red from a recent spanking, were held apart by a slim, rectangular frame of metal, the cross-struts of which were holding in place a gleaming cylinder that disappeared into the dark depths of her anus. It was said that when Jem played the dominant role she delighted in exploring and tormenting the deep canyon between Julia's buttocks, and that she had had made a set of instruments for the purpose, but this was the first time that Talia had seen evidence that the rumours were true. Julia seemed to enjoy her mistress's ministrations, however, as the lips of her sex, held apart by the wide base of a phallus that was embedded in her vagina, were glistening with wetness.

The Supreme Mistress, who had been kneeling beside Julia, stood and turned to face Talia and the guard. Unlike Julia, who was tossing her head in frustration, Jem Darke seemed pleased to have visitors. As always, Talia was momentarily taken aback by the delectable, impish prettiness of the Supreme Mistress. Her blue-green eyes, set in her heart-shaped face and fringed by her red-gold tresses, lighter than Talia's own titian hair, seemed to promise everything: they hinted at a devilish inventiveness whenever she was in control of you, but they danced with a mischievous invitation, a suggestion that she wanted to be punished for her naughtiness. She was wearing a green satin corset that cinched her tiny waist and emphasised the curves of her hips and breasts.

'Yes?' she said, and smiled as though she expected Talia and the guard to join in her games.

'I'm sorry to disturb you, Mistress,' the guard stammered, 'but Talia has an urgent report for Mistress Julia.'

'Julia's rather busy at the moment,' Jem said, and giggled. She turned and smacked Julia's upraised bottom twice. 'I was just about to make her come again.'

'I can come back later, Jem,' Talia said.

'I won't hear of it,' Jem replied. 'It will do Julia good to wait. I haven't seen you for ages, Talia, my dear. Come here.' She opened her arms to welcome Talia into an embrace.

It was always a pleasure to cuddle the Supreme Mistress. As Talia pressed her body against Jem's, the perfect pink bow of Jem's lips opened under Talia's kiss. Talia sighed as she felt Jem's hands wander down her back and on to her hips. Jem's nimble fingers soon pulled up the back of Talia's short skirt.

'Your bottom's hot,' Jem whispered between kisses. 'And I can feel the marks of a cane.'

Talia murmured and nodded. 'But I can take more, Mistress,' she whispered, 'if you want to punish me for disturbing you.'

'And what's this?' Jem said, breaking away from Talia's kisses but leaving her hand between Talia's thighs. Her fingers were tugging gently at the clip attached to Talia's sex.

Talia gasped, and gathered her breath to reply. 'It's a keepsake from Anne, Mistress. I've just seen her off.'

'Of course,' Jem said. 'She's going back to college today. You poor thing. I certainly won't smack you, then. I'm sure you'll want to remember only Anne today. Anyway, I should save my strength for Julia. I'm keeping her from her duties, but I'm determined to give her lovely bottom my thorough and prolonged attention. I suppose it's almost time for you to return to the forest, isn't it? Your people will need you now that the summer's nearly over.'

'I should go back, Jem,' Talia said. 'I've enjoyed my training, and I've learnt a lot, but I can't stay. The House will just remind me of Anne.'

It was true that Talia wanted to leave the House as soon as possible. Already she had found that everywhere she went she imagined that Anne would appear on every staircase, along every corridor, in every mirrored room. But the prospect of returning to the forest had little appeal. She missed the foresters, of course, and she missed the tall trees and the smell of woodsmoke and leather and horses, but she knew that no one in the forest could satisfy the urges she had discovered in herself, or submit her to the perverse practices that she had learnt in the House. In the depths of the forest, as she organised the hunters and the leather-workers and the wood-turners, she would pine for Anne.

'While I was saying my final farewell to Anne,' Talia said, no longer whispering, 'I saw Olena being kidnapped.'

Jem frowned. Talia heard a muffled exclamation from Julia.

'Kneel beside me,' Jem said, 'so that Julia can hear. Tell us everything.'

Talia and Jem knelt next to Julia's bound body. Jem used her fingers to comb Julia's long tresses from her face, and stroked Julia's bottom while Talia talked. Talia described exactly what she had seen.

'Untie me, Jem,' Julia said when Talia had finished her account. 'I can't think like this, let alone act.'

'Don't be silly, Jules,' Jem said soothingly. 'I haven't finished with you yet, and you can be perfectly decisive even though you're tied up. You told me that you saw a young woman from Olena's home community?'

'Yes,' Julia said. 'This morning. Just before I came here. She had Olena's colouring, and she was wearing one of those heavy robes that Olena wears. She said that she had a message for Olena. A member of Olena's family has fallen ill, apparently, and Olena has been summoned home.'

'It would be easy to invent such a story,' Jem said. 'Olena is extremely desirable and still quite innocent of the world. I hope you didn't let her go on such a flimsy pretext, Julia. If you did I'll keep you tied up all day, and I won't be at all gentle with you.'

'Of course not, Jem,' Julia said angrily. 'The young woman brought a token from Olena's family. It was a carved wooden emblem. I showed it to Olena. She said each family's was unique, and she certainly recognised it. It convinced her that the message was genuine.'

Jem turned to Talia. 'It seems as though the summons to Olena really was from her family,' she said. 'Are you sure that she was dragged into the car by force? Perhaps she was just reluctant to leave the House, and needed to be persuaded to get into the car. After all, you must admit that when you witnessed her abduction – if that's what it was – you were preoccupied, to say the least.'

Talia couldn't deny that it was true. She had thought that Olena had looked alarmed. But maybe she had merely been surprised. She had been some distance from Talia's vantage-point in the bushes.

'We ought to check,' Julia said, twisting her neck to look at Jem. 'Olena is a valuable prize. It will be a simple matter to send someone to her village. If she's there, or if her family is expecting her, then we can be sure that the message was genuine. I'll brief an agent. Once you've finished with me, Mistress.'

'Send me,' Talia said. She had blurted out the words before she had even considered the consequences. Now she rapidly summoned arguments to support the idea. 'It will help to take my mind off Anne,' she suggested. 'And it won't take long. I'll be back in the forest in a matter of days.'

'Talia,' Julia said, impatiently, 'you've had no training as a field agent. You haven't even served in the guards.'

Talia felt her face flush with sudden anger. 'Your guards were no match for my foresters,' she retorted, 'when I led them in raids against the House. And I can hunt and track better than most of my people. I seem to remember that you needed my help when you were captured by the Whipmaker.'

'Talia has a point, Jules,' Jem said mildly. 'Hush, both of you. I'm thinking.'

The Supreme Mistress stroked Julia's flanks as she gazed searchingly at Talia.

'You may go to Olena's village, Talia,' Jem decided. 'They are a quiet, isolated, rural community. It won't be very different from being in the forest. And I'm sure that even without an agent's training you will have no difficulty in discovering whether the message did truly come from Olena's family. In all likelihood you'll find Olena there, and I'm sure you'd rather put your mind at rest yourself than expend the time of one of our agents. And you, Julia,' Jem added, placing her hand over the base of the phallus that protruded from her lover's sex, 'can forget all about the matter, and concentrate instead on what I'm doing to you.'

'Thank you, Mistress,' Julia murmured. She lowered her head to the floor and lifted her bottom. It seemed to Talia that the chief of the guards had already dismissed the subject of Olena from her mind and was ready to submit herself once more to Jem's torments.

'You don't have to leave immediately,' Jem said to Talia. 'You're welcome to help me play with Julia.' She caressed Julia's glowing buttocks. 'I think I'll give her another spanking, and then put a larger plug in her anus, before I start bringing her to another climax.'

It was a tempting invitation. The embers of Talia's arousal were still warm, and were being fanned by the scent of female sex in the room. But she knew that if she stayed to watch Julia's bottom being chastised, held open and penetrated, she would become so excited that she wouldn't be able to tear herself away. And, she thought, the sight of Jem and Julia at play might remind her of the games that she and Anne had enjoyed only that morning.

'Thank you, Mistress,' she said, 'but the sooner I leave, the sooner I'll be back.'

'Very well,' Jem said. She kissed Talia's lips, and then stood beside her and looked down at Julia. 'Isn't she adorable? Should I use a strap or a cane, do you think?'

'A strap,' Talia replied automatically. 'Then you can still use a cane, later, if you want to, to mark her with stripes.'

'That would be the usual procedure,' Jem agreed. 'But I like to surprise her. It encourages her to surprise me when

17

I let her take charge of me. I expect she'll punish me particularly severely,' she added, in a whisper, 'because I invited you to stay and help me.' She smiled in anticipation.

Talia followed the guard towards the door. She sniffed back a sob. It was all so unfair. Jem and Julia were so happy together. Why did she have to be separated from Anne?

She straightened her shoulders. At least she had a mission to perform. She would set off immediately to find Olena.

Barat looked once again in the driving mirror. The blinds were, of course, still pulled down inside all the windows of the passenger compartment. He didn't need to reassure himself that Olena was still with Madame and Kym. He forced himself to concentrate on driving the vast, old-fashioned vehicle. The city streets were crowded and narrow, and he had only recently learnt how to drive.

The important thing was that Madame had captured Olena. And it couldn't have been done without Barat's knowledge and assistance. The dusky, voluptuous beauty was Madame's now, but Barat would receive a reward for his help: he would be allowed to have Olena, once she was ready, as often as he wanted, in as many ways as his imagination could devise, until he was tired of her.

Two years previously he had been on the point of seducing Olena when she had been taken from him. He had then suffered indignities beyond measure at the hands of the Chatelaine, the imperious mistress of the Chateau, the most disciplinarian of the many establishments of the Private House. He had found himself enjoying his servitude, it was true, and in Madame la Patronne he had found a new mistress almost as severe as the Chatelaine. But he had never forgotten Olena. He nursed for the dark-haired, big-eyed, coffee-coloured, curvaceous girl a passion that had burnt more and more brightly through the months of separation.

He had waited this long; he could wait a little longer. Madame would want to inspect her new acquisition, and test her to see whether Barat's claims about her perverse desires were true, and keep her to herself for a while. But Madame had promised Barat that when Olena was ready to be used for the pleasure of others, Barat would be the first to have her.

He took one hand from the steering wheel and inserted it into his robes. His manhood had been stiff since he had driven away from the Private House, because his mind had been constantly full of images of the things he planned to do with Olena. He held the hot bar of flesh in his fist. It would be a triumphant achievement: he could imagine the sensation of pushing his hard, sensitive staff into Olena's yielding flesh. But that would not be the best moment. The most satisfying part of the act would be when, with his manhood deep inside her, he threw back the hood of his robe to reveal his face.

She had abandoned him to a life of slavery in the Chateau. She had made no appeal to try to save him. She had sent no word to him. Perhaps she had forgotten him. Well, he would have his revenge. He imagined the look of shock and outrage that would appear on her face when she realised that it was Barat who was fucking her. He imagined her cries of protest. He imagined her resignation, followed by her reluctant enjoyment, as Madame made it clear that she was to submit to every carnal act that Barat required of her.

And all through her ordeal Olena would be expecting at any moment to be rescued by those interfering bitches from the Private House. Barat gripped his penis more tightly and grinned. Olena would not be rescued. He and Madame had planned Olena's capture meticulously, and had laid a false trail for anyone sent to look for her.

Anyone who comes searching for Olena, Barat thought, will be pulled into a world of bondage and torment beside which Madame's house is no more than a children's nursery.

Two

Outside, Talia knew, the ochre stone of the village's cottages was glowing in warm sunshine. A few shafts of yellow light fell through the shutters, but did little to illuminate or heat the room in which she sat, surrounded by the members of Olena's family. She shivered. She could understand why Olena's people covered themselves with heavy robes. She felt chilly in her leather skirt and bodice. And she was uncomfortably aware that everyone sitting around her was staring at her exposed arms and legs.

Until now she had felt entirely confident. It had been several years since she had last ventured beyond the bounds of the vast estate that surrounded the Private House, but she had had no difficulty in buying a ticket for the railway, and later changing trains on to the branch line that terminated only a few miles from the isolated hamlet in which Olena had been brought up. She had realised that her skirt was rather shorter than those worn by other women travelling on the trains, and it had occurred to her that outside the House it was probably customary to wear underclothes. On more than one occasion she had caught people staring at her. But her attire was only a little more revealing than what she saw others wearing, and she hadn't thought it necessary to change her clothes or to cover herself with the coat that was folded inside her leather travelling-bag.

Now, however, she felt almost naked. Olena's mother, brothers and sisters were all swathed in thick coverings, so that it was difficult to tell them apart. All she could see of their faces was their eyes, staring at her as if she was an alien creature.

She kept her head lowered, and gripped the hem of her skirt to ensure that it couldn't slip any further up her thighs.

Olena's mother seemed to be friendly, though. She spoke with such a thick accent that Talia had difficulty understanding everything she said, but she patiently answered each of Talia's questions.

Olena hadn't returned to the village; that was immediately clear. But her mother wasn't concerned. As far as Talia could make out a young man named Barat, who had once been Olena's chaperone, and who had been away from the village as long as Olena, had recently visited the cottage. It was Barat who had asked Olena's mother for the carved wooden emblem of the family: he had said that he wanted it to show to Olena, so that she would trust him. He had hinted that Olena had fallen among sinful people, and that he intended to bring her home. It was clear that Olena's mother trusted Barat.

Talia didn't know what to think. It sounded as though Barat and Olena were old friends. On the other hand, if he was as conservative and prudish as everyone else from the community, it was possible that he would resort to force in order to liberate Olena, as he might see it, from the wickedness of the Private House, even if his intentions were good. And then there was the possibility that his intentions were not at all good, and that he had deceived Olena's mother into parting with the family emblem.

'Do you know how I can find Barat?' Talia asked.

'Of course,' Olena's mother said. 'He wrote down his address. Now, where did I put it? Umara, look in my sewing box.'

One of the smallest of the robed figures rose, bowed slightly to Talia and then to Olena's mother, and padded into the darkness in a corner of the room. Talia endured an uncomfortable silence and the unrelenting gaze of Olena's family.

Umara, whom Talia presumed was one of Olena's younger sisters, returned with two slips of paper and a pencil, sat down in her place, and laboriously copied the words from one piece of paper to the other. She then leant forward and offered one of the slips to Talia.

'Thank you,' Talia said. She tucked the paper into her bag. She had no more questions to ask. 'I'd better be on my way,' she said to Olena's mother. 'The trains are infrequent. Thank you for your help. I'll let you know if I find Olena.' She got to her feet, being careful not to let her skirt ride up her legs.

Olena's mother snorted. 'Olena used to be a good girl,' she said. 'Now, I don't know. She's old enough to care for herself, anyway.'

'Of course she is,' Talia said. 'It's just that – Well, I'll let you know what I find out, if anything.' She turned and opened the door, flooding the room with sunlight.

A figure, covered in robes like everyone else in the village, stood in the doorway. Talia thought it was a man. Olena's father, perhaps.

'You,' the man said. He glanced at Talia's body, and then averted his face as if it had been struck. 'Sinful,' he muttered. 'You must come with me. The elders wish to see you.'

Talia smiled. 'I'm afraid I don't really have the time,' she said. 'The trains, you see.'

The man's right hand shot from the folds of his robe and closed around Talia's wrist.

'Ow!' she said. 'That hurts.'

'You must come with me,' the man repeated. 'The elders will judge you.'

The only good thing about being back in Madame's house, Kym thought, was that she no longer had to wear that heavy, rough robe. She hadn't waited for Madame's permission, but had marched off to her room, pulling off the robe as she went, as soon as the car had stopped in the underground garage. She had opened the jet in the shower as far as she could, and for a little while, as she stood under the streaming water, she had felt refreshed and free.

But she knew that her employer would soon summon her. She was given little time to herself. She had dressed hurriedly in her uniform, and now she was waiting for the ring of the bell that would call her to Madame's side.

She didn't like the uniform. It was a symbol of her lowly status in the household. She placed herself in front of the full-length mirror and scowled at her reflection.

She hated grey. It matched her eyes, and went well with her short, white-blonde hair, but it was so drab. Everything was grey: the little pleated skirt, the thick stockings, the short, tailored, military-looking jacket that left her midriff bare. Even the leather collar around her neck was grey. Only her sensible shoes were a different colour – and they were black.

If the uniform had only been a more interesting colour it might almost have been acceptable. It was, after all, rather sexy. Kym twirled in front of the mirror, and glimpsed her naked bottom and hairless sex as the skirt lifted. She liked to taunt Barat in this way, although she hated it when he tried to grope her. Madame la Patronne had dozens of little rules about how to dress and behave. They drove Kym to distraction, because she was always forgetting them. But she couldn't help obeying Madame's injunction to wear no knickers: there were none in the house. And she didn't mind shaving off her pubic hairs: it felt nice, and it saved having to dye them blonde.

The jacket was as firm and tight as the skirt was light and flyaway. It supported and lifted her breasts, which pressed against the two button-down flaps on its front. The flaps were positioned so that whenever Madame wished to punish Kym for a minor offence – and that was often – she had only to instruct Kym to unbutton one of the flaps and a nipple was bared, ready for Madame to smack or pinch.

Kym didn't mind the punishments. They made her feel sexy. Sometimes she would disobey an order or break a rule in order to get the attention of her pretty employer. Occasionally Madame would summon her last thing at night to the main bedroom, or to one of the special rooms that were kept locked, and the two women would have an hour or two together. Kym knew how to please a woman with her tongue, lips and fingers, although she preferred to have a woman pleasing her. She had come to enjoy the taste and smell of Madame, and as Madame usually let Kym have some pleasure, too, Kym had even come to appreciate the erotic spankings and penetrations that Madame inflicted on her. Sometimes Barat was in the room, too, and that was all right since usually he was there because Madame intended to punish him, so he was tied up and on his best behaviour.

It gave Kym an extra thrill to know that Barat was watching her and Madame play, and that he was helpless even to touch himself. Increasingly often Madame had Kym assist her when she was entertaining the well-dressed toffs who came to visit, and who provided, Kym suspected, Madame's considerable income. These wealthy business-men usually came to be tied up and chastised, and Kym enjoyed watching them grovel and plead under Madame's whip.

So, all in all, Kym thought, there were some compensa-tions for working in Madame's tall, dark, immaculately furnished house. Apart from the dull uniform, and the stifling silence of the place, the main problem was that Kym had to do all the work. Barat was forever cutting corners, dodging his duties, and complaining to Madame that it was Kym who was lazy. When, Kym wanted to know, was the last time that Barat had made the laundry list, or ordered the groceries, or polished the brass door-handles and banisters?

Now there was a fourth member of the household. Kym couldn't decide whether Olena's arrival would make mat-ters better or worse. There would be another pair of hands to share the work. In the car it had been impossible to tell what Olena looked like under her robes, but Barat was obviously obsessed with her, which meant that Kym might get some relief from his wandering fingers. On the other hand, if Olena was as desirable as Barat claimed, Madame might prefer her to Kym, with the result that Olena would be the one who helped Madame with her visitors and shared her bed, while Kym would end up with even more skivvying.

Kym sighed. She unbuttoned one of the flaps of her jacket and played idly with her nipple, studying the spread of the flush of arousal on the face and neck of her reflection in the mirror. After a while she used her other hand to lift the hem of her skirt, and she inserted a finger along the denuded slit of her sex.

Being Madame's maid, Kym thought, was always strange and sometimes difficult. But at least it was more interesting than working in a factory or a shop. She pinched her nipple, and shivered. Now that Barat's plan to capture Olena had succeeded, he would be in favour with Madame, at least for a while, and so Kym could not expect to have the satisfaction of watching him being punished that night. But perhaps Madame would want to play with Kym alone. Kym's finger pushed upwards, into the wet channel of her cunt.

I'm going to smell of sex by the time Madame rings for me, Kym said to herself. But she'll probably like it.

Barat felt his cock stiffen and twitch as he climbed the staircase. He wasn't yet in sight of the door of Madame's bedchamber, but already his body was betraying his excitement. He cursed as the tender skin of his swelling shaft brushed against the harsh interior of the metal contraption that he had fastened over his genitals when the bell in his room had summoned him to his mistress. He began to recite to himself one of the many liturgical texts he had had to commit to memory when he had been studying to become one of the elders of his community. The effort of remembering the repetitive prayers, meaningless to him now, distracted his attention from licentious thoughts, and his erection subsided. He knew, however, that the relief would be only temporary.

'Enter,' Madame called when he knocked on the dark oak door. She was waiting for him, standing in front of her dressing-table, wearing only a translucent peignoir. He saw through the thin material the curve of her hips and, when she turned to face him, the dark shadows of the areolae of her round breasts. He felt his penis surge with blood. He knew that from now until she dismissed him the best he could hope for was continuous discomfort.

'Come here, Barat,' she said, beckoning him with a crooked finger and a knowing smile. 'Take off that robe and let me look at you.'

'Yes, Madame.' The air in the bedchamber was suffused with her perfume. Once he had discarded his robe he was naked, but for the metal device that gripped his testicles and hooded his penis. Her scent, and her gaze inspecting his body, were enough to excite him. If she were to touch him, or make him kneel with his face close to her sex or her breasts, he knew that he would be unable to control the lengthening and thickening of his manhood. He tried desperately to think of anything but her.

'Turn round,' she said.

He obeyed, and there was a silence. He heard her bare feet padding across the thick crimson carpet. He felt her breath on the back of his neck. He uttered a wordless prayer. The shaft of his cock was already pressing against the roof of its covering, and the pressure, thanks to the ingenious design of the device, was tightening the cords around his testicles.

'I should have taken Kym's advice,' Madame whispered. 'Next time you're disobedient I will use the heavier cane.' Her fingers brushed against his right buttock. 'But you're not here for punishment. Follow me into the dressing room and help me dress.'

As Barat trailed his mistress he tried to avert his eyes from the swaying of her bottom. He tried to close his ears to the rustle of the voile against her skin as she walked.

Once they were in the dressing room it was futile for him to try to avoid looking at her. The narrow room was lined on both sides with mirrors. She shrugged off the peignoir and stood naked before him, and he was once again so enraptured that he forgot for a moment about the restraints around his manhood. Madame la Patronne was petite, but perfectly proportioned. Her waist was narrow, her breasts and buttocks were high and round, and the V of her sex, hairless but for a neatly trimmed line of black curls, was plump and inviting. It was no surprise that men worshipped her.

Barat was relieved to see that she had already selected the garments in which she wished to be clothed. Hanging over the back of one of the armchairs were a narrow corset, stockings, and a dress of dark blue *crêpe de chine*. Lying across the seat of the chair was a riding-crop. Barat knew that he was not permitted to touch Madame's skin while dressing her, and that he could expect immediate punishment if he did so.

Keeping his eyes lowered so that he would not be excited by the reflections of his naked mistress, Barat took up the corset. His cock was almost entirely rigid now, but by concentrating his attention precisely on the task of dressing Madame without touching her he thought that he could avoid any further stiffening of his member. The cords tugging on his balls were a constant reminder that he had to remain calm and controlled.

'I want to discuss Olena,' Madame announced, while Barat struggled to tighten the laces of the corset without allowing his thoughts to dwell on the soft, perfumed flesh his efforts were constricting. 'How do you think we should proceed?'

For a brief moment Barat was elated: Madame still needed his help and advice, and that meant that she could hardly intend to renege on her agreement that he could have Olena once she had submitted to Madame's authority.

Then he realised the plight he was in. Dressing his mistress, with his fingers so nearly caressing her pearly skin, was enough to make him almost entirely erect. Thinking and talking about Olena was too much. Images flashed into his mind of Olena's perfect breasts, too large for her narrow ribcage, and of her lush, spherical buttocks, and of her soft, quivering lips and dark, liquid eyes. His manhood expanded, pushing against the metal hood that tugged fiercely on the cords around his balls, while pressing the sensitive, silky skin of his glans into the narrow cone, lined with cruel spikes, at the front of the hood.

This was his punishment for becoming too aroused. He cried out and leant forward, trying to ease the pressure of his hardness. He heard Madame laugh.

'Are you uncomfortable, Barat?' she asked. She put her hand under his chin and lifted his face until he was looking at hers. 'This little contraption is supposed to prevent you becoming too excited,' she added, using her other hand to stroke the metal hood that protruded from his groin.

'It's working, Madame,' Barat gasped. His erection had shrunk a little, and he was able to stand upright. But he knew that it was only a matter of time – particularly if Olena was the subject of conversation – before the delicate bulb of his penis would be burrowing once again into the wickedly painful cone. He had found on previous occasions that if his mistress kept him aroused he began almost to welcome the pain and discomfort.

'Good,' Madame said. 'Pay attention to dressing me, then, and talk to me about Olena. What do you recommend? Will you attend to her, or shall I?'

'It should be you, Madame,' Barat said. Had his mistress already forgotten everything they had planned? 'Olena is to be yours: a gift from me to my mistress. You will find that she will learn quickly to love and obey you, if you follow my advice. And remember, I will watch and remain hidden. She must not recognise me until the moment that you choose to reward me by letting me have her. I have waited years to possess her, and I yearn to see her face and hear her hopeless protestations as I use her.'

He doubled over again as his anticipation of the delights to come made his manhood thrust forward.

'One thing,' he gasped. 'Just one request, Madame, I beg of you. When we go to Olena; when I watch you inspect her, and test her, and discipline her; please, Madame, may I be relieved of this restraint on my cock?'

'Don't you like it, Barat?' she said, teasing him. She put her hand beneath the hood and flicked her fingernails against his tightly bound testicles. She stroked the veined underside of his solid, hard shaft. He sobbed as the cone seemed to close around the exposed plum of his penis. 'Oh, very well,' Madame said. 'You've done well, Barat. Your plan to secure Olena has worked precisely as you predicted. I'm pleased with you. You may remove the device now. And then you will kneel before me and lick me for a while, before we have our first meeting with my new possession.'

Olena felt calmer now. She felt as though she had been made to run a gauntlet of emotions, ever since Julia had summoned her and, with the emblem of Olena's family lying in the palm of her hand, had told her that a messenger from her community had arrived at the House to take her away to see her mother. It seemed like an age had passed since then, but it could have been only a few hours.

Olena had been anxious at first, about the message from her family and at the thought of leaving the House. Then, when she had seen that the vehicle in which she was to ride contained no one from her village, but instead a sinister woman and a girl disguised as one of Olena's people, she had been suspicious, and then alarmed and frightened when the woman had grabbed her and the car had sped away. Then the piercing attention of the woman who liked to be addressed as Madame had embarrassed and aroused her. And as for the realisation that the heavily robed driver of the vehicle could be Barat, the guardian who had desired her: she hadn't known whether to be reassured or even more worried.

Now that she had been left alone in one of the upper rooms of Madame's tall, elegant house, Olena felt less anxious. She knew she was a prisoner, even though she had not been restrained and the door was not locked. She realised that no one at the Private House knew that she had been abducted. It might be weeks before Mistress Julia began to be concerned about Olena's absence, and more weeks before the House's agents found her and rescued her. She had no doubt that she would be rescued, but she also knew that she would have to endure a long incarceration as Madame's guest. Whether or not Barat was involved, she was sure that Madame wanted her for some specific purpose.

It was warm in Madame's house, but Olena didn't relinquish her all-covering robe as she explored the confines of her room. She pulled aside the heavy curtain to reveal a view of russet-leaved trees and tiled rooftops: an attractive prospect, but not informative. There was a door to a bathroom, all white and blue tiles and brass metal-work. There Olena had disrobed for a few moments to refresh herself, even though there was no lock. The bed, with a headboard of brass struts and linen of *broderie anglaise*, was more than big enough for two people. Olena took care not to look closely at the framed prints on the walls or the leather-bound books on the shelves: she suspected that they had licentious themes, and she wanted to avoid anything that might inflame her undisciplined passions.

It was difficult for her to suppress the lewd thoughts that rose in her mind, unbidden, simply at the idea of being Madame's captive. How, she wondered with a sob of shame, could she be so wicked and dirty? At a time such as this she should be thinking of nothing but the peril of her situation, but instead she found her hands wandering towards the sensitive, most private parts of her body, and her imagination straying into daydreams about the things that Madame might require her to do. Even if Madame, against all expectation, proved to be kind, and had no intention of imprisoning her, Olena realised that she would have to ask for at least one punishment, just because she had been unable to control her filthy thoughts.

There were footsteps in the corridor. Then a knock on the door, which opened before Olena could reply. Kym, the young woman who had pretended to be one of Olena's people, entered the room, carrying a small bundle of clothes. She glanced at Olena, and scowled.

'Madame won't let you wear that old robe,' she said. 'Take it off. You're to wear these.'

Olena gazed at Kym. In the vehicle the young woman had been swathed in a robe like her own. Now Olena could see her pretty, round face, her eyes ringed with black make-up and her plump lips rouged, her spiky blonde hair, and her shapely figure barely covered by the grey uniform she was wearing. Her skirt was so short that Olena could see pale bands of skin between it and the tops of her thick stockings. It was the kind of costume that would not have looked out of place in the Private House, and it made Olena once again aware of the tingling excitement in her sex. Meanwhile Kym simply glared at her, as if daring her to defy her instructions.

'This robe is the traditional attire of my people,' Olena said.

'Don't give me that,' Kym said. 'Madame's told me all about that house you've been living in. You know how to behave, and you know what you'll get if you don't.'

'Yes,' Olena said. There was no point in resisting. She began to untie the fastenings of her robe. She was wearing no underclothes, and so Kym would see her naked as soon as the robe fell to the floor. Olena knew that it would be modest to turn her back on Kym, but she couldn't help wanting to watch Kym's face. She knew from long experience of being told to undress that she could expect Kym's eyes to widen with surprise and appreciation as her body was revealed. She knew that the effect she had on people was evidence of her impurity, and that taking delight in watching their reactions was even more sinful. But although she lowered her head and averted her face, from under the curtain of her hair she glanced towards Kym as the robe slid from her shoulders, fell from her body, and pooled around her feet.

As Olena had expected, Kym stared, and her lips parted. She breathed a blasphemous oath.

'All right,' Kym said. Her manner was abrupt, as if she hadn't enjoyed being discomfited by the lush beauty of Olena's form. 'I can see why her ladyship was so keen to get her hands on you. But you'll get no favours from me just because you've got tits like melons.' She looked down at the scraps of clothing she had brought with her, and thrust them towards Olena. 'I thought these were going to be too big,' she muttered. 'Now I just hope they're big enough.'

Olena wondered whether Kym's aggressive attitude represented her true feelings, or whether it was a façade to conceal her discomfort at being attracted to Olena. Kym's gaze, Olena noticed, kept returning to Olena's breasts, and to the V of closely trimmed dark curls on her pubic mound. Olena was used to being admired by both men and women, but she knew that in the world outside the Private House many people suppressed the desirous feelings they felt for others of their own sex. If only, she thought, as she had wished countless times before, if only I could suppress those lewd feelings.

The clothes – a blouse and a skirt – were, indeed, barely adequate to cover her. Both garments were made of soft voile of a golden yellow that complemented Olena's dusky skin. The material was almost transparent, and when stretched across the generous curves of Olena's breasts, hips and bottom it concealed nothing that it covered. The blouse was short, like Kym's grey jacket, and was secured at the front only by knotting together a ribbon under the gap between Olena's breasts. The two halves of the garment didn't meet, and the inside crescents of Olena's breasts were exposed. The skirt, no more than an expanse of material designed to wrap around the wearer's lower body, was long and apparently modest: the waistband was ample for Olena's slim waist, so that it rested on her hips. However, the swelling curves of Olena's bottom and hips were too much for the material to cover, and Olena found that taking just a small step opened the parting in the skirt, revealing her right leg from ankle to hip.

As she dressed, Olena tried to distract both Kym and herself from the tight hardness of her nipples by asking Kym questions. How had Madame acquired the emblem that belonged to Olena's family? Who was the man driving the vehicle that brought her here? What did Madame want with her?

Kym countered every enquiry with a muttered, 'I haven't got a clue,' or 'No one tells me anything, do they?' And, Olena noticed, Kym kept glancing at the front of Olena's blouse, as if she didn't believe that breasts so large, round and firm could possibly hang on a frame as slender and delicate as Olena's.

'Come on, if you're ready,' Kym said. 'I'm supposed to take you to see the boss.'

The village elders ignored all of Talia's protests. Grim-faced, four of them concentrated on tying her wrists and ankles, keeping their eyes averted from her, while the others stood around the perimeter of the circular room and stole furtive glances at her.

The elders, assembled in their council chamber in a ring of dark robes and glowering male faces around Talia, had taken less than a minute to conclude that her attire and demeanour were offensive to the community, and that she should be tested for lewdness. They had crowded about her, and although she was lithe and strong, her struggles had been futile. Now her wrists were tied together above her head by a rope suspended from a roof-beam, and the four elders were busy lashing her ankles to the bases of two wooden pillars.

Red-faced, and shielding their eyes lest they catch a glimpse of Talia's bound, stretched form, the four elders stumbled back to join the circle of their peers. Talia writhed in her bonds, but was helpless to move her limbs. Her bodice felt tight against her chest, and with her legs held apart her skirt had risen up her thighs so that she was sure her bottom and sex were visible. She cursed her thoughtlessness: she should have realised that when visiting this isolated, conservative community she should have worn clothes that covered her completely. And she should have worn some underwear!

Talia struggled, and cursed, and pleaded with the elders to be reasonable as she was merely a visitor. The circle of robed men remained impassive.

To make matters worse, Talia knew that there was something exciting about her predicament. She had discovered her taste for submission when she had fallen in thrall to Robert, the Whipmaker, and although her passion was now reserved almost entirely for her darling, pretty, adorable, mischievous, insatiable Anne, she had lost none of her appetite for being rendered helpless and being disciplined. The Whipmaker and his friend, the mysterious hooded man, had worn robes not unlike those of the elders, and Talia had often found herself in the Whipmaker's cabin, naked and bound, trembling with trepidation and anticipation, while the two men gazed at her and discussed calmly how they intended to punish her and use her for their pleasure.

Now Talia's situation, and the smells of wood and leather and men, brought back memories of all the indignities and whip-strokes she had suffered and enjoyed in that lamp-lit cabin. She couldn't help becoming aroused. She and Anne would often take turns to tie each other up, but it was a long time since she had felt as defenceless as this, with her legs held wide apart and with no idea what the elders intended to do with her. She hoped that they would chastise her, but she knew that once she had been whipped she would want the men to use her, toy with her and penetrate her, and she feared that their strict moral code would prevent them from so much as touching her.

'Lead Cobal to her,' one of the elders said.

Talia tried to look over her shoulder to see what was happening. Two of the elders were leading a third by the arms to where she was bound in the centre of the circle. As they steered the robed figure towards her she saw that he was being supported not because he was frail but because he was blind. In the shadows of the hood of his robe his eyes shone milky white.

'The harlot is in front of you, Cobal,' one of the elders said, and the two who had led the blind man retreated to the perimeter of the room. 'Begin the inspection, Cobal. Brother elders, turn away. We should not witness this.'

As one, the elders turned to face the walls of the chamber. Cobal drew back his hood. His pearly eyes gazed unseeingly in Talia's direction. She gasped and drew back, as far as the ropes would allow, as his hands groped towards her face.

She shuddered and closed her eyes as his stubby fingers touched her cheek, and then cried out in protest as his hands roamed across her face, prodding into her ears, fingering her lips, and rubbing her jaw and forehead.

'Hush, slut,' Cobal muttered, and through half-closed eyes Talia saw a lascivious smile appear on his round face. He raised his voice to announce, 'The harlot has a smooth face. No doubt she works indoors.' He managed to imbue this apparently innocuous comment with suggestive and insulting meaning.

'That's not true,' Talia protested. 'I'm the leader of the foresters.' But even as she cried out she told herself that, between tuition and playing with Anne, in recent weeks she had hardly been out of doors.

'Her lips open readily,' Cobal said, once again conferring a second, lewd meaning on a simple sentence. The elders, still facing away from Talia and Cobal, murmured.

'Her hair is long and unrestrained,' Cobal said, running his fingers through Talia's titian tresses. 'An obvious sign of lewd, immoral, undisciplined behaviour.'

Talia sighed and slumped in her bonds. There was no point in trying to refute Cobal's ridiculous comments, just as it was useless to try to evade his grasping hands and poking fingers. She would just have to put up with it. She had no doubt that the blind elder would feel every part of her body. Her breasts and sex felt very vulnerable.

'She's a skinny thing,' Cobal announced, having squeezed her arms and pressed his hands against her waist. 'I was told she was clothed. Nothing of her seems to be covered. I can't believe that she had the effrontery to enter our village almost naked. Ah! I have found something.'

Cobal's fingers had encountered the leather bodice that covered her breasts, and were nimbly untying its laces. 'A whore's garment,' he commented, and Talia saw him almost snarl with pleasure as his hands fell on to the exposed mounds of her breasts.

He was silent as he palpated the soft flesh and Talia wriggled helplessly. His fingers closed around her nipples and squeezed them mercilessly. 'Thick teats,' he declared, and Talia uttered a wordless cry of protest. 'As hard as flint. A sure sign of lewdness.'

Talia had no doubt that the sightless elder was enjoying his inspection of her body. With his brother elders looking away, lest they be contaminated by the sight of Talia's naked breasts, Cobal took full advantage of the opportunity to play with them. He grinned as his hands gripped and rubbed the soft hemispheres and their tender tips.

The problem, Talia realised, was that she couldn't help enjoying it too. However much her rational mind rebelled against being held captive and being pawed by this crude, unattractive old lecher, her instincts and her body revelled in being tied up and toyed with in a room full of men.

Talia became aware of the silence in the chamber. Each small sound – Cobal's heavy breaths, her own gasps and moans, the shuffling of the feet of some of the elders – seemed to resonate from the walls and ceiling.

Someone cleared his throat. 'Brother Cobal?' one of the elders said.

The blind man released his grip on Talia's breasts and shook himself. 'She is lascivious,' he said hurriedly. He dropped to his knees in front of her. 'I shall inspect her legs.'

Instinctively Talia tried to draw together her legs as Cobal's hands groped for and then grasped her calves. It was no use: there was nothing she could do to deny him access to the insides of her legs, and she felt herself trembling as violently as Cobal's fingers as his hands slid inexorably upwards.

'There's no fat on her,' Cobal reported. 'She's all sinew,' he added, kneading the insides of her thighs. 'Is the harlot wearing no covering at all on her legs?'

Talia knew that it was only a matter of seconds until his short, shaking fingers would touch her most intimate parts. She knew that she should be revolted by the thought, but she couldn't help wishing that he would hurry. His rough handling of her breasts had aroused her, and she wanted her sex to be subjected to the same treatment.

Cobal's questing hands reached her skirt. 'She has some sort of covering around her hips,' he announced in a thick voice. 'It is utterly immodest. It doesn't cover her shameful parts.'

Talia closed her eyes and tried to control her trembling as his hands explored her hips and belly.

'No underclothes,' Cobal stated, like a judge pronouncing a sentence in court. 'She is completely uncovered. And –' he went on, his voice faltering as his fingers crept across the mound of her pubes, '– she has no hairs. None at all. Brothers, can my fingers be deceiving me? Surely she is not so young? She has the bosom of a grown woman.'

The pressure of Cobal's fingers, so near to the hood of her clitoris, was making Talia writhe with pleasure. 'I'm shaved there,' she said, and the shocked intake of breath from around the room provoked her to continue. 'My girlfriend likes me to be smooth. She kisses me there.' Talia let her words tail off into a moan of desire at the memory of Anne's caresses.

'We've heard enough,' one of the elders cried.

'No,' Cobal said. He was enjoying himself too much to be interrupted now. 'I must complete the inspection.'

Talia tensed her body, and felt his fingers pressing down and into the furrow of her sex. As she had suspected, she was wet, and his fingers slid easily into her. She tried to grip with her internal muscles to keep his fingers inside her, but he recoiled as though bitten.

'Whore!' he exclaimed. 'Brothers, she is as hot as an oven and she is dripping like the inside of a foul well. There can be no doubt. She is utterly lewd and sinful. She can have no redeeming qualities.'

The blind man rose to his feet, wiping his hand on his cloak as if he had excrement on his fingers. He backed away from Talia as rapidly as he could. The elders turned from the wall, and now, Talia noted, they seemed to have lost their inhibitions about looking at her. She found herself surrounded by men's faces expressing lust, curiosity and contempt.

37

One of the elders approached Cobal and guided him away from Talia. 'You have done well, brother Cobal,' he said. 'Now we know she is nothing but a lascivious whore, we need have no fear of her. We know how to deal with her. We must eject her from the village immediately. Two of you, go and fetch the cart and the rod. While we're waiting for the horse to be harnessed, any of you who have never before seen the depths of wickedness to which a lewd woman can descend should inspect this one for yourselves. Touch her womanly parts, and see how she delights in the sinful pleasures of her body. Don't be concerned that she appears to be enjoying herself: her pleasure only proves how sinful she is, and it will be only temporary. We can be assured that her ride from the village will be anything but enjoyable for her.'

The cool leather of the helmet pressed against Barat's face. The rubber sac inside his mouth wasn't inflated, but he was so tense with anticipation that it seemed almost to choke him. Sometimes Madame la Patronne secured his head inside the helmet when she summoned him to serve her, but today he was wearing it to conceal his face. With his body covered from neck to toes by his robe, and the hood pulled over his head, he could not be recognised and, he hoped, he looked menacing and mysterious. He had come to associate wearing the helmet with those sessions in which Madame, sometimes assisted by Kym, would chastise him, and then tease his private parts while he was smarting and helpless. The feelings induced by the helmet, and the knowledge that soon he would watch his mistress's first inspection of Olena, had combined to arouse him: under his robe his right hand was clenched around the rigid staff of his manhood, and he once again gave silent thanks that Madame had agreed to release his genitals from their restraints.

He stood in the shadows at the edge of the drawing-room, a few paces behind Madame's thronelike chair. She was sitting in a pool of light cast by a lamp on the table beside her. He could see her legs, crossed, and the sheen of her stockings; her hands, resting on the arms of the chair;

the dark blue of her silk dress; her profile, as she leant forward, as if listening for the sound of footsteps in the hallway. He wondered whether she was as excited as he was at the prospect of seeing Olena. He knew she was aroused: she had made use of his lips and tongue. The taste of her sex mingled with the tang of rubber in his mouth.

The room was silent, but for the ticking of the art nouveau clock on the mantelpiece and the barely audible strains of a Debussy symphony emanating from the gramophone concealed in a corner cabinet. It was dark outside now, and the heavy velvet curtains covered the long windows. Opposite them embers burnt in the fireplace. Barat could smell only leather and rubber, but he knew that the drawing-room's aroma of woodsmoke and old upholstery would by now be overlaid with Madame's perfume. The room was calm, and dimly lit. Madame did not want anything to alarm her new guest. There would be plenty of time to introduce her to the special rooms, in the basement and on the upper floors, that were usually kept locked.

Facing Madame's chair was a two-seater sofa, on which Olena would be invited to sit, and on which she would later be inspected and, perhaps, given her first whipping in Madame's household. Barat could hardly wait to see Olena's luscious rump bent over and parted, and to hear her sobs of mortification as the stripes appeared on her buttocks and as her sex opened and moistened with each stroke.

He was startled from his reverie by a knock on the door.

'Enter,' Madame called.

Kym, wearing her grey uniform, opened the door, and led Olena into the drawing-room.

Barat gasped and gripped his erection. Even though for two years not a day had passed when he had not thought about Olena, he had forgotten just how startlingly desirable she was. When he had accompanied her to the city, before she had been drawn into the Private House, she had been still in her teenage years. She had had the most sensual body that he had thought possible, with flawless, white-coffee-coloured skin and high, spherical, jutting breasts and buttocks that had seemed exaggeratedly large on her slim frame.

She had developed since then. The flimsy skirt and blouse she was wearing did nothing to conceal the swelling curves beneath. Even her pubic mound was so pronounced that it pressed against the thin material. Barat could see that her pubic hair had been trimmed to a neat line of dark curls. He wondered how often, since he had last seen her body, she had presented her breasts and her bottom to the lash; to how many men and women she had offered her mouth, her sex and her anus for penetration. It was unfair: he should have been enjoying her all that time. Soon, he consoled himself: soon Madame would let him have her.

He was pleased to see that she had not cut any of her long, wavy hair: it still fell in tumultuous cataracts down her back, across her shoulders, and around her wide, strong face. And he was delighted to find that, despite all her experiences in the Private House, she was still demure and shy. Her large, luminous dark eyes were shining with excitement, but they were downcast; on her cheekbones, which were now more noticeable than ever, her skin was blushing dark red. As she stepped timidly across the carpets towards Madame's chair she tried and failed to cover her breasts with her slender arms.

'Olena,' Madame la Patronne said, 'it's a pleasure to have you in my house. Please be seated.' She indicated the sofa in front of her.

'Thank you,' Olena said, and Barat noticed that her voice was steady, and that a smile appeared briefly on her lips as she sat facing Madame. Perhaps she was not, after all, still the naïve and guileless girl that he had known. But the smile faded from her face as she made futile attempts to cover her exposed thigh, and Barat was reassured: she had, after all, been brought up in the same community as he had, and he knew how deeply ingrained her sense of sin and shame must be.

Kym took up a standing position behind the sofa. It occurred to Barat that since Olena had entered the room he had not even glanced at Madame or at Kym. Both were attractive women; both could easily arouse him. But Olena's lush beauty eclipsed them: they might as well not have been there.

'Why have you brought me here, Madame?' Olena said. Her words were direct, but she spoke with her head lowered, glancing shyly towards Madame.

Madame laughed. 'Don't worry, Olena,' she said. 'There's nothing sinister to worry about. I just wanted to meet you, and to get to know you. You have become rather celebrated, you know. People talk about you. And I can see why.'

Olena smiled, but her blush deepened and she tried to shelter her face behind her hair.

'You had my family's emblem,' Olena said.

Madame spread her arms. 'I confess, that was a ruse to extract you from the clutches of the Private House. I used to be associated with that remarkable organisation, my dear, and I know how jealously the Supreme Mistress hoards her treasures. It was the only way I could think of to attract you away. I'm sorry I had to resort to a trick. But I'm not sorry it worked. I had assumed that the reports about you were exaggerations, but I can see now that if anything they did not do justice to you. If your behaviour is as pleasing as your appearance, then I'm sure I'm going to enjoy your visit. And as you've been trained in the Private House, I have no doubt that your behaviour will be impeccable.'

Barat's gaze was fixed on Olena. He saw her look up, with glittering eyes, as Madame spoke. He saw her lips part slightly, and the tip of her tongue appeared between them. He saw that her nipples had become so hard that they were almost pushing through the thin material of her blouse. She knows now, he thought; she must have guessed already, but now there can be no doubt. She realises that she is here to serve, to be tested and enjoyed. He tried to imagine the conflicting urges – trepidation, desire, anticipation, shame – that must have been surging through her mind.

'It won't be very different from the life you're used to in the Private House,' Madame reassured her. 'I'll carry out a preliminary inspection now. Over the next few weeks I'll test your skills and your responsiveness, and I hope I'll be able to teach you a few things that you don't already know. As we proceed we'll assess how much discipline you require.'

Olena leant forward. 'I need a lot, Madame,' she murmured. 'I can't control my sinful feelings. In fact I seem to get worse.'

'I can't believe that of a young woman as beautiful as you,' Madame said. 'I'll punish you, I suppose, if you need it. This gentleman,' she added, turning her face briefly towards Barat, 'will observe your progress. He is seeking a new female slave, and if he approves of you I will let him have you, for at least a time.'

'But I must return to the Private House,' Olena said. 'They will miss me.'

'Everything has been arranged,' Madame replied. 'I have notified the Private House that you are to stay with me for a while. And I very much hope that you enjoy your stay so much that you decide to remain here. I have a wide circle of acquaintances who would love to meet you. But we're getting ahead of ourselves,' she announced. 'The first thing is to inspect you thoroughly. Remove your clothes, Olena.'

While she still had the flimsy material wrapped around her, Olena had succeeded in maintaining her self-possession. Now, as the skirt flutteringly followed the blouse to the floor, she felt the walls of her self-control crumble before the onslaught of her pent-up lasciviousness and wickedness. Her breasts seemed to swell as she glanced up and saw Madame's gaze fixed on them; their tips tingled and sent electric signals deep into her body. She realised with shame that even here, far from the influence of the Mentors of the Private House, she had stood with her feet apart and her bottom pushed back. She could feel the lips of her private place peeling apart. She knew that they were sticky with the moistness that had been trickling down inside her ever since she had been made to remove her robe. Her bottom felt vulnerable, and she could already imagine the lines of stinging pain, the welcome heat and soreness that would do a little – but never enough – to assuage her shame and redeem her sins.

Perhaps, she thought, trying to catch Madame's eye, perhaps if I ask for punishment now, and it's hard and fast enough, perhaps then the wicked feelings will stop. But she knew that it was a futile hope. She knew that her body, with its ceaseless depraved lusts, could be relied on to betray her. Every punishment, from the mildest spanking to the most thorough whipping, served only to inflame her desires and sink her further into the pit of licentiousness. She was no longer surprised by this: nearly every day spent in the Private House entailed some sort of punishment, and she had become a connoisseur of the riding-crop and the tawse. She had soon learnt that being chastised for her wickedness was as stimulating as being ashamed of it, and now she accepted – indeed she welcomed – the waves of pleasure that swept over her when she was being displayed, and toyed with, and punished, and penetrated. But the shame never lessened: the more she abandoned herself to her sinful urges, and the more she enjoyed the pleasures they led her into, the deeper the depths of wickedness and filthiness she discovered within herself. In her home village a girl who revealed the lower part of her leg to a man would rightly be called a slut. Olena knew that there was no word sufficiently vile for what she had become.

The worst of it was that as she stood there, naked, with the eyes of Madame, and Kym, and the masked man on her, her lustful urges were not her only sinful feelings. She couldn't help feeling proud, as well. She knew that most people regarded her body as perfectly formed for sex, and she had become accustomed to the fact that whenever she was in a crowd, hands would clutch at and caress her breasts and buttocks. Women, watching her face while they caned her breasts, and men, gazing into her eyes as they pumped their seed into her mouth, had told her again and again of her beauty. It was said that in the Private House it was possible to trade a year's work on the kitchen rota for half an hour with Olena. The list on which guests and servants could request the use of her had become oversubscribed within minutes of being posted. When the replacement lists – one each for Olena's sex, anus, breasts and mouth – had been almost as quickly filled, the Supreme Mistress had abolished the system and had decreed that Olena would be made available only by lot, or at Olena's own request, or at the Supreme Mistress's discretion. Olena knew that she was special, and that she inspired passion in others. And while she knew that this was yet more evidence of her wickedness, she couldn't help feeling proud.

That alone, she thought, merits a whipping; pride is one of the worst of sins. She had been expecting a punishment that afternoon: two of the male guards had promised to take her down into the dungeons beneath the oldest part of the House, and to use a variety of whips on her bottom. She had agreed with them that if the whipping caused her to become aroused – and all three of them had known that it would – then she would allow them to repeat the punishment and to sodomise her. She had been looking forward to the rendezvous all morning, with a mixture of fevered anticipation and a dreadful, sickening awareness of her depravity. Now she felt acutely deprived of her punishment. Her bottom had received not a single smack all day.

'Breathtaking,' Madame whispered. 'Olena, you are even more desirable than I had been told. Do you enjoy showing your body like this?'

There was no point in denying it. Madame la Patronne clearly knew the methods of the Private House, and she would find out for herself that Olena was aroused. 'Yes, Madame,' Olena breathed. She had never found it easy to confess to her sins, and now that she knew something of the unplumbable depths of her wickedness it was even more difficult to admit how unspeakably dirty she was. 'I know it's wrong. I just can't help it. I deserve to be punished.'

'Later, perhaps,' Madame said. 'Turn around. Bend over a little more.'

Olena obeyed without even thinking of protesting. She had been well trained. But the blush on her cheeks spread across her whole body as she leant forwards, and felt the weight of her breasts as they hung from her ribcage, and felt her bottom lift and open so that Madame could see the parted lips of her sex and the deep funnel of her anus.

'I imagine you're very popular at the House,' Madame commented. 'Turn around again, and face me. Tell me, Olena, are you still intact, as they say, or have you been introduced to the pleasures of penetrative sex?'

Olena couldn't find the words to reply. How could she answer without revealing her sins? 'Yes. Yes, Madame,' she stammered. 'I let others use my body for their pleasure. And mine,' she confessed. 'Often,' she added, in a whisper.

'Do you let them penetrate your arsehole?' Madame asked, clearly relishing the coarse language, and smiling when she saw that it made Olena start with embarrassment.

'Yes, Madame,' Olena replied quickly. 'I prefer –' She stopped as she realised what she had been about to say. 'I find the sensations more intense,' she said. She looked towards the masked man. He hadn't spoken, or even moved, since she had entered the room. She was sure that he was Barat, and the fact that she had deduced his identity, when it was clear that he didn't want her to recognise him, had given her another thrill of sinful pride. She wondered what he was thinking about the transformation that she had undergone since she had been an innocent college girl and he had been her guardian. No doubt he desired her: most people did.

'I'd better have a closer look at you,' Madame said, rising from her chair. She was shorter than Olena, but imposing in her dark-blue dress and striking make-up. 'Kneel on the seat of the sofa, my dear, and present your bottom.'

In the relatively short time since she had discovered and had begun to enjoy exploring her taste for the more esoteric byways of sexuality, Talia had become quite accustomed to being held in restraints. This was, however, the first time that she had been placed in a set of stocks. Her neck and wrists were held in a line in three holes that had been carved, three semicircles in each, in two wooden planks whose ends were bound together by ropes. The two outer holes were small, and she could hardly move her hands at all; the middle hole was larger, and padded with leather, so that she could lift and lower her head, and even move it from side to side, with ease. All in all, she reflected, being held in stocks wasn't quite as uncomfortable as she had feared. But she was, nonetheless, entirely unable to free herself.

During her courses of training at the Private House, Talia had also become used to being put on display: she had quickly discovered that having an audience, whether for punishment, or pleasure, or both, intensified her feelings of excitement. She had never previously, however, been used as a mobile exhibition. Being driven through and out of the village on the back of a cart was, she decided, rather like being on a float in a carnival.

The spectators were not in a carnival mood. She had been able to see, while the elders prepared her in the cart at one end of the village's only street, that all the inhabitants of the cottages had lined the street, and that men and women were tramping in from the surrounding fields to join them. It was clear that the entire population of the settlement – men, women and children – had been summoned to watch her being expelled from their community. The faces she had been able to glimpse were hard with disapproval.

The elders had made ingenious arrangements to ensure that none of the spectators would be put at risk of seeing Talia's dangerously unclothed body. Only her head and hands were visible, protruding at the back of the cart through a tightly tied gap in the canvas sheets. A larger expanse of canvas was stretched over great hoops of bent wood, creating a high tunnel that covered the entire cart.

Only Talia and two of the most senior of the elders knew what the cart contained. Piled at the back of the cart was a mound of fleeces, across which Talia's body was stretched. Ropes around her ankles which were pulled tight to the sides of the cart kept her legs widely parted, and others, stretching from her knees to the cart's tailboard, ensured that her bottom was held open and uplifted. Her short skirt had ridden up to her waist, and her bodice was still unfastened. Her travelling-bag had been thrown into the cart beside her. Also in the cart, in the dim light under the taut canvas, were the two elders who had secured her, and a long, slender, wooden switch.

Talia wondered whether the villagers would know that she was being whipped as she was driven past them. The elders had hastily written a sign, which they had hung above her head from the rear of the roof of the cart. Talia felt that she should perhaps be grateful that she couldn't crane her neck far enough to read what the elders had written about her.

The wait at the end of the street seemed endless. At first there had been a long debate among the elders about which of them should travel in the cart – the private, enclosed space containing nothing but Talia's exposed and bound body – and administer the punishment. The only one of them who could be sure of remaining uncontaminated by looking on her body was Cobal, because he was blind; however, this same disability, it was pointed out, would prevent him from applying the rod with any accuracy. Then it was proposed that one of the elders who had bound Talia in the cart should be given the task of punishing her, as he had already been obliged to see her private parts. There was no reason, many of the elders said, to expose any more of their number to the sinful pollution that Talia embodied. But there was an objection: what if, in the seclusion of the covered cart, the chosen elder were to succumb to Talia's evil influence. He might begin to think unnatural thoughts; he might even be tempted to touch her. Two elders – the two who had tied Talia's ankles and knees – could be relied on to chaperone each other.

Once this decision was taken, however, it was necessary to delay the start of the drive until all of the farm workers

47

and woodsmen had returned to their families. At last, Talia heard one of the elders shout an instruction; she felt a jolt as the horse stepped forward, and the wheels began to turn slowly.

The whipping began immediately. The first Talia knew of it was a streak of fiery pain down the inner slope of her right buttock. She gasped, and although she knew it was futile she involuntarily tried to clench her muscles and move her legs together. There was nothing she could do to protect herself.

Suddenly she felt vulnerable. With her head held outside the cart's canvas covering she could hear the rumble of the wheels, the clop of the horse's hooves, the murmuring of the crowd – but nothing from inside the cart. She had no way of knowing when the next stroke of the rod was about to descend on her opened bottom.

The elder wielding the rod, with no room in the cart to stand beside her, must, she realised, have positioned himself behind her, between her widely parted ankles, so that the strokes he applied would fall vertically. It soon became clear that he was in fact aiming for the sensitive valley between Talia's parted buttocks. His aim was not always true, because the trundling cart jolted from side to side on the rutted track: soon both of Talia's slim buttocks, the delicate skin around her anus, her perineum and the folds of her sex were blazing with hot pain. Talia found that she could not suppress the little cries and gasps that rose in her throat with each lash and, as she tossed her head from side to side, making her long titian tresses swing behind the cart, she realised that the villagers lining the street must have been aware that she was being punished. Some of her louder cries were met with answering shouts of pious approval from the villagers nearest to her.

Even in these trying circumstances Talia found that, as usual, being tied up and punished was making her feel very aroused. Her breasts, pressed into the scratchy softness of the fleeces, had tips as hard as nuts. She felt her sex, still moist and warm from the elders' inspection, become wetter and more open. Now, instead of trying to clench her

48

buttocks together and close her legs, she couldn't resist lifting her bottom so that more of the strokes could land on or near the delicate membranes of her sex.

Halfway along the street the cart slowed and then stopped. The villagers stepped forward from their cottages and crowded at the rear of the cart. The whipping stopped, too, and for a moment Talia and the villagers simply gazed at each other. But the respite was not long.

Now that the cart had stopped moving, Talia was given notice, in the form of the hiss of the rod as it swished through the air, of the first stroke of her continuing punishment. She held her body rigid, and lifted her head in readiness.

Now the elder using the rod was able to aim every stroke. And, as he no longer had to worry about keeping his balance in the swaying cart, he was able to put more strength into his work. The rod fell harder and faster, until Talia could hardly draw breath between her cries, yelps and drawn-out wails.

Even the Mentors in the Private House had not whipped her this hard. And although Anne liked to torment her lover's most intimate parts, most of the mutual punishment she and Talia enjoyed was relatively gentle spanking. Talia had not been whipped this mercilessly since she had escaped the clutches of the Whipmaker. She became entirely lost in the sensations of pain and arousal, both carrying her upwards, away from the everyday world, through the clouds and into the clear, harsh light where there was nothing but the feelings in her nerves and the abrupt summit from which she would fly when she had climbed to the point of orgasm.

In a brief moment of clarity she realised that the elders wouldn't even touch her once they had driven her to the edge of the village. And, tied as she was, she couldn't adjust her position so that the rod would fall near her clitoris. Her frustration grew as the whipping took her closer towards the brink of an orgasm. As soon as I'm free, she promised herself, I'll find somewhere private and I'll make myself come. I'll clip Anne's keepsake to my sex lips,

I'll put two fingers into my poor, sore anus, and then just a touch will be enough.

The anticipation of a climax only increased the level of Talia's arousal, and when the whipping stopped she was at first too distracted to notice. When she felt the waves of her lust begin to ebb, she groaned and slumped in her bonds. As the cart began moving forwards again, more rapidly now, towards the end of the street, she realised that two pairs of hands were exploring the tender flesh that had been stung by the rod. Some of the children followed the cart, and threw handfuls of dirt at Talia's head.

Talia shook her hair, and hoped that the dust and muck would be easy to clean off. Basically, though, she felt satisfied. The cruel whipping had prepared her for a spectacular climax, which she intended to enjoy as soon as she was released from the cart. In her travelling-bag she had the address of Barat, the man who had taken the emblem that had seduced Olena from the Private House. Talia thought that her detective work was going well.

Does Barat realise, Kym wondered, what an idiot he looks in that helmet and that robe? She'd been trying not to look at him, in case she couldn't stifle a fit of the giggles. Madame wouldn't like that: she was particular about her servants maintaining the decorum of her household. So if Kym did utter a spluttering laugh, she knew she could expect a titty spanking, at the least.

Mind you, Kym thought, that wouldn't be so awful. It always makes me feel sexy when her ladyship does my tits. And almost anything would be more fun than this: standing about while Madame pokes and prods her new toy, and trying not to look at Barat.

The new girl, Olena, had been kneeling on the sofa for a while now. She wasn't really Kym's type – too curvy and dark – but Kym grudgingly admitted to herself that Olena had a stunningly lush body and a beautiful face. As for Olena's personality, Kym couldn't fathom it. Olena acted as though butter wouldn't melt in her mouth. Kym had never met anyone so naïve and strait-laced. As soon as she had met Olena she had dismissed Barat's wild stories about Olena being the hottest, most sex-hungry she-devil he'd ever encountered.

Even now, having been stripped and made to display herself for Madame, Olena was sobbing with embarrassment, blushing with shame, protesting her innocence, and pleading to be punished for her wickedness. The trouble was – as Madame's explorations had revealed – it was clear that Olena was enjoying every moment of her shameful exhibition and every touch of Madame's clever fingers. The smell of female sex was filling the room. Kym felt the unmistakable little thrills of her own arousal, deep in her belly, and a warm, sinking sensation that told her she was getting wet in her cunt. She hoped Madame would instruct her to assist when the time came, as it inevitably would, to give Olena a spanking.

Kym realised that she had stopped feeling resentful of the newcomer, even though it was obvious that Madame was besotted with her. Kym tried to analyse her emotions. Usually she felt resentful about everyone and everything. It was an attitude she had nurtured during her teenage years, and she was sure she'd pretty well perfected it. Cynicism and self-concern had protected her during the years she'd spent in schools that couldn't handle her and then when she'd been living rough. It had been a long time since she'd let anyone get to her, but there was something about Olena that prevented Kym from disliking her.

I must be going soft, Kym told herself. I mean, Olena's utterly gorgeous. I ought to be madly jealous. And it's obvious she'll be Madame's favourite. Her ladyship can't keep her hands off. But Olena just looks so beautiful – even more so when she's getting worked up. I have to admit I wouldn't mind having her all to myself. Look at her swivelling her hips! She's covered Madame's hands with her juices.

Surreptitiously Kym allowed her right hand to stray along the hem of her skirt, and then under it. The tips of her fingers brushed the smooth mound of her sex, and then pressed at the top of her slit. She glanced at Barat. His eyes, glittering in the eyeholes of the helmet, were fixed on Olena. Kym pressed again, and shivered with pleasure. Madame would punish her if she saw her playing with herself. But Madame, too, was preoccupied with Olena. Kym caressed herself and watched with a contented smile as her employer, kneeling beside Olena on the sofa, continued to probe Olena's cunt and arsehole with her fingers.

Three

Olena woke to the sound of sparrows twittering outside the window above her bed. Grey light seeped around the edges of the heavy curtains. The room, with its high ceiling and heavy furniture, was already familiar; the towers and corridors, the parkland and the Gothic pavilions of the Private House seemed distant in her memory.

She knew that it was early, but she would not be able to sleep again. She was restless, and beset with a hazy sense of anxiety. Then she moved her right hand, and felt a pulse of pleasure when her fingertips brushed against the damp warmth of her private place. With a guilty gasp she pulled her hand away. She was not to touch herself there – not without being given permission, and not until after a punishment.

Now she understood the reason she was feeling troubled. She had not been given so much as a light spanking during the whole of the previous day.

It had been a long time since she had endured twenty-four hours without any punishment. Very occasionally, when she had displeased her Mentors, the Supreme Mistress had decreed that she was to remain untouched for a day. Once, the isolation had been extended to two days. It had been explained to her that sometimes she needed to be reminded that the cauldron of unspeakably vile desires that simmered inside her was prevented from bubbling over only by regular chastisement. And if Olena did sometimes forget, amid the pleasures of the House, that she was utterly wicked, a day without spanking made her acutely aware of it. As the hours without discipline crawled by, her thoughts turned to memories and fantasies of increasingly depraved acts. No amount of solitude, or company, or exercise, or quiet contemplation, could prevent her sliding into the corrupt pit of her lascivious imagination.

Punishments, no matter how severe, could not cleanse her. She knew that from bitter experience. The pleasure she took in her humiliations and sufferings, and in being penetrated, and in the glorious climaxes with which she was usually allowed to finish her chastisements, was irrefutable evidence that her sinfulness was ingrained. At least the regular application of corporal discipline, the ritual of being displayed, whipped, and pleasured, seemed to keep her licentiousness under control. And it was all so completely, sinfully, deliciously enjoyable.

Once again she had to check the straying of her hand towards her sex. She told herself that she had only a few hours more to endure. Madame had hinted that Olena's evident arousal during the previous evening's inspection was enough to merit a minor punishment; Olena vowed to do everything she could to convince Madame that she deserved more. But even a mere spanking would calm her. She curled on her side under the quilted covers, hugging her warm, sensitive breasts, as she anticipated the ignominy of being made to undress before the mistress of the house, probably with Kym in attendance. She put a hand behind her back and caressed the firm, soft globes that soon might feel the warming sting of Madame's hand, at least, if not a strap or a lash.

Somewhere in the back of her mind she remembered that she should be trying to think of a way to escape from Madame's tall, silent, dark-shadowed lair, or at least to send a message to the House. Later, she promised herself: later, after I've proved to Madame that I'm irredeemably wicked, and after she's punished me and made me beg to be allowed to have a climax, then I'll be able to concentrate on getting away.

In any case, she thought, the House will send someone to find me. I only have to wait.

* * *

It was only as Talia counted out the money on to the counter at the reception desk that she realised that her one night's stay in the hotel had used up almost all of the allowance that Julia had given her.

'This is rather more expensive than I had expected,' she said to the uniformed clerk, and placed her finger firmly on the bill that he had presented to her.

The clerk, a young man whose manner of supercilious boredom was so practised that he was unmoved even by the appearance before him early in the morning of a young woman with tumbling tresses of dark-red hair, lustrous eyes, and a slender body barely covered by a leather tunic and short leather skirt. He raised an eyebrow. 'This is a five-star hotel, miss. Conveniently located in the centre of the city.'

'I haven't been to the city before,' Talia said, shrugging as if to say that she didn't care very much for it. But she knew that she should have been more careful with the funds that had been allocated to her. She should have realised the previous evening, when the porter threw open the door of her room to reveal a four-poster bed, and a bathroom with a vast, sunken bath, that the hotel would prove to be expensive. But the sight of the bath and the soft luxury of the furnishings had driven from her mind everything but the prospect of pulling off her clothes and soaking her aching limbs and her sore bottom.

Well, there was no point in arguing. She had stayed in the room, she had eaten dinner in the lamp-lit dining room and, although she could scarcely believe its price on the bill, she had drunk most of the bottle of red wine that she had ordered. She could hardly refuse to pay for everything now. She pushed a sheaf of banknotes across the counter. She had only a few coins left.

The clerk picked up the money and riffled through it. 'Thank you, miss,' he said. He coughed discreetly. 'Service is not included.'

Talia stared at him. 'Oh,' she said. 'Of course.' She emptied her purse on to the counter. 'I'm afraid that's all I have. Do you think I could look at a map of the city before I leave?'

The clerk sniffed, collected the scattered coins, reached under the counter, withdrew a road map, and then turned away. But he kept glancing at Talia as if he was concerned that she might make off with the map.

It took Talia only a few moments to find on the map the street named on the slip of paper she had been given by Olena's mother. Getting there, though, would be a problem. She had underestimated the size of the city. She had made for the centre, the commercial heart of the metropolis, and she had assumed that from there she would be able to walk to almost any address in the city. But the street she had to find was, according to the map, hardly in the city at all: it was a narrow thoroughfare leading from the main street of a suburb, so far from the centre that the map indicated fields and parkland nearby. It was too far to walk, and in any case Talia knew that she would never be able to find the street without a map; thanks to her extravagance, she had no money with which to buy one. She couldn't afford a train or a taxicab, either. She didn't even have a few coins for a ride on a public omnibus.

She sighed, and picked up her travelling bag. She noticed that the porter, who had been so keen to assist her when she had arrived, was nowhere to be seen now that she had run out of money.

Mistress Julia had given her a list of the names and addresses of all of the agents of the Private House who were living in the city. The sensible thing, Talia knew, would be to find the nearest one. She would receive whatever funds and assistance she required. But she was determined to find Olena all by herself. To seek help would be an admission of defeat. And she hadn't failed yet.

In fact, as she strode across the expanse of green carpet between the reception desk and the gleaming doors of the hotel, she felt confident. She was alone in the city, on an exciting mission of rescue. The sumptuous hotel room and the excellent dinner she had eaten had been expensive, but they had refreshed and fortified her.

As she looked from side to side she saw that although few of the hotel's guests were up at this early hour, every one of them, dressed in conservative, restrained suits, glanced more or less surreptitiously at her as she walked past. She tossed her head, drawing attention to her glorious titian curls, and smiled.

They admire me, she thought, but not one of them knows that my sex is naked under my skirt. None of them could guess that my bottom is still tingling and marked with fading lines from the whipping I took yesterday.

She had brought herself to a climax three times since the village elders had released her from the stocks and told her never to return to their community. As soon as she was alone she had found an isolated spot, just off the track that led from the village, and she had pulled up her skirt and squatted in the shade of a copse of low trees. Her bladder had been full, and she had been wanting to pee for some time. But she had held it in, and had enjoyed caressing her throbbing buttocks, and touching the sore, raised lines left by the rod. At last, with a long sigh of contentment, she had released the pent-up stream of urine. The release had felt almost as good as an orgasm. But she had wanted more, and while the jet of fluid was still hissing on to the bed of fallen leaves the fingers of her right hand had begun to press at the apex of her slit while her left hand had burrowed into the sopping-wet opening of her sex. The whipping alone had brought her near to the brink of a climax, and the pressure of her fingers had been enough to propel her over the edge. A vision of Anne's face had appeared briefly before her, but she had been so swept up in the whirlwind of sensations that she had been able to think coherently about nothing. She had fallen forward on to her knees and had come, her body shaking in starts and her voice uttering raucous cries, even before the last drops of urine had fallen from her urethra.

Later she had played with herself in a leisurely way, stroking her breasts and touching her sex and her anus, while she lazed in the vast bath in her hotel suite. She had managed to delay the moment of climax until she was standing under the shower, rubbing a bar of the hotel's soap between the lips of her sex and with the jet of warm water playing over the hood of her clitoris.

Finally, she had masturbated again that morning, before dressing. She had been feeling a little guilty that she hadn't been thinking of Anne as often as she should, so she had set out to have an orgasm while thinking only of her pretty lover. She had arranged the mirrors in the room around the bed; she had clipped the lock of Anne's blonde hair to her sex; she had positioned herself on all fours on the bed, so that she could watch her reflection. Then, using the belt that she had last used to smack Anne's perfect breasts, she had whipped her bottom lightly, to make her buttocks blush and to bring out the colour of the few stripes that remained from the previous day's whipping. She had imagined that Anne was watching her – that she was performing according to Anne's instructions – and she had soon become very aroused. She had almost come while she pushed the handle of her hairbrush inside her, first into her vagina and then into her anus, and she had remained on the bed, with her face pushed into the covers and her bottom, still holding the brush, raised for Anne's imaginary inspection, while her trembling fingers had plucked at her sex and her clitoris. She had gasped, 'Anne, I love you,' over and over again as the tremors of her climax shook her. When she had recovered she had found that her cheeks were wet with tears, even though she didn't feel at all sad. She had then kept the hairbrush handle inside her bottom for as long as she could, while she completed her preparations for departure, because it reminded her of the games that she and Anne liked to play.

Talia guessed that not one of the hotel guests had had as many as three orgasms since the previous day. She felt very pleased with herself, and very definitely damp between her thighs, as she pushed through the tall doors and marched into the city streets.

Naked, and with his arms and torso bound inside the rough linen of a straitjacket, Barat was struggling for breath in his mistress's bed. He had slept, fitfully, on the floor, wearing the straitjacket all through the night. Madame had woken him with a kick and, before he had

had time to gather his thoughts, she had ordered him to clamber under the sheet. Blinking the sleep from his eyes he had found, once he had scrambled awkwardly on to the bed, that Madame had parted and lifted her legs, ready for him to begin serving her with his mouth. Now, under the dimly lit tent of the lifted sheet, Madame's soft, scented thighs were pressed against his head, and his nose and mouth were embedded in the yielding, moistening folds of her sex.

'Lick me!' he heard Madame cry. He felt her hands pressing on the top of his head. 'Better than that, Barat. What's the matter with you this morning?'

The matter, Barat thought as he gasped for air while extending his tongue, is that I'm not ready. I'm still half asleep. It isn't fair to expect me to perform without any warning at all.

Barat, restless in his bondage, had been dozing, and daydreaming about Olena. He knew that she was to be punished that morning, and he was sure that Madame would allow him to watch. The thought was almost too exciting to bear, and although he needed to relieve his bladder his penis was upright and painfully hard.

Madame's legs released their lock on his head. Her hands pushed him away from her sex. 'Stop, Barat,' she instructed him. 'You're bristly, you're incompetent, and I don't believe you're trying. Get off the bed and stand beside me.'

Barat cursed as he made his ungainly progress off the bed. She was displeased. He would have to submit gracefully to whatever punishment she imposed, or she might bar him from watching Olena. And he would put up with almost anything to see Olena being disciplined. He stood at the side of the bed, and willed his erection to subside before Madame noticed it.

'What's this, Barat?' Madame said. Her painted finger-nails reached under the hem of the front of the straitjacket. He gasped and wriggled as she found his rigid stem. She pinched the skin of the pulsing shaft.

He should have known that he couldn't hide his arousal. Madame la Patronne seemed to have a sixth sense that could detect the slightest hint of sexual interest. He wished, not for the first time, that he could have found himself a mistress who was less physically attractive than Madame. He couldn't prevent his body responding to her, even though he told himself, against all the evidence, that it wasn't in his nature to enjoy submitting to a woman.

Madame, wearing only a short black negligee that barely covered her breasts, was lounging on the bed and leaning towards him, her dark eyes glittering with mischief as she toyed with Barat's erection. It was hardly surprising that he was aroused. If only he wasn't trussed up in this jacket! Then he'd jump on to the bed beside her and make her submit to him. He'd show her what he could do to please her.

But even as he struggled against his bonds he knew that he had no choice but to submit to her. She was the mistress of the house, and she had Olena. And he would put up with any indignity in order to possess the beautiful girl he had desired since he had watched her growing up in their village. The trouble was that Madame knew how much he wanted Olena, and he had no doubt that she would use that knowledge to extract from him ever more extreme expressions of his servility to her.

'What's the matter, Barat?' Madame repeated, squeezing his shaft. 'You're not being a good boy this morning. I don't like it when your mind wanders from the tasks I set you. Are you thinking of someone else? The lovely Olena, perhaps?'

'No, Madame,' Barat lied quickly.

Madame laughed, and moved her hand down to cradle his testicles. 'You know you'll have her only if you're completely willing and obedient, Barat.'

He felt trapped and vulnerable. He wished that his balls would contract and that his erection would subside, but he remained resolutely aroused. 'I'm utterly devoted to you, Madame,' he said.

'See that you stay devoted,' she said, with a hint of steel in her voice. Then she was playful again. 'I'm glad I didn't have you shaved, after all, Barat,' she said, tugging at the wiry hairs of his scrotum. 'It means I can punish you like this.'

She pulled harder, and Barat gasped with pain as she plucked a few hairs from the sac. 'Remain silent,' she told him, and proceeded to grasp and pluck out another bunch of hairs, and then another. Barat gritted his teeth. The pain was excruciating, and he felt hot tears gathering in the corners of his eyes. But still his penis remained upright, and harder than ever.

'You see?' Madame said, running a fingernail up the underside of his shaft. 'You do like it when I teach you how to behave.' She withdrew her hand from underneath the jacket, and Barat breathed a sigh of relief – which was stopped in his mouth when he saw her reach for the bell-rope above the bed. He heard the bell ring, distantly, on the landing.

Madame had rung for a servant and, as he was already with her, that could only mean that she intended to summon Kym. Barat could bear to be humiliated when he was alone with his mistress: she treated him despicably, and she usually made sure that his submission to her was degrading and uncomfortable, and often painful. But when they were alone together, and there was no one else to witness his shame, he found that serving her was inexplicably exciting and strangely satisfying.

But he hated it when Kym was present. The young woman took full advantage of the opportunities Madame allowed her to be insolent to him, and to play up to Madame. In the few weeks since Kym had joined the household Barat had tried every trick he could devise to get Kym into trouble with Madame, in the hope that Kym would be severely punished. He hoped to be able to watch or, even better, to assist Madame in chastising the surly girl. But his plans always went awry, and although he knew, from Kym's frequent complaints, that Madame sometimes disciplined her, he had not witnessed Kym receiving anything more than a few smacks.

The situation would have been more bearable if Kym had responded with any interest at all to Barat's advances.

He couldn't understand why she didn't want to while away the little spare time they had together with some sexual games. He was young, and reasonably fit, and not ugly. Madame, after all, liked to make use of his body. What was wrong with the girl?

There was a knock at the door. It flew open, and Kym rushed in. Barat was surprised, and relieved, to see that she was not dressed in her uniform. She was wearing a short cotton nightdress, and her spiky hair was even more unruly than usual. Perhaps this time Madame would punish her.

'I'm sorry, Madame,' Kym said. 'I overslept. And I thought that Barat was attending you this morning.' She threw a venomous glance in his direction.

'He is, as you can see,' Madame said, and she lifted the hem of the straitjacket so that Kym could see Barat's erection. Barat closed his eyes with mortification as he saw Kym's grin.

'But that's no excuse for lazing in bed,' Madame continued. 'Come here and expose your left breast.'

Kym scowled, but she slouched to the side of the bed and pulled down one of the shoulders of her nightdress until one breast, looking pale and vulnerable, was revealed.

Madame turned away from Barat to face Kym. She knelt on the covers and reached to fondle Kym's breast. Her negligee had ridden up almost to her waist, and Barat was given a view of her round buttocks and the valley between them. Madame rarely allowed him to penetrate her, and he had never been permitted to so much as finger her anus, although he was often required to kiss and lick it. She had occasionally hinted that access to her most intimate orifice would be his reward for being particularly obedient, but he was beginning to think that she would never consider him sufficiently servile. He was sure that her display this morning was not accidental: it was intended to provoke him.

'Hands behind your back,' Madame told Kym, 'and lean towards me.'

Kym tutted with exasperation as she positioned herself. Barat had noticed that the young woman liked to make a show of independence, even when she was performing as instructed. She glared at Barat over Madame's shoulder, and stuck out her tongue at him.

'Keep still,' Madame said, as she lifted her right arm. Her hand slapped down on to Kym's exposed breast, and she knelt back to watch the pendant hemisphere jiggle and blush.

Barat wished that he could touch himself. His erection was iron-hard. It was almost worth the humiliation of having Kym present while he served Madame to be able to watch her spanking Kym's titty. The expression on Kym's face interested him. Her eyes and mouth were almost closed, and she had thrown back her head. If Barat had not heard her state, frequently and vehemently, that she had no interest in the games of dominance and submission that Madame liked to play, he would have been sure that she was enjoying the punishment.

Madame leant forward and delivered another five smacks in quick succession, making Kym's breast bounce and redden. 'That will do,' she said. 'For now. I hope you'll remember in future that I expect you to be ready to attend me at any time.'

'Yes, Madame,' Kym said. 'Thank you, Madame.' Once again she caught Barat's eye, and smiled nastily at him. She had escaped with a minor spanking, and she guessed that she was about to watch Barat being especially servile.

'Fetch a small cane,' Madame told her, 'and stand at the foot of the bed.' She rolled towards the centre of the bed and propped herself against the pillows with her legs parted. She beckoned to Barat. 'Now get back on the bed and lick me properly. Kym will encourage you with the cane. I said the small one, Kym, but it doesn't matter. That one will do. Don't stop, Barat, until I give you permission. Then you can help me take my bath. If you're not good I'll keep you in that jacket all day.'

'I'll be good, Madame,' Barat said. He would have to be. If he was made to wear the straitjacket under his robe he would be insufferably hot. More importantly, he wouldn't be able to touch himself while he was watching Olena being punished.

* * *

63

Kym was still smiling as she carried the tray and the bag up the stairs towards the new girl's room. It was worth getting a sore tit, she said to herself, just for the pleasure of watching Barat being put through his paces. The way Madame bossed him about was wonderful. Although the fact that she obviously liked playing with his cock and balls was a bit disgusting: Kym didn't much like men, and she thought male genitals were particularly repellent. Still, it had been fun watching his erection bob about while she had whipped his arse and he had tried to concentrate on licking out Madame's cunt.

Having her tit smacked hadn't been too awful, either. It was a mystery to Kym why she liked the little punishments that Madame handed out. It wasn't surprising that she liked being alone with Madame, and playing with her in bed: Kym had long known that she liked women, and although Madame wasn't of the type Kym usually went for, she was attractive and very skilful. But in the past Kym had found that she preferred to take the lead: she had always played the seductress rather than the seduced. And, although her experience was more limited than she liked to admit, she had introduced a few shy, skinny, waiflike girls to the pleasures of lesbian love.

So Kym was surprised to find that she didn't mind, as much as she had expected to, working for a female boss. And she quite liked being told what to do in bed. She had never really thought about games of tying-up and spanking, but her body responded to Madame's little punishments, and her imagination had begun to invent other, more interesting scenarios. Whacking Barat was amusing, but it wasn't stimulating in the way that made her feel hot between her legs. But she had imagined turning the tables on Madame, and ordering her about, and that fantasy had proved very exciting. Last night she had found herself wondering what it would be like to spank the new girl, Olena. That was weird, because Olena was just another of Madame's servants, Kym supposed, and Kym's potential rival in the household.

Kym stopped at the top of the stairs to gather her breath. She knocked once on the door and immediately opened it. Olena, naked, was at the window, standing on tiptoe to look out. She turned, and her mouth formed an O of surprise. Kym noticed that she tried to cover her breasts with her arms.

Kym kicked the door shut with her heel. 'Breakfast,' she said, lifting the tray, 'and clothes.' She swung the bag.

Olena didn't move from the window. She seemed reluctant to let Kym see any more of her body. Kym didn't see why she should be the one to break the awkward silence, so she stared at Olena and waited. It was an opportunity to let Olena know that Kym was not to be trifled with. And therefore, as Olena was obviously ashamed of showing off her body, Kym made no attempt to hide the fact that she was studying it.

I suppose, she thought, that Olena has the kind of looks that men can't resist. But then she had to admit to herself that anyone, of either sex and of almost any sexual persuasion, could hardly fail to find Olena attractive. She was slim and well proportioned, so that although she wasn't tall, her legs appeared long and her waist narrow. Her skin, the colour of milky coffee, was without a blemish. She had long, wild, wavy locks of shiny dark hair. And although her face was too wide to be pretty, with pronounced cheekbones and a broad, full mouth, it was so strong that it was beautiful. And so Kym had to conclude that Olena was more than ordinarily attractive – even before you took into account her remarkable breasts and bottom.

Kym had always reckoned herself to be shapely, but next to Olena she felt underdeveloped. Olena seemed to be made of swelling, gravity-defying curves of flesh. Her breasts – perfectly smooth spheres – jostled for space high on her ribcage, and were so large that they appeared like half-moons on either side of her narrow back when she lifted her arms. When, as now, she tried to conceal them, she had to hold her arms far out in front of her chest to try to encompass them. Kym had seen arses as big as Olena's only swaying behind the portly, dark-skinned women who lived in the south of the city. But Olena wasn't remotely portly, and her buttocks were as high, firm and round as an athlete's.

'There's no point trying to cover yourself,' Kym said. 'I saw everything yesterday, anyway.'

'Yes,' Olena whispered. 'I remember.' She lowered her eyes and her cheeks flushed.

I suppose it's what you'd call ironic, Kym thought, that she's got such a perfect body and she's ashamed to show it.

Kym placed the tray on a table, gestured towards it and, still holding the bag, brushed past Olena to stand at the window. She wasn't Olena's servant, and she didn't care whether Olena ate breakfast or not. When she glanced over her shoulder she saw that Olena was steadily eating her way through everything on the tray.

'The condemned girl ate a hearty breakfast,' she said. 'The thought of being punished obviously hasn't hurt your appetite.' She swore under her breath. She wasn't supposed to let Olena know that she was in for a spanking.

Olena looked worried, and blushed again. She put down the bread roll she was holding. 'You're right,' she said. 'I'm being greedy. I do try not to surrender to my lusts.'

'It doesn't bother me,' Kym said. 'Eat as much as you want. But if you're finished, you're to bathe, put on your make-up, and get dressed. Do you want me to help?'

Kym noticed that the blush on Olena's cheeks deepened, and the large, light-brown circles around her dark nipples began to crinkle and harden. Perhaps the thought of being helped in the bathroom had excited her.

'No, thank you,' Olena said. 'But,' she added, softly, 'perhaps you should watch me. It's very tempting,' she went on, forcing herself to confess, 'when I'm in the bath. I almost can't help touching myself.'

'Come on, then. Let's get you washed and spruced up.'

Bathed, dusted with talcum, perfumed, brushed, and with a few delicate touches of make-up, Olena was a vision of flustered loveliness. Kym had found it impossible not to assist, and had helped Olena with soap, towels, and with the dusting-pad. She now knew that Olena's skin was as silkily soft as it was flawless, and that she trembled every time she was touched. A brushing of Kym's fingers along the side of one of Olena's breasts was enough to make Olena gasp and shiver.

'You're incredibly responsive,' Kym had remarked, touching Olena again and watching her reactions.

'I know,' Olena had replied sadly. 'I'm very, very wicked. I can't help it.'

Kym didn't know what to make of Olena, but she understood why Barat was so obsessed with her, and why Madame was so keen to keep her. 'You're to wear these,' she said, emptying the contents of the bag on to the bed.

Olena uttered a long 'Oh' of surprise and recognition. She picked up an item from the pile of clothes: a collar, made of white leather, with metal rings set into its circumference. Her eyes shone with excitement. 'It's a slave collar,' she told Kym. 'I often wear one at the House.' She sighed with pleasure as she buckled it round her neck. 'I hope Madame lets me keep it.'

There were matching cuffs to go around Olena's wrists, but the remaining garments were less unusual. There was a crisp, white blouse, a short, pleated skirt, white ankle-socks, and sturdy sandals – which, Olena pointed out, were furnished with metal rings behind the heel so that her feet could be tethered.

Kym and Olena stood together in front of a mirror and studied their reflection. Olena's costume was perhaps a little less revealing than Kym's grey uniform. 'I suppose the idea is that you look like a naughty girl,' Kym said.

'I am,' Olena said.

Kym's hand went to the buttoned flap covering the breast that Madame had spanked. 'I know how Madame deals with naughty girls,' she said, and she held her breath with excitement as she dared to let her hand fall to her side and then steal under the hem of Olena's skirt. She watched Olena's face in the mirror as she let the tips of her fingers touch Olena's bottom. She saw Olena's eyes widen and her lips part, and she felt her tremble.

'What a lovely arse,' Kym said, caressing the silk-smooth spheres. It's going to be so sore, she thought, and she realised that the idea excited her.

Olena uttered a little cry, and Kym saw that her eyes were closed. Olena's body was shivering continuously as Kym stroked her. Kym was aware that she was herself becoming aroused, but Olena seemed to be almost ready to come. Kym let her fingers slip down the deep valley between the lower slopes of Olena's buttocks, and then into the gap at the top of her thighs. 'Bloody hell, Olena,' she whispered. 'You're sopping.'

'I know,' Olena murmured. 'I can't help it. I'm sinful and perverted.'

Kym remembered that Madame had told her that under no circumstances was Olena to be allowed to have an orgasm. She reluctantly withdrew her hand. 'I'm not supposed to touch you like that,' she said. 'Sorry. It's just that you're rather irresistible.'

Olena nodded. 'It's my fault,' she said. 'I need to be punished.' She turned to face Kym. There were tears in her eyes. 'Please?'

'We'll see,' Kym said. 'I really don't know what Madame has planned for you,' she went on, not entirely truthfully. 'Let's find out, shall we?'

As soon as Talia was outside the hotel her confidence began to falter. The wide road in front of her was an angry river of vehicles, and the pavement on which she stood, looking from right to left, was no less crowded. She took a few steps in what she thought was the correct direction, and was jostled and cursed by impatient pedestrians. She was suddenly aware of the skimpiness of her clothing. Passers-by stared, and young men shouted comments about her. She thought of pulling her coat from her travelling-bag, but to do so she would have to bend down, thus revealing her naked bottom. In any case the morning was becoming warm, and she would be too hot in her coat.

She made up her mind to walk to a quieter street. And, she decided, it made sense to set off towards the district which contained the street she sought, even though the distance was too great for her to manage on foot. But she realised that she was already disoriented: she didn't know whether to turn right or left. She tried to remember the details of the map she had seen in the hotel, and to ignore the crowds sweeping around her.

'Taxi!' The repetitive cry eventually impinged on Talia's consciousness. 'Oi, darling. You want a taxi?'

A shiny black vehicle had stopped at the kerb near her. Other vehicles hooted, and their drivers shouted, as they manoeuvred noisily around the stationary car. The driver of the taxi was leaning out of its window. Now that he had Talia's attention he stopped shouting, but his gaze travelled up and down her body.

The intensity of his stare made Talia shiver, but he was young, and he had a smile and a friendly face. 'Yes,' she mouthed, and she strode to the kerb and through the door that he had opened for her.

She pulled the door shut and leant forwards as she sat on the black leather of the bench seat in the back of the vehicle. The driver, now looking at her over his shoulder, made no attempt to hide his interest in her long, bare legs.

Talia thrust the slip towards him. 'That's where I have to go,' she said. 'The problem is that I have no money.'

'That's quite a way from here,' the driver said, running his fingers through his unruly mop of black curls. 'Normally I'd offer a special price for a run like this, but if you've got no cash at all ...' His voice trailed off and his gaze moved from the paper and slid slowly up Talia's legs. 'I'll have to think of a very special price,' he said, with a wide grin. 'What can you offer me?'

He turned away, and concentrated for a moment on the controls of the taxi, making its engine roar as he drove it into the thick of the traffic streams. Talia looked around her, amazed at the speed and numbers of the vehicles surrounding the taxi. She caught sight of the driver's eyes, reflected in the driving mirror, watching her.

It had been several months since Talia had had a man. In recent weeks she had been entirely taken up with her beloved Anne, but even when she had been in the forest, among her own people, she had preferred to play with women. But the whipping she had received the previous day had aroused her to such an extent that even three self-induced orgasms had not satisfied her. She wanted more. She wanted to do things with another person. And this taxi driver would do.

'I don't know what you mean,' she said. 'I haven't got anything that you might want.' But as she spoke she uncrossed her legs and pulled her skirt up to her hips. She wondered, briefly, whether he thought she was a prostitute. She had heard that in the city there were women who exchanged sexual acts for money. Talia had never seen one, as far as she knew. She didn't know whether she could be mistaken for one.

'I'm sure you'll think of something,' the driver said. 'You can pay me when we get there.'

Of the many emotions that were swirling through Olena's thoughts as she followed Kym from her room, the one that afflicted her most often was anxiety. She was nervous. The fact that she was dressed up as a schoolgirl made the feeling stronger: it was as though she was about to face her first day in a new school. She recognised the symptoms: a fluttering in her stomach, a tightness across her chest. She remembered feeling like this on the first day she had attended college in the city, and again when she had been presented formally to the Supreme Mistress of the Private House.

During her two years in the House everyone there had come to know about her. After a while it had not been necessary for her or the Mentors to explain that, although she seemed a polite, diffident, and pleasant young woman, she was in fact so corrupt, dissolute, depraved, and stained with sin that there was no act so perverse that she did not take pleasure in it, and no amount of punishment that could redeem her. The Private House had become her home because its denizens accepted her, despite her wickedness. They helped her to explore the depths of her

70

degeneracy, and there was always someone willing to satisfy her need for strict discipline. Olena could never forget that her heart and soul were rotten with lust, and her sense of shame grew as she discovered more and more about the black desires that festered within her, but the people of the Private House didn't judge or criticise her, and she had come to feel at least partly content.

Now she was in Madame's house, among strangers who didn't know her, and who would inevitably find out her dark, shameful secrets. As she walked behind Kym, along corridors and up stairs to parts of the house that must surely, she thought, be in the loft, she knew that within a few minutes Madame would discover that her new guest was once again wet and open, as lascivious as a bitch on heat. And that would be only the start of Olena's humiliations.

Olena also knew that she was almost as excited as she was nervous. She had come to accept, and even to take pleasure in, the fact that her sense of shame was intimately connected with the arousal of her lustful urges. Once it had seemed to her grossly unfair that those emotions that should have chastened her and helped her on to the path of righteousness in fact had the opposite effect. Now she knew that in her perverse nature the humiliation of, for example, a public flogging would never fail to fan the flames of her lust.

The thought that she might be on her way to a session of punishment was almost insupportably exciting. Olena had learnt that corporal discipline, if applied sufficiently often and thoroughly, and especially if she was allowed a sexual climax during or after the punishment, could temporarily satiate and dull her lustful appetites. But the anticipation of the degradation she would suffer and of the physical sensations she would endure had the opposite effect: sometimes, if she was kept waiting for a promised chastisement, her private place would become so wet that it dripped.

As she climbed the steep stairs to the landing on which Kym was waiting for her, she felt the wetness that had already seeped from her private lips and on to the insides of her thighs.

'This is it,' Kym said, opening the door behind her. 'One of the special rooms. You're honoured.'

Olena could see no daylight through the doorway. The room beyond was illuminated with the soft glow of lamps. She took a deep breath and stepped past Kym.

Madame la Patronne was standing in the centre of the room, and behind her, in the shadows, was the masked man. Kym followed her into the room and closed the door. The entire household was present to witness Olena's performance.

The room was unlike any Olena had yet seen in Madame's house. The walls were plain, and around the carpets the floorboards were bare. There was no ceiling: the walls rose up to the rafters of the house. The furnishing was sparse and utilitarian: an armchair; a sofa; a couch with adjustable, padded parts edged with leather straps; an upright, square, wooden frame with loops of rope at its corners; a desk on which was displayed an array of disciplinary implements. It was a punishment room, similar to several of the chambers in the Private House. A wave of relief swept through Olena: she was in no doubt, now, that she was at last about to receive at least a spanking.

But Madame was in no hurry to start. She greeted Olena, and complimented her on her appearance. She guided Olena round the room, stopping at each item of furniture to explain the various positions in which a miscreant could be bound to it, and which parts of the body would thereby be presented for punishment. Olena was entirely familiar with everything that Madame told her, and she was sure that Madame knew it. Nonetheless Madame's voice, describing calmly and politely the dozens of ways in which Olena might be secured and made ready, had the effect of making Olena ever more desperate for the punishment to begin. She became increasingly aware that her breasts, with their nipples as hard as nuts and pressing against the stiff cotton of the blouse, and her bottom, beneath which her sex was becoming so tingly that it was almost an unbearable itch, were still covered. Her desire to expose the private parts of her body was as sinful as it was urgent, although not, she thought, as wicked as was the pleasure that she was experiencing as tremors and thrills in her breasts and her private place. She wondered whether Madame had any idea of the cauldron of bubbling, boiling lust inside her. Olena's friends at the Private House were genuinely not offended whenever she couldn't help revealing the disgraceful depths of her depravity. She hoped that Madame would be as tolerant.

'Often,' Madame said, 'I find that it's enough to secure the culprit in a demeaning position for a while. Both Kym and –' She paused, and Olena guessed that she had been on the point of saying Barat's name, '– and my manservant,' she went on, 'have spent some time tied up in here, and it's usually sufficient to persuade them not to misbehave again. At least until the next time.'

'Oh,' Olena said. 'I see.' Surely, she thought, Madame must be teasing her? Surely she hadn't been brought to this room merely to be bound for a while? The frustration would be unbearable.

'Occasionally, though,' Madame said, moving to the desk, 'I find it's necessary to add an element of corporal punishment. I don't like having to do it, and they don't like receiving it, but sometimes it's the only way to instil discipline. I'm told that there are people who take pleasure in that sort of thing. It's difficult to believe, isn't it?'

Olena could only shake her head miserably. She was sure, now, that Madame was being provocative, but she couldn't deny that it was true: normal people weren't so wicked and full of lust that they deserved punishments; normal people tried to avoid the pain and humiliation of being spanked or whipped, and found the experiences hateful.

'I have a small collection of implements,' Madame said. 'I've arranged some of them here, on the desk. Purely as examples, you understand.'

Olena stared at the array. She felt her heart beat faster, and she stood with her legs close together for fear that the wetness might begin to drip from her sex. She saw two slender dowels of different thicknesses, a riding-crop, a two-tongued tawse, a simple leather strap with a wooden handle, and a whip with a multitude of short leather thongs. As she looked at each item she imagined what it would feel like on her bottom or her breasts. She couldn't help uttering a little moan of desire.

'I know, my dear,' Madame said. 'It's distressing even to look at these things, isn't it? Now, I know that you told me yesterday that you deserved to be punished, but I'm quite prepared to forget all about it. You've been perfectly well behaved ever since you arrived yesterday, you know. I can't think of a single reason to punish you.'

Olena felt a stab of doubt in the pit of her stomach. She had become convinced that Madame would not have brought her to this room if she hadn't intended to chastise her, and that Madame's apparent reluctance to use her collection of implements was merely a game to tease Olena and fuel her wicked desires. But perhaps it was true: perhaps Madame wasn't going to punish her at all. The idea was insupportable.

'Please, Madame,' Olena said. 'You said yesterday that I would be spanked, at least.'

Madame took a step back. She looked at Olena with an expression of amused surprise. She was wearing a long, soft, button-through dress of dark green jersey, and as she stood with one arm cradling her breasts and supporting her forearm so that the fingers of her left hand touched her cheek, she looked the epitome of sophisticated elegance. 'Did I?' she said. 'Well, I may have hinted at something of the sort. But I'm in a much better mood today. You're here for pleasure, Olena. Yours, and mine, among others. I wouldn't dream of hurting you.'

'Please, Madame,' Olena said again. She was worried now. How could she make Madame realise that she needed discipline? 'You said yesterday that I deserved to be smacked. It's true. I do deserve it.'

'You were adorable yesterday,' Madame protested. 'But,' she added, as she went to the armchair and slid into

74

it, 'if you've been naughty you'd better tell me all about it. And make sure you keep your voice up. The others should hear your confession, too, if you've done something truly bad.' She crossed her arms and looked up at Olena with an expectant smile.

Olena realised that for Madame and her staff this was merely a game. She understood, in that moment, that Madame had intended all along to punish her. It didn't matter. Olena wanted to explain; she wanted to make Madame understand the utter vileness of her nature.

'It isn't what I've done,' Olena said. 'It's what I am.' She felt her face blazing with embarrassment. How could she make this charming, friendly woman understand that she had brought a monster into her house?

'Don't slouch, dear,' Madame said. 'And do try to speak clearly.'

Olena was used to obeying instructions. The leather band around her neck reminded her that she had been trained to serve. But it was the costume she was wearing that filled Olena with shame: its simplicity, its redolence of innocent schooldays were so much at odds with the body it clothed. Her breasts, swollen and sensitive with desire, pressed outwards with every deep breath against the white cotton of the blouse; under the covering of the simple skirt her sex was naked, hot, and weeping the sticky evidence of her licentiousness.

'I have tried all my life to be good,' Olena sobbed, 'and when I was a girl I managed to ignore, or suppress, the strange urges and imaginings that came into my mind and afflicted my body. But as I changed from a girl into a woman, as my body changed, the sinful desires came upon me more and more often. I couldn't tell anyone. Only I knew that beneath the modest robes I wore in the village I was turning into a thing of lust and filth. I found myself admiring my body, and congratulating myself when I saw the village boys and men looking at me. I should have talked to my mother; I should have thrown myself on the mercy of the elders. But I did nothing. I added the sins of pride and deceit to the lust that pervaded my thoughts. I

75

had no rest even at night: my dreams were full of depraved acts, and I would wake in horror because I had been enjoying them. I knew then that I was thoroughly corrupt.'

'Don't upset yourself,' Madame said. 'Olena, it's entirely natural to begin to think of such things as you're growing up.'

Olena shook her head. How could she make Madame understand? 'That's what I came to believe,' she said. 'When I came to the city to study at college, my guardian was a young man named Barat.' She succeeded in not looking towards the masked, robed figure. 'He explained that it was normal for a young woman to take a little pride in her appearance, and to experience strong feelings about men. He was very kind to me. He encouraged me to wear less clothing, and to talk to him about my desires. He was prepared to sacrifice his innocence on my behalf.'

Despite her embarrassment, Olena found it difficult to stifle a giggle as she mentioned Barat. It had been obvious, as soon as they had arrived in the city, that his only ambition had been to use her for his pleasure.

'But then,' Olena went on, 'Barat and I were taken, by mistake, to a place called the Chateau.' She noticed that Madame's eyes widened: she had heard of the isolated, strictly disciplined establishment in which Olena had been held captive. 'The people there tested me,' Olena said. She hung her head, remembering the daily humiliations she had endured as each test uncovered more evidence of the seemingly bottomless pit of Olena's wickedness. 'In the Chateau I found out what I'm really like, Madame. I'm like a frozen pond: there's a thin layer that's white and pure, but underneath the waters are black and deep, and swirling, and filthy, and full of ravenous creatures whose appetites are never satisfied. I'm sorry. I will understand if you would prefer me to leave your house.'

'I won't hear of it, my dear. Please continue with your story. I still don't see why you're so sure that you deserve to be punished.'

Olena moaned with frustration. It was so obvious to her. Perhaps Madame didn't believe that she could be as bad as she claimed. But Olena knew that no description could do justice to the corrupt reality of her nature. Only Olena experienced the terrible truth, day after day: that there was scarcely a waking moment when she was not thinking about the sinful pleasures that she so guiltily enjoyed.

'I was rescued from the Chateau and taken to the Private House,' Olena went on. 'Everyone there was kind to me, and they didn't condemn me even though my desires became no less wicked. They taught me how to be obedient,' she said, touching the collar, 'and they encouraged me to take pleasure in the things I desired, and in the shame I felt about them, and even in the punishments that I was given. They told me that I should balance the pleasure against the shame. My mental anguish was eased, and I became more content.'

Madame was still staring at her. Olena didn't know what else to say. It must have been obvious by now that she was worse than a trollop, and that she deserved more punishment than she could ever hope to receive. She glanced at the desk and its array of rods and canes, and felt a lurch of desire in her loins.

'Yesterday, Madame,' she burst out, 'when you inspected me, you found that I was wanton, didn't you? I was, I know I was, wet,' she stammered, 'in my private place. Isn't that all the proof you need?'

A smile spread slowly across Madame's carmine lips. 'And what about today?' she said. 'Are you aroused now? I think that might be considered a little naughty.'

Olena closed her eyes and nodded. She had known that Madame would find out sooner or later.

'Kym,' Madame said. 'Have you touched Olena? I know what you're like when I leave you alone with a young woman.'

Kym stepped forward. 'No, Madame. I followed your instructions.' She exchanged a glance with Olena, no doubt fearing that Olena would denounce her as a liar. But Olena was too preoccupied to concern herself with such trifles. And in any case, Kym had merely discovered her excitement, she hadn't caused it.

Madame beckoned to Kym. 'Lift Olena's skirt,' she said, 'and put your fingers between the lips of her sex.'

Olena knew that by now she should have become used to this experience. But, as was usual whenever her lubriciousness was about to be revealed, she merely wished that the ground beneath her feet would open and swallow her. She closed her eyes and, when she felt Kym lift the back of her skirt, she leant forwards, as she had been trained, to offer her bottom and her private places.

She knew that she couldn't blame the training that she had received. The slight forward movement, the sensation of her bottom lifting and opening – these were, as much as the wetness of her sex, the irrefutable evidence that her nature was base and lascivious. The knowledge that Kym's gaze was on her naked bottom was so embarrassing that she felt as though her whole body was blushing red, and the shame made her breath catch in her throat, but at the same time she couldn't stop trembling with thrills of pleasure, and she could feel more wetness trickling inside her private place. But overriding everything, so urgent that it was like physical hunger, was the need for a long, hard spanking and an orgasm.

Kym's fingers slid between the tops of her thighs, and Olena gasped. Gently the fingers prised apart her outer lips, and pressed upwards between them. Olena's breathing became ragged as she felt the muscles inside her clenching rapidly, trying to close around the intrusive fingers. She knew that she was already very close to at least the beginning of a climax.

'Bloody hell,' Kym breathed, 'you're wetter than ever.'

'Come here,' Madame told Kym. 'Show me.'

Kym's fingers withdrew, and when Olena opened her eyes Kym was standing beside . Madame's chair. Olena could see, even though she was several paces away from Madame, that most of Kym's right hand was slick with moisture.

Madame's eyes narrowed, and her smile seemed to have become frozen on her face. 'I see,' she said. 'Am I to conclude, then, Olena, that you are responsible for the condition you are in? This,' she added, flicking a red-painted fingernail against Kym's hand, 'is all your own work?'

'I can't help it,' Olena cried. She lowered her head. 'I'm very bad.'

'The point is,' Madame stated, 'that I do not permit anyone in my house to touch their own sexual parts, or those of another person, without my express instruction. I know that you come from a community in which self-restraint and purity of thought are highly regarded. I therefore would have expected you, of all people, to understand the necessity of controlling your sexual urges.'

'I do try, Madame,' Olena said. She was close to tears: Madame's words had summed up her own sense of failure and shame. 'I need discipline. I can't control myself. I need help.'

'Oh, very well,' Madame snapped. 'If you insist, I'll punish you. Go the desk and choose an implement.'

'Thank you, Madame,' Olena said. She was so relieved that she almost ran to the desk. The skin of her bottom, brushed by the material of her skirt, felt as taut as a drum-head and as tingly as her nipples. She could hardly wait to feel the first stinging lash, but when she gazed down at the array of implements she was unable to choose. The strap or the tawse would provide the most instant gratification; one of the canes, though, would sting more and lingeringly; while the whip, with its many tails, would reach particularly sensitive places.

'Madame,' she said, 'I'm sorry to be a nuisance. But may I have the strap first, and then a caning? Please, I beg you. I need such a lot of discipline.'

In Barat's imagination Olena had already endured, over and over again, punishments beside which a strapping and caning seemed no more than mild rebukes. He had endlessly revised and refined the plans he intended to put into effect when Madame finally gave Olena to him. In this imaginary time there was not a moment, night or day, when he would not be with her. When he was not using her luscious body for his pleasure he would be administering the strict discipline that she craved, concentrating on her most sensitive parts and using a variety of instruments so diverse that sometimes he couldn't remember which ones he had already dreamt of. When he became too exhausted to continue he would watch while his servants and guests enjoyed her.

But that was all in the future. Now, he was about to see Olena punished – not in his imagination, but before his very eyes.

He was delighted to see that despite her years of indulgence in carnal pleasures Olena still found it desperately embarrassing to undress in public. When Madame had told her, 'You'd better take off your skirt and blouse,' Olena had looked momentarily surprised, as if it hadn't occurred to her that being punished would entail her revealing her body. With her face blushing scarlet she had glanced from Madame, to Barat, to Kym, while fumbling with the buttons of her blouse.

Now she was naked, standing nervously before Madame's chair, and Barat leant forwards a little to make room under his robe for the sensitive head of his stiffening cock. He could no longer resist the temptation to hold it, and to slide his hand up and down the shaft, as he surveyed the peerless, bountiful beauty that would soon be his to enjoy.

Madame stood up, but she didn't immediately walk to the desk to pick up the strap that Olena had chosen. As Barat knew well, Madame's approach to discipline was to tease her victim. Olena would be made to wait a little longer.

Barat could see Olena's body quivering as Madame circled her like a lioness around her prey. Olena tried to hide her breasts and her sex with her hands, but one tremulous nipple was entirely uncovered, and there was nothing she could do to conceal the jutting moons of her bottom.

'Bend over,' Madame said, and she watched in silence while Olena leant forwards and placed her hands on her knees. Barat noted that despite her embarrassment she curved her back inwards, so that her bottom was lifted up, and she stood with her legs apart. It was remarkable that two years of training had made her outward behaviour so automatically lewd while leaving her sense of sin and shame as entrenched as it had been while she had been growing up in the village.

Madame studied Olena's bottom for some moments. Her purpose, Barat knew, was to increase Olena's anticipation of the impending punishment, and to give her plenty of time in which to think about the revealing position she had voluntarily adopted. But in Barat's opinion Olena's lush hindquarters merited lengthy inspection for their own sake. When she's mine, he said to himself, I'll have her hold her arse-cheeks apart and I'll make sure she knows I'm looking at her before I instruct her to so much as touch herself.

At last Madame broke the silence. 'Charming,' she said, placing a hand on Olena's left buttock and making Olena start. 'Eminently spankable. It was the strap first, wasn't it? On the armchair, then, for the time being. I won't have you tied down just yet. Kneel on the seat, my dear. Knees apart, of course. You can rest that magnificent bosom on the back of the chair. That's it. Now cross your hands behind your back.'

Only now did Madame make her way to the desk to collect the strap. Barat saw Olena's head turn so that she could watch every step of Madame's leisurely progress: as Madame returned Olena's large, dark eyes were fixed on the leather tongue dangling from Madame's hand. As Madame moved behind her Olena lowered her head and lifted her bottom higher.

Still Madame did not begin the punishment. Instead with her free hand she gently stroked the proud curves of Olena's bottom. Barat heard Olena make a whimpering moan. He was as impatient as she was for Madame to administer the first lash.

'I had better make sure you still need this, my dear,' Madame said, and she placed the wooden handle of the strap under the overhanging roundnesses of Olena's bottom. She pushed it up, and Barat saw Olena's whole body shudder as the handle touched her sex.

The tip of the leather tongue brushed against the seat of the chair as Madame moved her hand back and forth. The only other sound was Olena's breathing, which had become deeper.

Madame withdrew the strap. 'Wetter than ever,' she commented, and with a show of distaste she curled her fingers around the sticky handle. She drew back her arm and swung the strap with a speed and vigour that took Barat by surprise.

With a loud crack the leather landed across Olena's right buttock. Olena uttered a gasp, and then a long sigh. A pink stripe appeared where the strap had struck her skin. The leather tongue was not narrow, but Olena's bottom was so full and round and generously proportioned that the mark it made looked almost insignificant. It would take a long time, Barat realised, and many strokes of the strap, to bring every part of Olena's bottom up to a consistent, glowing redness.

It was clear that Madame relished the challenge. She swung the strap hard and fast, aiming entirely at one side of Olena's bottom, and pausing so little that the quivering buttock had no time to come to rest between lashes: Madame, with a smile on her face, made the swelling flesh jump and dance.

Olena's face was lowered, and entirely obscured from Barat's view by the curtain of her dark hair. From where he was standing he could see Olena's bottom, but he wished that he could watch the expressions on her face. He wondered whether he could ask Madame for permission to move, but he decided that she wouldn't like to be interrupted. He would have to imagine that he was standing behind the chair, and that he could see Olena's half-closed eyes, and the little frowns and winces that must surely be appearing on her face as the strap continued its remorseless rhythm. He pictured her broad, full lips parting to release small gasps and cries. He would have only to step forward, and open his robe, and he would be able to push the bulb of his cock into her mouth. His hand was pumping furiously now, but he no longer cared if Madame or Kym noticed the movements under his cloak.

Madame had begun on Olena's left buttock. Barat had missed his chance to ask Madame for permission to move. There had been a brief interlude during which she had rested her arm and adjusted her position in readiness for the second onslaught.

Now the other half of the luscious split peach of Olena's arse was slowly attaining the colour of its sister. The crack of the lash on Olena's flesh resounded from the walls like rapid, regular pistol-shots. Barat was grateful that Madame had never punished him as thoroughly as this; he was also, he realised with dismay, a little jealous. Since the punishment had started his eyes had not moved from the reddening spheres of Olena's bottom, but now he glanced at Kym. The young woman, her mouth slightly open and her grey eyes unusually bright, was staring at Olena as fixedly as he had been. Her hand, he noticed, was resting on the breast that Madame had smacked that morning. Even the icy and sardonic Kym, it seemed, was interested in this.

Madame stopped, and nursed her right arm while she surveyed the results of her work. Barat was grateful: he had seemed unable to stop touching his erection during the punishment, and he was dangerously close to an orgasm. He didn't care to imagine what Madame might do to him if he reached a climax without her permission.

The individual marks made by the strap could not be seen: Olena's twin, round hills were entirely coloured, varying from a pink blush on the lower slopes to a fiery red across the peaks. Madame moved behind the chair and whispered something to Olena. Barat saw Olena press her ribcage against the back of the chair as she curved her spine inwards even more. Her glowing buttocks lifted and parted, so that even from a distance Barat could see the open lips of her sex, glistening with her lubriciousness.

Barat had assumed that Madame had positioned Olena for the second part of her punishment: the caning. But when Madame began again to strike Olena's rear, she was still using the strap. The strokes were slower now, and were delivered with an upswing. Madame was aiming for the backs and insides of Olena's thighs, and the lowest, innermost slopes of her buttocks. Olena kept her arms crossed behind her back, and Barat saw her hands clench and unclench as Madame's lashes increased in speed and force.

'That will do,' Madame announced at last. She placed the strap on the seat of the chair and ran her hands over Olena's bright-red buttocks. 'She's ready for the cane. Kym, fetch a jug of water and a few tumblers. I'm thirsty, and I'm sure Olena would like a little refreshment before we start again. And bring a small towel, too. It's clear that all this discipline is making our guest more and more aroused. Do you see, Kym? She's actually dripping.'

Once the taxi was threading its way through the traffic Talia quickly agreed with the driver that her payment for the trip would be half an hour of sexual servitude. She also readily agreed to remove her skirt for the duration of the journey: it excited her to know that the driver could see her, naked from the waist down, in his mirror, and she always liked the sensation of sitting on leather.

She was aware that her readiness to consent to the driver's requests had surprised him, but she was looking forward to rewarding him for his help and she saw no reason to haggle. In any case, now that she was safely inside the taxi she felt that she could relax and enjoy the trip through the city streets. Talia had become a creature of the woodlands, and it had been several years since she had been in a town, let alone a city as vast and populous as this. She admitted to herself that she found the noise and the crowds slightly intimidating, and she thought that the long drive would help her to become accustomed to the sights and speed of urban life.

And so she sprawled on the long seat, with her legs apart for the benefit of the driver, with one hand resting in her lap so that she could keep her sex warm and moist and tingling, and she stared at the vehicles, pedestrians, shops and houses that the taxi carried her past.

When the streets were busy with traffic she kept her feet on the floor of the taxi, so that from the point of view of passers-by she would look just like a respectably dressed passenger; in quiet, residential avenues she would lift her heels on to the seat and, having made sure that the driver's eyes in the mirror were on her, she would use her fingers to open her sex and to tease the hood of her clitoris. She was pleased that there was still no hint of stubble pushing through the delicate skin of her mound and her sex-lips. To judge from the number of times that the driver had to pull on the steering wheel to avoid driving into the side of the road, he also admired the perfect smoothness of Talia's sex.

As the taxi motored from the centre of the city towards its suburbs the shops and busy streets became fewer, and there were more and more roads lined with trees and rows of similar houses. Talia spent more and more time with her hands busy between her thighs. For the last few weeks she and Anne had attended to each other's intimate toilet, and touching her delicate, depilated skin summoned delicious memories of time spent with her pretty blonde lover. Talia had found it surprisingly easy, in the short time she had been in the world outside the House and the forest, to obtain a sound spanking and a sexual partner. It would be more difficult, she thought, to find someone who would shave and pluck and pamper her sex as gently and thoroughly as Anne did.

Talia was so lost in memories of Anne that she didn't notice, at first, that the taxi had stopped. She opened her eyes to find that the motor had stopped and that the driver was looking at her over his shoulder with a wide grin on his face.

She looked out of the windows. 'This can't be the place,' she said. 'There's nothing here.'

The taxi had stopped at the end of a narrow cul-de-sac. On both sides rose the sheer brick walls of warehouses; in front of the taxi there were the arches of a low railway bridge. The warehouses were derelict, with broken glass in most of their windows. The vaults under the railway arches were black, gaping, and empty, or had been boarded up with rough planks. There was not another vehicle or person in sight. For a moment Talia was unnerved, and a little frightened. Then she reminded herself that while most of her forest skills were useless in the city, she was almost certain to be able to best the taxi driver in unarmed combat, or a knife fight, or, if it came to it, running.

'Don't worry,' the driver said. 'The street you want is just over there.' He pointed towards a footbridge that crossed the railway line. 'But I thought I'd better stop somewhere private so you can pay your fare.'

'Where do you want to go?' Talia said. She peered again through the taxi's window. The late summer sun had been obscured by grey clouds, and the swirling of litter along the alley suggested that there might now be a cold wind blowing. None of the warehouses or archways looked welcoming. Talia was aroused and keen to play games with the driver, but she didn't want to be uncomfortable.

'We'll stay here,' the driver said, and he climbed into the passenger compartment. 'I've been watching you fingering yourself, darling, and I can't wait any longer.'

When she had been alone in the back of the taxi the space had seemed generous. Now it was suddenly crowded. The driver was taller and leaner than she had expected, and he smelt of leather and soap. His eyes were as black and shiny as his curly hair. 'Excuse me,' he said, leaning across her to pull down a blind over one of the side windows. He did the same on the other side. 'That's a bit more private,' he said. 'Now then,' he went on, looking at his wristwatch. 'We've got half an hour. Why don't you take your top off, and then sit with your feet up, like you were before, and play with yourself a bit more.' He perched on one of the small seats facing hers.

Talia pulled her heels up to the backs of her thighs, so that the driver could see her anus as well as her shaved, open sex. He whistled appreciatively. Talia unbuttoned her tunic and pulled it off. Now she was naked except for her ankle boots.

'You've got good tits,' the driver said. 'Lots of skinny women are as flat as pancakes. Yours are on the small side, but nice and round. Play with your nipples.'

Talia's nipples were already erect, but when she caressed the tips of her breasts with her fingers she shivered as she felt the crinkled skin swell and harden even more. The taxi driver's manner was abrupt and coarse – his instructions were even more direct than those she had received from the Whipmaker, when she had been in thrall to him – but she found it exciting. In any sexual situation she was excited by being told what to do.

She wondered whether the taxi driver realised that she enjoyed obeying his rough commands. It was obvious, from the growing bulge in the front of his trousers, that he was becoming increasingly aroused. Perhaps he was as stimulated by the idea that he was in control of her as he was by the sight of her naked body. It was possible, she supposed, that he would be less excited if he knew that it pleased her to obey him. As far as he knew she was penniless, and dependent on him, and obliged to do whatever he told her. She had to admit that she also found that fantasy seductive.

'Pinch them,' he said, and his gaze remained fixed on her nipples as he began to undo the belt around his waist.

Talia cupped her breasts in her hands and held each nipple between a finger and thumb. As she tightened her grip she felt the thrills of pleasure in her body begin to pulse in a slow rhythm. She licked her dry lips and watched the snake of leather as he drew it through the loops of the waistband of his trousers. There was something powerfully arousing about the sight and sound of a belt being unbuckled and pulled free. It implied that private parts were about to be revealed; an implement of punishment was being made ready.

'Pinch them harder,' he said. His voice was low and urgent. 'Stretch them. Pull your tits towards me.' He unbuttoned his trousers. His engorged penis, russet-skin-ned and lazily upright, rose into sight. He put his hand around the shaft, and pulled down the foreskin to reveal the purple plum of his cock-head. The shaft immediately stiffened into a vertical pole. 'Now twist them,' he said. 'Twist them until they hurt.'

Talia had already pulled her breasts into cones of taut flesh that felt as though they had a core of tingling electricity. As she held the hard tips and twisted them slowly she watched the driver's hand sliding up and down his erect manhood. She gasped and closed her eyes when she felt the first pang of pain. Her eyelids fluttered open for a moment, and she saw that he was now staring at her face. She continued to move her fingers, and stopped when the pain in her nipples had become a steady throbbing that sent pleasure signals pulsing along the thread that seemed to stretch through her breasts and down to her sex. She heard herself gasping with each breath, and it occurred to her that the driver probably didn't care about her enjoyment: he wanted to see that she was prepared to cause herself pain on his command. She turned her pants of pleasure into winces of anguish.

'Does it hurt?' he asked.

Talia nodded.

'But you like it really, don't you, you little tart? Tell me you like it.'

Talia realised that it wouldn't do to be too honest. 'I like it,' she whispered. 'But it does hurt terribly.' She managed to make her voice sound very small and tremulous.

'All right,' he said. 'You can stop now. I want you to play with your cunt. Hold it open and put your fingers in.'

The driver was content to watch and to stroke his erection while Talia performed for him. He was surprisingly inventive, and his instructions were precise. Her right hand was used to pinch and twist her labia, and to keep them parted; to pinch, rub and pull back the hood of her clitoris; to touch and squeeze the clitoris itself; to tickle the entrance of her urethra; to pull on her inner labia; and to dip into the wet hole of her vagina. Her left hand, once it was lubricated, went under her thigh and its fingers were used to stroke her perineum, to pinch the delicate skin around her anus, and to penetrate the tiny hole.

Although Talia had to concentrate on the driver's complicated instructions, she very soon reached the level of arousal from which it would have been easy to reach an orgasm. Occasionally she opened her eyes to find that his gaze was unwavering and his hand was still moving up and down his shaft, but most of the time she was in a private world, riding the waves of pleasure that her fingers created. She could hear her own gasps and cries, and the liquid suckings and slidings of her hands. She had become very wet. The air in the confined space of the taxi was heavy with the scent of her arousal and the musk of the driver.

'Stop,' he said. 'Now use this.'

She stilled her fingers, but kept them pressed against the hot, sensitive, moistened skin. She couldn't bear not to touch herself at all. She opened her eyes and saw that he was holding an empty bottle made of dark-brown glass. She supposed that it had contained beer, or some other drink that he had consumed while driving. The bottle was squat, but wide. The top, where once the cap had been, was a narrow neck, but it widened so that most of the bottle consisted of a fat cylinder.

'Put this in your cunt,' he said, holding it towards her. 'Don't worry, it's clean.'

Talia took the bottle. The glass was cool and smooth. It would feel wonderful inside her. But she remembered that she should appear unwilling. 'It's too big,' she said. 'I can't.'

'Do it,' he said. 'We've got a deal, remember?' He looked at his watch. 'Still ten minutes to go. Or do you want me to drive you back to the centre of the city and leave you there?'

'No,' Talia said, feigning reluctance. 'I'll try.' She held the neck of the bottle at the entrance of her vagina. When the cool glass touched her skin she shuddered. She supported the bottle with one hand and placed the other over its base, so that she could control the angle and speed of entry. The sensation of the bottle sliding into her was exquisite, and she wanted to make it last.

She had no doubt that she would be able to take the bottle inside her. The Whipmaker had liked to put things into her; her courses at the Private House had included sessions with artificial phalluses of several shapes and sizes; and she and Anne had made a collection of smooth, long objects to play with together. Once, when she and Anne had been playing lazily together, Anne had, almost without thinking about it, inserted her hand, up to the wrist, into Talia's vagina. The bottle would stretch her, Talia judged, and it might feel uncomfortable – but it would be an exciting discomfort.

The neck of the bottle was inside her, and its shoulders were stretching apart her inner labia as she pushed the base towards her. It was certainly wide. She groaned and tossed her head. She wouldn't have been able to take it if she hadn't been so thoroughly aroused. But it was sliding in, little by little, filling and stretching her.

'Stop a moment,' the driver said.

Talia shook her head to clear it. She was so close to coming that the merest caress of her clitoris would have been enough to send her into ecstasy. She looked at the driver: he was sitting on the edge of the small seat, leaning forwards, with his erect phallus standing straight from his opened trousers. She looked down: the bottle was about halfway into her. Its thick base protruded obscenely from between her stretched sex-lips.

The driver consulted his watch. 'Only a few minutes left,' he said. 'Hold the bottle where it is. Get off the seat and kneel in front of me. I'm going to use your mouth.'

Talia clambered from the seat on to the floor. Her limbs felt clumsy and boneless. She was shaking with desire. The Whipmaker and the hooded man had liked to put their penises into her mouth. She associated the act with being punished and humiliated. It had been some months since she had last done this for a man, and she was surprised how much she wanted it.

She knelt between his legs. His penis smelt of maleness and the imminence of semen. She reached to hold it.

'No,' he said. 'Don't touch. Just your mouth. And kneel with your arse closer to the ground. So the bottle's resting on the floor. That's it.'

Talia shuddered again as she lowered herself, the bottle touched the floor, and the thickness of it moved inside her. Her lips brushed the velvet hardness of the driver's glans. She licked the bead of clear fluid that had seeped from the slit of his urethra.

'Get on with it,' he growled, and he grasped a handful of her dark-red hair and pulled her head on to his erection.

He fucked her mouth without finesse, so that she had little opportunity to use her lips and her tongue to please him with the techniques she had learnt. Perhaps, she thought, he's worried about the half-hour ending; perhaps he thinks I'll stop as soon as the time expires.

There was no question of it. With the bottle in her vagina and his penis in her mouth, and with every one of her nerve-endings throbbing with pleasure and crying out for the release of orgasm, stopping was the last thing on Talia's mind.

The driver's thrusts became more and more frantic, so that Talia had to struggle to keep her teeth from grazing his sensitive skin and his powerful lunges from hitting the back of her throat.

He uttered a wordless cry, and pulled on Talia's hair so that she was obliged to release his penis from between her lips. He held her still with one hand, and with the other he pumped his shaft, pushing the soft head against her lips. He shouted again, and a jet of sperm fell like hot rain across Talia's face. She closed her eyes, opened her mouth, and pressed down on the bottle as more of his semen spurted over her. She tasted it in her mouth; it fell on her cheeks, her lips and her eyelids.

'That was good,' she heard the driver say. She opened her eyes and saw that he was once again looking at his watch. 'Two minutes over,' he said. 'Sorry.' He tucked his rapidly shrinking penis into his trousers. 'I'd better be getting back,' he said. 'I'm not likely to pick up a fare round here. Do you want to borrow my handkerchief?'

During the short time that Kym had been in Madame's employment she had seen Madame administer several punishments to the smartly dressed, outwardly respectable guests who came to the house for discipline. Some of the men and women meekly accepted whatever Madame imposed on them; others struggled and cried out, and had to be put in restraints. But none had received a strapping as prolonged as that which Olena had just endured, and none had responded, as Olena had, by drifting into a state of languorous arousal.

During the strapping Kym had felt sympathy for Olena's suffering, and grateful that she wasn't in Olena's place. Now, however, she could only be envious of Olena's glowing sensuality. It was as if the fiery heat that had been applied to her bottom had lit a slow-burning furnace within her. She was standing, leaning against the back of the chair, with a distant smile on her face and with her naked body seeming to radiate the warmth of her desire.

'And now it's time for the cane,' Madame said. 'Are you ready, Olena?'

Olena appeared to wake from her reverie. 'The cane,' she said. 'Oh, yes, please, Madame. Where should I kneel?'

Madame smiled. 'You have been kneeling long enough, my dear. I think I will allow you to lie down. Come here. Lie on your back on this couch. Kym, would you assist me, please.'

Kym realised that she had been hoping that Madame would ask her to help with Olena's punishment. It had been surprisingly exciting to watch Olena being whipped with the strap. Kym hurried across the room to join Madame and Olena beside the couch. She wanted to be close to Olena during the caning. She wanted to watch the thin lines appear on Olena's already reddened buttocks, and to hear Olena's gasps as the cane struck her.

The couch consisted of four sections, all of which were thickly upholstered and covered in black hide. Each section could be raised, lowered, tilted, or removed altogether. The first task that Kym was given was to shorten the couch by taking away the fourth section.

Kym was puzzled. She had seen the couch in use, and she knew that it was hardly long enough for a person to lie on even when all four sections were present.

Madame, however, seemed to know exactly what she was doing. 'This will act as a headrest for you,' she said to Olena as she adjusted one of the end sections so that it was slightly tilted. 'Kym, tilt the other end up a little, in the same way, and then fetch a cushion.'

When Kym returned with a cushion she found Olena lying on the couch. Her head was resting against one tilted section; her shoulders were on the flat central section; and her spine was curved upwards so that the small of her back was resting at the raised end of the third section. Madame was holding her ankles aloft.

'Put the cushion under Olena's back,' Madame told Kym. 'She should be supported in this position.'

Kym had not seen anyone arranged in this way for a punishment, but she could appreciate that it was practical. Olena's sore bottom was raised up and looked very vulnerable. Olena obviously agreed, as she was vainly trying to reach around her hips to cover her sex and her bottom with her hands.

'I can see that we're going to have to tie you down,' Madame said. 'Kym, would you strap Olena's wrists to the sides of the couch?'

Like most of the furniture in the room the couch was fitted with restraints. Olena offered no resistance as Kym took her hands and tied them. When Olena was secure Kym lingered beside the couch. With her fingers she combed back a stray tress of Olena's long, dark hair and then, on impulse, she leant forwards and kissed Olena's lips. She felt Olena's mouth respond to hers, and as she pulled away she let her hand caress one of Olena's proud, round breasts. Olena trembled and gasped.

'You see?' Olena whispered. 'I'm so wicked that my body inspires sinful thoughts in others.'

Kym was mystified. Did Olena enjoy being punished or not? Did she even enjoy her sexual arousal?

'Kym, that's enough,' Madame said. 'You still have work to do. Hold Olena's ankles while I fetch the cane.'

Kym stepped back and took Olena's ankles from Madame's hands. She wondered whether Olena's legs would have to be restrained, as well as her hands. She had seen Madame use an adjustable metal rod to hold apart the ankles of one of her guests, and the couch had plenty of straps and rings to which ropes could be tied.

Kym was standing beside Olena's uplifted bottom, and she couldn't help looking at it. Even this close it was impossible to see any individual marks made by the leather strap. Kym leant towards Olena: she was sure that she could feel the heat emanating from the glowing buttocks, and she could certainly tell that Olena was very aroused. It had been only a few minutes since Olena, blushing furiously, had dabbed at her sex with a towel in order to dry herself. But Kym could see that Olena's sex was already wet again. The outer lips were slightly open, and the space between them was filled with glistening fluid.

'Bloody hell, Olena,' Kym said. 'Have you got a lake inside your cunt?'

Olena sobbed, and kicked her legs so that Kym had to struggle to hold them.

'I don't think she wants us to see her naughty bits,' Kym said to Madame as she returned with a cane.

'She's a well-brought-up young woman,' Madame said, swinging the cane through the air experimentally. 'But she knows she has to show us everything. It's these parts of your body that get you into trouble, isn't it, my dear?' Madame rested a hand lightly on the mound of Olena's sex. 'Don't fret,' she added, patting the sticky, split purse. 'The caning is about to begin. I chose a light one, because I want to be able to continue for a long time, without having to worry about causing bruises or weals. It would be a shame to damage such soft skin.'

The punishment did not start immediately. Madame had more instructions for Kym. 'I will hold Olena's ankles for a moment,' she said. 'I want you to stand at the other end of the couch.'

When Kym was standing with the top section of the couch touching the front of her thighs, and the hem of her skirt brushing Olena's hair, Madame was still not satisfied. 'Step forward, Kym,' she said, and then, when Kym did not understand how she could advance through the couch, she said, 'I want you to stand astride the couch, so that your skirt is covering Olena's head. You'll have to stand with your legs wide apart.'

It wasn't easy to adopt the position that Madame required. The couch wasn't wide, but even so, once Kym had moved her feet apart she could only shuffle forwards with her knees slightly bent. She lifted the front of her skirt as she moved into position straddling Olena's face.

Kym was once again impressed with Madame's perverse imagination. Kym was, as usual, wearing nothing under her skirt, and so Olena's head, supported on the tilted section of the couch, was enclosed in a tent of grey material and her face was almost touching Kym's sex. With her legs held apart, Kym knew that her sex-lips were parted. Olena, she thought, must be able to see that I'm getting wet; she can probably smell my excitement.

'That's where I want you,' Madame said. 'Now I want you to hold Olena's ankles. Take one in each hand, that's right, and pull them towards you. Hold them wide apart.'

Olena, who had been in an undignified and revealing position, was now utterly and obscenely displayed. With her knees pushed almost up to her shoulders, and with Kym holding her ankles at the full sideways extent of her reach, she was doubled up with her glowing, tautly rounded buttocks and her wide-open sex lifted and prominent. Kym had never seen a woman's cunt and arsehole exhibited so brazenly.

'Now we're ready,' Madame said. 'I think this is the best position for a woman who needs to be caned. I can stand on either side of her bottom, to make sure that both sides are treated equally, and later I'll move to stand behind her, when I want to concentrate on caning the insides of her thighs, and her vulva and her anus. You'll find it tiring to stand like that, Kym,' she added, 'but you can rest by lowering yourself on to Olena's face. You might need to do that anyway, later on, if she starts to make a noise.'

Experimentally, Kym bent her knees a little more. She could feel the warmth of Olena's breath on the delicate membranes of her open sex. A little further, and she felt her moist skin nudged by Olena's nose and the lower, inner curves of her bottom settling on Olena's forehead. She shivered with pleasure. She was sure that she was going to enjoy helping Madame to punish Olena. She could hardly wait to see the first bright-red stripes appear on the curvaceous expanse laid out before her. She found herself wishing that she had a cane of her own. And it was bliss to feel a woman's face so close to her cunt. Madame enjoyed playing lesbian games with Kym, but she was always in charge and while she was happy to receive Kym's attentions she never reciprocated. It had been some time since Kym had been kissed and licked properly. She was looking forward to using Olena's face.

'Ready, Olena?' Madame said. 'I thought it would be a good idea to give you Kym's private parts to look at while you're being caned. The sight will remind you of the source of your own sinfulness, I expect.'

The punishment began. The narrow cane hissed through the air. A ladder of red lines began to appear on Olena's tight, swollen, quivering, pinkly glowing buttocks. Kym, driven by an impulse to add to Olena's embarrassment and humiliation, dipped her body in time with the cane-strokes, wetting Olena's face with the viscous fluid that seeped ever more plentifully from her sex.

Madame maintained a regular, rapid rhythm of wristy strokes. She paused only to rest her arm and to move around the end of the couch. The proud round curves of Olena's buttocks were covered with bright lines that became so numerous that it was impossible to differentiate them. Kym could feel Olena's gasps become quicker and louder, until she was panting and crying out continuously.

'This is for your own good, Olena,' Madame said sternly, breathing deeply from her exertions. 'It gives me no pleasure to have to be so strict with you,' she added, but she gave Kym a smile that belied her words. 'You'd better sit on her firmly, Kym,' she said. 'It's time to start on the most sensitive parts.'

Kym lowered herself gratefully on to Olena's face, and wriggled until she was comfortable. She held Olena's ankles as wide apart as she could, and then she rocked her hips gently and watched through a haze of pleasure as the cane fell smartly, again and again, on to the sopping wet, split-open mound of Olena's sex.

Olena hardly noticed when the caning finally stopped. The individual stinging stripes had long since merged into a continuous, ever-expanding flowering of gloriously painful heat, and the relentless tattoo of the cane striking her body had been overlaid by and lost within the pounding throb of desire that rippled from her private place.

As she had found so many times before, prolonged punishment had the power to make her forget, for a while, that she was flawed and sinful. All of her pain and shame and lustful desires had combined and been sublimated into a state of ecstasy. She felt as though she was floating, adrift in the clouds, and as she rose higher and higher she knew that at any moment she would emerge into the endless heavens where her entire being would be drenched and suffused in the unbearable, brilliant light of an orgasm.

With her face smothered against the heat of Kym's private place, every breath she took was alive with the scent of sex. Her mouth was flooded with the taste of arousal. Her lips and tongue were sticky with the nectar of lust. Nothing existed except the sensations that made her body vibrate with desire. It would take just the merest touch to lift her into the shuddering release of a climax.

But then the pressure on her face eased, and the source of the nectar was taken away. She blinked in the unexpected light, and shut her eyes tight. She felt her legs being gently lowered, and her wrists were untied. She heard voices, but she didn't try to understand the words being said to her. She felt hands holding her shoulders, and she allowed herself to be helped to her feet. Her legs were unsteady, and she was grateful for the body beside her against which she could lean. As she floated downwards, away from the bright sun of her beckoning orgasm, she began to realise that her bottom and her private place were on fire with pain. She had had the strap and then the cane.

The memory of the punishments was enough to start lifting her once more into her personal world of sensual delight.

She opened her eyes. For a moment she was disoriented. She had expected to see one of the familiar rooms in the Private House. Then she remembered where she was. Someone was speaking to her again. Madame la Patronne. The owner of this house. The wielder of the strap and the cane.

'Olena, my dear, are you all right? Kym, give her a drink of water.'

Olena sipped from the glass that was held to her lips. 'Yes, thank you, Madame,' she said. 'That was wonderful. Thank you.'

'Kym, run and fetch a mirror. I'm sure Olena would like to see how well I've coloured her bottom.'

Although her body was still trembling with unsatisfied desire, Olena felt strong enough to stand unaided. She looked over her shoulder into the long mirror that Kym was holding. Madame had whipped her well. Her buttocks seemed more pronounced and protuberant than ever, and although their redness covered a spectrum from pink to dark scarlet, there were no individual marks. She slid a hand down her hip and on to the hot, sore skin, and shivered with lust.

'That's what you wanted, isn't it?' Madame asked.

'It's what I need,' Olena said. 'Thank you, Madame. It's perfect.' She looked around the room. Madame, Kym and the masked man who must surely be Barat were all looking at her. They had all watched her expose her most intimate parts and submit to a long punishment. And now they would all witness an even more humiliating performance. Just the thought of it made Olena blush with shame and shiver with desire. 'Madame,' she whispered, 'there is just one more thing I have to ask for.'

Madame sat in the armchair, crossed her legs, placed her hands on the arms, and looked up into Olena's face. 'And what is that, my dear?'

Olena knew that of all her sinful thoughts and deeds, the most abominable was to achieve and, worst of all, to enjoy the state of blissful release that she had been taught to refer to as an orgasm or a climax. She was aware that others, men and women, could have orgasms without a twinge of guilt: they came as easily as they breathed. Olena had learnt how to enjoy her climaxes, but she could not do so until she had been properly punished, and she needed someone else's permission. If someone else took the responsibility for authorising her to unleash the vilest part of her nature, then she could allow herself to enjoy the shattering waves of pleasure.

'Please, Madame,' Olena said, 'may I be permitted to have an orgasm? It's usual,' she added, her voice faltering as she admitted her frailty and vice, 'after I've been punished.'

'Of course you may,' Madame said. 'But I'm glad you asked me. No one is allowed that pleasure in this house without my permission. You may go to your room, if you want privacy.'

It had been a very long time since Olena had been allowed to have an orgasm alone. Sometimes she was brought to a climax while she was being whipped; sometimes she came afterwards, while still bound and held open, or while being penetrated. Even when she was freed, and instructed to use her own fingers, the humiliation of opening herself, and knowing that spectators were watching her hands at work in her private place, added to both the punishment and the pleasure she was allowed to take in it.

She was tempted to accept Madame's offer. Alone in her room she could do whatever she chose. She could smack her sore bottom, to revive the searing pain that could be relied on to take her to the edge of her climax. She could push something into her little hole, and hold it stretched open as a constant reminder of just how depraved her desires were. She could hurt her nipples, perhaps with the bristles of her hairbrush, because she knew that her breasts were almost as much a sign of her sinfulness as were her bottom and her sex, and her breasts had so far received no punishment at all.

But she knew that to have an orgasm alone would be selfish. She was aware that people took pleasure in watching her, and she had to admit that she liked to have an audience: she deserved to be made to feel ashamed.

'I'd prefer to show you, Madame,' she said.

Madame looked at her and smiled. 'How sweet of you,' she said. 'Well, we'd better gather round and watch, then. Come and kneel at my feet, and do as I tell you.'

Olena knelt in front of Madame's chair and waited for instructions. Now that she knew her climax was not to be delayed much longer, her entire body was once again trembling with anticipation.

'Put your left hand behind your back,' Madame told her, 'and play with your anus. Put your right hand over your pretty little mound, my dear, and put your fingers into your vagina. You can press the heel of your hand against your clitoris. Very good. You may begin.'

As soon as Olena's hands touched her sensitive places she began to feel stabs of breathtaking pleasure. It wouldn't take long for her to come. She realised that until a few moments ago she hadn't thought about the Private House for hours, and even the familiar act of masturbating for a small audience didn't make her homesick. But she knew that she was in the wrong place, and that she had to return home.

'What will you do, Madame,' she said, gasping and catching her breath as she pressed her fingers into herself, 'when people from the Private House come looking for me?'

Madame ran her fingers through Olena's hair. 'Don't worry about that,' she said, and laughed. 'No one will find you here. We've laid a false trail. Anyone who tries to look for you will be led directly to Edmund. And no one escapes from Edmund's menagerie, unless I ask him very nicely.'

Talia, with the taste of the taxi driver still in her mouth, and with unsatisfied desire buzzing like sleepy bees in her sex and her nipples, had walked past the address written on the piece of paper she held in her hand. She shook her head, and told herself to concentrate on her mission: the day was drawing to an autumnal close, but there was still time to find and rescue Olena.

She retraced her steps, and stood on the pavement outside the building with the correct number. At one end of the narrow alley she could see the lights and bustling traffic of the suburb's main shopping street. Here, only a short distance from the jostling crowds and rumbling vehicles, there was only windswept silence. Many of the small shops were closed, and some had boards nailed across their windows. Some of the houses appeared to be derelict. The building in front of which she stood, however, seemed to be still in use. It was the largest premises in the alley, occupying the space of several houses. The gaudy paintwork was faded, but relatively new, and the doors and windows were in good repair.

But this can't be the right place, Talia said to herself. It was a shop, and she didn't think it likely that the man she was looking for, Barat, who had been brought up in the village from which she had been so memorably ejected, would take up residence in a shop.

Well, I can't stand out here, she thought. I have to do something. The wind is getting colder, and I'm not dressed for poor weather. I've come all this way, so I suppose I'd better go in and make some enquiries. It's a strange place, though.

As she strode towards the shop's entrance she glanced up at the sign hanging above the door: EDMUND'S TOYS & AMUSEMENTS.

There was a picture of a teddy bear and a blonde-haired doll. In the fading light it looked to Talia as though the doll was kneeling, with her face in the bear's groin. Very odd, she thought.

Four

On the morning of her first day in Edmund's house of toys and amusements, Talia woke suddenly and remembered at once where she was.

Her cottage in the forest; the room in the Private House where she and Anne had moaned and panted their vows of undying love; even the hotel room in which she had spent the night before last – all of these seemed as distant as a dream. But she was surprised to find that she felt curiosity rather than foreboding.

She was in a little room high in an attic, with a dormer window that gave her a view only of the city roofs. She was warm and comfortable under a thick quilt. The room was sparsely furnished, but it was clean and the whitewashed walls were bright with morning light.

The door was closed. She couldn't remember whether she had closed it herself before clambering gratefully into the soft bed. She looked at the door-handle. She was sure that if she went to the door and tried to open it, she would find it locked from the outside. She had guessed the previous evening, even as she had allowed herself to be ushered into the depths of the building, that she would not be permitted to leave as easily.

Yesterday, the little man behind the counter of the shop – so short that she had not at first noticed him watching her – had recognised the name Barat, and had clearly been expecting her to arrive. As he stood on tiptoe and extended his stubby arm to shake her hand, his face had creased into a cheerful grin. He had looked scarcely less grotesque than the masks and mannequins that had leered at her from the dusty display cases, but his manner was nothing but friendly.

He had beckoned her to follow him through the doorway at the back of the shop, and as he had led her along garishly painted corridors she had heard snatches of music, and declaiming voices, and laughter, from distant parts of the house. Coloured lights flickered around the edges of some of the closed doors that she passed.

'Where are we going?' she had asked. 'Does this place go on for ever?'

'It's a whole world of entertainment in here,' the little man had replied. He had turned to her and tapped the side of his bulbous nose. 'Edmund owns half the street, although you wouldn't know it from the outside. All the properties are knocked together, connected by passages and doorways. Even I get myself lost sometimes.' He had laughed, and had set off again through a door that led into another corridor.

Talia strode after him. 'Is Barat here?' she had asked. 'It's rather urgent.'

'You'll have to speak to Edmund himself about that,' the little man had said. 'In the morning.'

Talia had hesitated only a moment. She had sighed, and had decided in that instant to accept the implied invitation to spend the night in the strange house, even though she had known that she might have been allowing herself to be ensnared. But what choice had she had? To find Olena she had first to find Barat, and it was obvious that he was known in Edmund's house.

Once she had seen the cosy attic room, with its temptingly soft bed, she had felt overwhelmed by tiredness. By that time she had realised that even if she had wanted to leave she doubted whether she would have been able to retrace her steps through the labyrinth of corridors and doorways. But in any case the warm, clean room with its inviting bed had seemed entirely preferable to braving once again the cold, gritty streets of the city. Through the little window the evening sky had looked dark and threatening, and she could hear the autumn wind whistling over the tiles.

She had been given a meal, with a small glass of wine, which she had consumed in her room. She had been left alone. Noises from the house below floated occasionally into the room: bursts of music, wilder than previously, and once again voices, raised in laughter or excited shouts.

She couldn't remember falling asleep, but she recalled fragments of dreams that were filled with images of circus entertainers and fairground rides.

She told herself that until she tried to turn the handle on the door she could not be sure that she was a prisoner. She pulled back the covers, and swung her feet to the floor. She enjoyed a delicious shiver as the air in the room caressed her naked body.

Still she didn't go to the door. Instead she ducked under an exposed roof timber and into the tiny bathroom. The house was entirely quiet now. The previous night it had seemed to contain hundreds of people; now it might have been deserted, but for her. As she performed her ablutions she felt herself becoming more excited and tense, but still not in the least concerned: as soon as she was washed and ready, something would happen. Either she would leave the room, and go to seek answers as she continued in her quest to find Olena; or someone would come for her, and lead her away, to provide her with information or for some other purpose. Something was about to happen, of that Talia was sure.

All that remained was to pull on her clothes. Then she would have no excuse to delay any longer: she would have to try the door. She could hear noises, now, from below: voices, and the sounds of people climbing stairways. Still naked, she checked her reflection in the tall mirror that stood next to the window. Her long hair was still damply dark, but she had brushed it out and she knew that as it dried golden highlights would appear among the shining auburn waves. Her high, round bottom showed not a trace of the whipping she had received in Barat's village. The pink tips of her breasts were hard. She brushed the tips of her fingers across the top of her freshly shaved sex: she knew she was damp inside.

She turned to face the door. Now she would discover whether she was a guest or a prisoner. She took a step forward.

The door opened. Talia stood, frozen with surprise, with one arm outstretched towards the door-handle, as the three remarkable men who filled the doorway invaded her room. She stepped back until she felt the bed against the backs of her knees and then, with a gesture that she had long thought had been trained out of her, she drew her arms together in an attempt to shield her nakedness.

She would not have felt so bashful if the men had said anything, or if they had not stared at her so intently, or if they had not looked so unusual. One of them, dressed in overalls and carrying coils of rope, was as short and crumpled-faced as the little man she had met the previous evening; the second was a broad-shouldered, muscular giant, wearing only a pair of trunks, who had to stoop to enter the room; and the third was wearing the grotesque make-up and harlequin costume of a clown.

'Hello,' Talia began, but before she could say another word the tall man stepped forward, grasped her shoulders, spun her round as if she was no more than a doll, and gripped her wrists together behind her back in one of his enormous fists.

'Be silent,' he said, in a voice that reverberated from the rafters.

'On the bed,' the clown said. 'Hold her down.'

Talia could only flail her legs as she was lifted into the air and deposited on the rumpled quilt. She tossed her head, trying to catch her breath and to protest, but she was helpless in the giant's grasp.

There was, she realised, no point in trying to converse with the men while she was in such an undignified position, and so she merely uttered wordless exclamations as the giant held her arms, and turned her this way and that, on her front and on her back, while the dwarf held her ankles and the clown carried out a thorough inspection of her body.

'Thin,' the clown said, 'but pretty enough. We can always use another redhead. Tits on the small side, as well, but good and firm. Shapely little arse, good and resilient. Already shaved, too – that'll save a bit of time. She'll do,' he concluded. 'Collar her.'

Talia was pulled to her feet. The giant bent her over, pressing his bulging shorts into her bottom, while the dwarf buckled a collar around her neck. The giant pulled her upright.

'Tie her,' the clown said. 'I've an idea this one's a fighter.'

Talia struggled, but she could do nothing to break the giant's steely grip. The dwarf looped rope around her wrists, and tied them tightly together. Then she felt him busy at her ankles.

'Not too close together,' the clown said. 'Hobble her so she can walk.'

When she realised she was helplessly bound, Talia stopped struggling, blinked, and tried to steady her breathing. The clown was standing before her, holding something in front her face. It was the key to the door of her room.

'Number Forty-one,' he said.

Talia realised that the key, like that of a hotel bedroom, had a number engraved on the plate above the stem. The previous evening she had noticed a plaque, carrying the number forty-one, on the outside of the door to her room.

'Come along, Forty-one,' the clown said. 'Step carefully and you won't trip.'

Propelled by a push of the giant's hand, Talia stumbled forwards. By taking small steps she was able to walk with a little dignity, although she could do nothing to stop the dwarf reaching up to jiggle the tips of her breasts. She followed the clown out of the room.

'Leave her alone, Emilio,' the clown said to the dwarf when they were all in the corridor. 'We'll play with her later. Now then, Forty-one,' he went on, leaning close to Talia. She could smell the sweet greasepaint on his face. He held up the key once again. 'This is yours,' he said. 'Your key to your own little room. As you've no pockets, I'll put it somewhere you can't lose it.'

He hooked his index finger in the metal ring at the front of Talia's collar and pulled her even closer. Talia watched his face as he concentrated on fiddling with the key and the ring. Under the make-up, she realised, he was quite good-looking. She heard a click.

'There,' the clown announced. 'Your key is safely locked in place.'

'How do I unlock it?' Talia asked.

The clown's face made a red-lipped parody of a sorrow-ful smile. 'One: don't speak unless you're spoken to,' he said. He nodded to the dwarf, and even as Talia realised what was about to happen she felt a swishing length of rope draw a line of fire across her bottom. 'I would have thought they'd have trained you better in the Private House. Two: you don't unlock your key. You'll get it once you've earnt it. You're here to work, Forty-one.'

Bound, collared, and with her buttocks tingling from the smack of the rope, Talia hobbled along the corridor with her bizarre captors. Even now she felt no presentiment of danger. On the contrary: her sex was quivering inside as she imagined what price she might have to pay for the information she required. Talia was still enjoying being a detective.

Kym stood outside the door to Olena's room. She smoothed imaginary creases from the pleats of her short grey skirt. Should she knock? she wondered. It went against her nature to be polite. And she had as much right as Olena to go anywhere in the house – anywhere except the rooms that Madame prohibited. But Olena had never done or said anything to annoy Kym – she was almost irritatingly sweet-natured.

Kym knocked on the door, and waited a couple of seconds. She had turned, and was about to stride away, when she heard Olena's voice saying, 'Come in.'

Kym almost cursed. She couldn't back out now. She took a deep breath and opened the door.

107

Olena was naked, but she had pulled a sheet from the bed and was holding it in front of her. It did nothing to conceal the swell of her breasts.

'Oh,' she said. 'Good morning, Kym. Does Madame want me to attend her?'

Now what can I say? Kym asked herself. The fact was that Madame hadn't asked her to fetch Olena. The visit was entirely her own idea. She wasn't sure why she was there, in Olena's room, breathing in Olena's spicy, chocolatey perfume, transfixed once again by the sight of Olena's exuberantly curvaceous body and her innocent, open face.

'Madame will want to see you later,' Kym said. That was a certainty. 'I'm here to help you get ready.'

Kym was pleased with her explanation. She hadn't specified that she was acting under Madame's instructions, but she'd made it sound as though she wasn't merely offering her assistance as an act of kindness.

'Thank you, Kym,' Olena said. She ducked her head, and looked at Kym from behind a curtain of her glossy, dark locks. She wound a corner of her sheet around her fingers as she allowed it to slide from her body. 'I know it's naughty, but I can't help liking it when someone watches me. I'm going to take a shower next. I suppose you'll want to help me.'

Kym could only nod. She followed Olena into the bathroom. Her eyes didn't stray from the sway of Olena's hips and the tiny quiverings of her luscious buttocks.

Like all of the bathrooms in Madame's house, Olena's was spacious. It had a shower cubicle, as well as a large bath with a shower hose attached to the taps. Olena stood uncertainly on one of the rugs. She looked shyly at Kym. She seemed to be waiting to be told what to do.

'Shower in the bath,' Kym said. 'I want to be able to see everything you do.' A thrill swept through her as she said the words. It was the kind of thing that Madame would say.

Olena, holding the shower head in her hand, played warm water over her milky-coffee skin. Kym said nothing but merely nodded encouragingly whenever Olena looked at her. Kym tried to analyse her feelings. She could be in no doubt that she was thoroughly aroused. Her sex, naked under her short skirt, was as warm and wet as the water that was cascading down Olena's curvaceous body. Her nipples, as firm as walnuts, were pressing against the buttoned-down flaps that covered them.

But why, she wondered, was she so excited? It was undeniable that Olena's body was spectacularly well developed. Although she was still only in her early twenties, and her waist, shoulders and limbs had the slimness of youth, her tits and arse were quite simply the biggest and roundest that Kym had ever seen. Glistening and glowing under the stream of water, Olena's body was what Kym imagined to be every man's ideal. That was the odd thing. Kym didn't usually go for overtly feminine women. She liked boyish girls, with small breasts and slim hips.

'Shall I wash myself now?' Olena asked. Kym looked up and met the up-and-under gaze of Olena's wide, guileless eyes. Another tremor of desire shot through her, and again she could only nod.

I could tell her to do anything, Kym realised. And she'd do it. I could tell her to wank herself off while she's cleaning out her arsehole with her fingers, and she'd do it, just like she spreads herself open so that Madame can play with her and smack her. She'll do anything for me, here and now. I could make her suck my tits, and then lick me until I come.

If only Madame didn't have such strict rules about when orgasms were permitted, Kym thought. I can't even bring myself off without Madame's say-so.

Nonetheless she let her left hand, behind her back, pluck up the hem of her skirt so that her fingers could nudge between her buttocks, into the space between the tops of her thighs, and touch the hot, sticky membranes of her parted sex. 'Do your tits again,' she told Olena, 'and then squat down so that you can soap your cunt and your arse. You know Madame will expect you to be thoroughly clean.'

Kym's fingers pressed upwards into the wet warmth, and she suppressed the shivering of her body. Bloody hell, she thought, it felt marvellous telling Olena what to do. As Olena massaged her breasts with the sponge, her face revealed every nuance of emotion she felt: outrage, arousal, submission, shame.

'Madame's going to test you again today,' Kym said, 'and punish you.' She was surprised to realise how much she wanted to be present during Olena's ordeal.

'I hope so,' Olena said. 'I know it's wrong, but I like it.' She held the sponge against her bosom and stared appealingly at Kym. 'If we're to be friends, Kym, you must understand how utterly wicked I am. It's not just that I'm naughty and sinful. It's far worse than that. I actually enjoy the wicked things I do. It seems that the more vile and unspeakable the thing is, the more I like it. I even enjoy being punished. So you see there's no hope for me.' Tears were standing in her eyes.

Kym stepped forward. Standing in the bath, Olena towered over her. Kym reached up, took the sponge from Olena's hands, stroked Olena's damp hair, and tugged Olena's face towards hers. They kissed. Olena's lips parted in response to Kym's pressure. Kym caressed the pendant globes of Olena's breasts, and felt her shiver with pleasure.

'It's all right,' Kym said. She stepped away from the bath. She had been about to say something really soppy. 'Come on, get on with washing yourself. That's right, squat down, facing me, and keep your legs wide apart. No, don't use the sponge. I want to see you do it with your fingers. Now hold yourself open and wash. Very slowly, very thoroughly.'

Sobbing, smiling, and red-faced with embarrassment and pleasure, Olena washed her vulva.

As she watched Olena's performance Kym wondered what Madame intended to do with her. It didn't seem possible that Madame could let Olena go. She would surely want to keep her.

* * *

The three men enjoyed Talia in a storeroom. They didn't discuss the matter: the giant simply pushed her into the dark room when the clown held open the door.

The clown lit a lamp, illuminating rows of shelving but not enough to allow Talia to identify the strange contraptions that were stored there. The dwarf made towards the shelves, but the clown called him back. 'No time for that, Emilio,' he said. 'We have to be quick.' He undid the bow at the waistband of his oversized trousers and they fell around his ankles, almost covering his equally oversized shoes.

The giant pulled down his trunks. The dwarf undid enough of the buttons of his overalls to release his erect member. His was the largest although, Talia supposed, perhaps it looked particularly massive because its owner was so small.

Talia sighed. Even though the love of her life was the delicious Anne, she liked being penetrated by men's cocks and she was ready for sex. However, she doubted whether these three would take much trouble to give her pleasure. And she had become accustomed to receiving quite a lot of corporal punishment before penetration and orgasm. None of the men, she noted ruefully, was wearing a belt. The best she could hope for was a spanking.

In fact she received not even a single slap on the bottom. When the giant, without undoing her bonds, bent her forwards and nudged her legs as far apart as the rope between her ankles would permit, she hoped that she was about to be smacked. Instead he simply stood behind her and thrust his hard penis into her sex.

Talia gasped, and then moaned appreciatively. Anne was endlessly inventive with phalluses, vibrators, her fingers and her tongue, but Talia still liked to feel the hot, throbbing hardness of a man inside her from time to time.

'She's wet,' the giant grunted.

The clown stood in front of Talia's bowed head. He collected her long hair in his hands and impaled her mouth on his erection. 'She's from the Private House,' he said, thrusting his hips back and forth. 'She's already half trained.'

111

The clown and the giant held her still and said nothing as they pushed inside her. The dwarf was content to stand beside her and let her swinging breasts buffet the monstrous dome of his penis.

Talia concentrated on enjoying the sensations, but she knew that she wouldn't come. If only the dwarf would play with her nipples, or if the giant would just reach around her hip and press his big fingers near to her clitoris. Instead, the clown and the giant were pumping methodically and rapidly, intent only on their own satisfaction. They came almost simultaneously: Talia had started to suck and swallow the jets of sperm that filled her mouth when she heard the giant exclaim, and felt him stop moving, as her insides were flooded with an explosion of heat.

Panting, the two men stayed inside her while the dwarf took hold of his vast member and thrust it more determinedly against Talia's breasts. His hand moved more and more quickly on the thick stem, and then he uttered a cry. Talia felt a splash of warm semen against her skin; another; and another; and another.

Still the dwarf's hand was moving, and still heavy spurts of sticky heat were issuing from the tip of his enormous erection.

'Finished, Emilio?' the clown said.

The dwarf gasped and grunted. 'Not yet,' he muttered, and he continued to deposit spurts of semen on to Talia's breasts.

'Finished now,' the dwarf stated at last. 'Very good,' he added as he stepped back and pushed his member back inside his overalls.

I wish I was finished, Talia thought. I've hardly started.

She couldn't contain a little whimper of frustration as the clown and the giant pulled their penises out of her. She remained bent forwards, hoping that one of them would do something else to her.

'Stand up, Forty-one,' the clown said. He was behind her, untying her hands. 'There's a sink in the corner. Get yourself cleaned up. And be quick about it. We'll be late if we don't hurry.'

Although the three men half carried and half dragged Talia, still dripping cold water from her breasts and face, along the corridors in their haste to deliver her on time, once they reached their destination there seemed to be no cause for hurry.

Until now Talia had seen the inside of only three rooms in the vast warren that was Edmund's domain: the shop, which was the public entrance; her bedroom; and the storeroom in which the three men had used her. She was intrigued to find herself taken into a large, windowless room that was clearly a workshop. Electric lights strung along the metal girders that supported the ceiling threw harsh illumination on rows of benches, on which scores of complicated mechanical and electrical devices were arrayed in various stages of construction. Talia had lived for years among the forest people, and she knew very little about engineering or electronics. She thought she recognised some of the devices as motors, but otherwise she knew only that she was looking at coils of wire, and wheels and cogs, and lengths of tubing, and here and there a mannequin's face or arm. Stacked along the walls were wooden boxes, neatly labelled: one contained a jumble of toothed wheels; another was overflowing with cloths in bright colours; a third contained nothing but coloured light bulbs.

She could hear the sounds of people working in the far reaches of the room, which she guessed was a basement that extended below several of the properties in the street. The only people she could see, however, were the two who were waiting for her to be delivered.

They were dressed identically in brown cotton coats with pens clipped into the breast pockets. Both had short, dark hair and were wearing round, black-rimmed spectacles. Both were carrying clipboards. It was a few moments before Talia realised that one of them was a man and the other a woman.

'You're late, Markov,' the woman said to the clown. She looked at the watch pinned to her lapel. 'Six minutes. And for goodness' sake untie her ankles before you go. Tethering is entirely unnecessary.'

113

The clown gestured to the dwarf, who knelt at Talia's feet and untied the rope. 'This one's new,' the clown said. 'Number Forty-one.'

The woman looked at him over her glasses. 'She's obviously new, Markov. And I can read.' She flicked the key that was hanging from the front of Talia's collar. 'You and your friends can leave us now. I'm sure you have other duties to attend to. We'd like to get Forty-one finished with before Edmund arrives to see her.'

The clown, the giant and the dwarf left the room. Talia was alone with the two technicians. She felt very exposed as they walked around her naked body, making occasional notes on their clipboards but saying nothing.

'I'm Freda,' the woman announced at last, and she tucked her clipboard under her arm. 'This is Fredric. We have to measure you. It's more efficient to take a complete set of figures now, right at the beginning.' She smiled, and Talia felt a little more at ease.

'I'm Talia,' she began, but Freda stopped her with an abrupt gesture.

'You are Forty-one,' Freda said gently. 'It will save a lot of confusion if you use only your number. Of course, you may be given temporary names, for certain performances. And one day, if you're good, your owner may allow you to have a name all of your own. But we're getting ahead of ourselves. You haven't even been measured yet, still less trained.'

'Follow me,' Fredric said. 'We have to find the appropriate frame for your size. A Two D, I'd have said,' he added to his colleague.

'Perhaps an E,' Freda replied. 'But we'll start with a D.'

'Aren't you worried that I'll try to escape?' Talia asked as she followed the two technicians between rows of benches. It felt strange and uplifting to be able to take normal strides.

They stopped in front of her and turned to face her. 'Not at all, Forty-one,' Freda said. 'Please remember not to speak out of turn. You will be punished for disobedience. There is no possibility of escape. You are naked, and you have no idea where you are. You should concentrate on doing your best for Edmund now that you are in his employ.'

'Oh,' Talia said. She had looked over Freda's shoulder, and she had seen the line of person-sized contraptions that Fredric and Freda were leading her towards.

Each one looked like an incomplete suit of armour suspended on wires and pulleys inside a boxlike framework of wooden struts. Talia thought that they looked like nothing so much as medieval instruments of torture.

'Two D,' Fredric said. 'That one.' He pointed to one of the contraptions. It looked to Talia no different from the others.

'Don't worry, Forty-one,' Freda said. 'They are merely measuring devices. Two D is, we think, the closest approximation to your height and shape. Once you're installed in it, we'll make adjustments to arrive at the precise figures.'

'What do they measure?' Talia asked. As she was led towards the frame that the technicians had chosen, it looked no less sinister.

'Everything,' Fredric replied. 'Length of arm, width of foot, circumference of neck, waist and thigh. Once we have your measurements, we can fit you with whatever costume or appliance is required. Please enter the frame, and place your feet on the footplates.'

Plates of shaped, cold metal embraced the backs of Talia's legs as she took up the required position. The technicians set to work, scarcely looking at her as they shortened this and lengthened that, tightened screws and adjusted hinges, and fitted more shaped plates around Talia's limbs.

It was, in fact, just like being fitted with a suit of armour. Soon Talia's feet, legs, arms and hands were encased in a metal exoskeleton that fitted so precisely, and was so artfully hinged, that she could move almost as freely as when naked. The only words that Freda and Fredric exchanged were the measurements that they took as they fitted new pieces and made adjustments. They noted every figure on the papers attached to their clipboards.

It was as well that the metal suit allowed Talia to move. Every piece had at least one anchor-point, and the technicians attached hooks and wires, and metal struts, to ever more of them as they worked.

Soon Talia discovered why her metal suit was festooned with connections to the outer framework. By turning handles and moving levers, the technicians were able to move Talia's limbs. This was important, Freda explained briefly, because the soft tissues of Talia's body adopted different shapes depending on her position. Her breasts, for instance, took on different shapes depending on whether she was upright, leaning forwards, or lying on her back.

Talia was wondering how the technicians were going to measure her breasts in all these different positions when she felt her entire body being lifted and turned. It was clear that inside the frame she could be hoisted into any position that the human body could adopt. She protested helplessly as she found herself suspended on her back, with her legs up and parted, while Freda and Fredric tried various metal cups on her breasts and buttocks until they found the ones that fitted exactly. Then they turned her over and measured her breasts and buttocks again.

The technicians saved the most demeaning measurements until last, however. Talia found herself suspended upright, with her thighs doubled up so that her knees almost touched her shoulders. By now her breasts, midriff, bottom and vulva were the only parts of her body not encased in metal, and they felt particularly vulnerable. While she was in this position Freda and Fredric quietly and efficiently found templates that fitted precisely to her hindquarters and her open sex, and they continued to make notes apparently oblivious to the fact that Talia was as exposed and helpless as a woman can be.

Why, Talia wondered with a little trepidation, was it necessary for Freda and Fredric to know the exact length of her sex-lips, external and internal, or the precise distance from the tip of her clitoris to the rear of her vagina?

These were not the last of their measurements. With Talia in the same position, Freda and Fredric inserted a

116

variety of cylinders and cones into her vagina and anus, in order, they said, to measure her internal dimensions. The helplessness of her position, and the unhurried attention that the technicians were paying to her most intimate and sensitive orifices, were making Talia very aroused.

At that moment Talia heard footsteps approaching.

'Let me out,' she appealed to the technicians, but Freda and Fredric merely smiled at her. Fredric gently pulled out the blunt-nosed cylinder that was in Talia's anus. 'Size six, girth C,' he said. Freda made a note. Talia felt something pressing against the delicate funnel of skin, and she relaxed the muscle so that it could slide inside her. 'I'm trying a size seven,' Fredric said.

Talia sighed with pleasure as she felt her anus being filled, but she also watched the tall figure who was approaching between the rows of benches. He was middle-aged, she thought, but slim and dark-haired. He walked with a confident stride. He was wearing a burgundy morning coat, immaculately pressed black trousers, and a floppy bow tie of black silk. He had an impressively curled moustache, like that of a circus ringmaster, and clenched between his even, white teeth was an empty cigarette holder. This must surely, Talia thought, be the proprietor of the entire establishment.

'Mr Edmund,' Fredric said. 'Delighted to see you this morning. This is Forty-one.'

The man stood in front of Talia. She couldn't meet his gaze as he narrowed his eyes and surveyed every inch of her suspended, doubled-up, exposed body. She realised she was blushing. She was acutely aware of the two objects – their flanged bases prominently visible – that were still embedded in her vagina and anus.

The man took the cigarette holder from his mouth. 'Edmund Jones,' he said. 'Master craftsman of toys and amusements, and owner of this emporium of entertainment. Glad to have you on the staff, Forty-one.' He flashed a vulpine grin.

'If I'm working here,' Talia said, 'what's my job?'

Edmund barked a laugh. 'First of all, Forty-one, you must learn to obey the rules of the house. And that means no talking back, as I'm sure you've already been told. Then you're to be trained.'

He stepped forward, and lent to inspect Talia's distended vulva. He tapped the end of his cigarette holder against the base of the phallus in her vagina, and watched her face as she gasped and blinked. 'I see you've had to use no additional lubrication here,' he remarked to the technicians.

'No, Mr Edmund,' Freda said. 'Forty-one was aroused when she was delivered to us. I suspect that Markov and his crew had a little fun with her. They were six minutes late. And she has become more excited during the measuring.'

'Excellent,' Edmund said. 'Very few of my people have come from the Private House,' he told Talia. 'I think in your case we'll be able to skip the initial training. But don't think that you'll find the work easy, Forty-one. I will expect particularly high standards from you. I fully intend that you will become one of my star attractions.'

He let the tip of the jet-black cigarette holder rest against the junction of her sex-lips, tantalisingly close to her clitoris. He rolled the thin, black cylinder very gently from side to side. Overcome with desire, Talia momentarily forgot that she was bound, and she moaned with frustration when she found that she couldn't push her sex forward to increase the pressure against it.

She heard Edmund's short laugh, and opened her eyes.

'My establishment is a little stricter than the Private House,' he told her. He withdrew the cigarette holder, wiped its end with the folded handkerchief that decorated the top pocket of his morning coat, and inserted it once again between his teeth.

'Filthy habit, cigarettes,' he said. 'Gave them up years ago. Got used to the taste of this thing, though.' The cigarette holder struck a jaunty angle from the corner of his mouth.

'Stricter than the Private House?' Talia asked. It didn't seem possible.

'I require complete obedience from all my staff, of course,' Edmund explained. 'But whereas, in the Private

118

House, I'm sure you were frequently allowed to indulge yourself and enjoy your own moments of pleasure, my palace of delights is dedicated to the enjoyment only of its patrons. Your task is to entertain and amuse. To perform well, to put on a show that will dazzle and delight – that requires dedication and unstinting hard work. I expect you to commit every fibre of your being to the enjoyment of the customers. You will not be permitted the self-indulgence of serving your own desires.'

'No pleasure for me?' Talia asked. 'No fun at all?'

'None whatsoever,' Edmund stated. 'Except, of course, the satisfaction of pleasing the public. Don't worry,' he added, when Talia opened her mouth to protest again. 'You won't be allowed to fail. Your education here is being sponsored by a valued customer who is also an old friend. You will become a star, Forty-one, no matter how long and arduous the road.'

Talia was bemused. 'Who has paid for me to be here?' she said. 'No one knows where I am.'

'You came here asking for a man named Barat,' Edmund said, and Talia's stomach sank as she guessed that she was about to discover that all her detective work had been in vain. 'No one here has heard of such a person, of course. But we were told that someone would arrive here asking for him, and I have been paid handsomely to hold that someone here and take her into my employment.'

He stepped back, let his gaze run once again up and down Talia's suspended and obscenely exposed body, and sighed with contentment. 'You're right, of course. Nobody knows you are here. Don't pin your hopes on escape or rescue. Apply yourself to your new job. If you work hard, at the end of the day the key to your room will be unlocked from your collar and you will be allowed to retire to your own little haven of comfort, rest and solitude. If you disappoint – Well, let's hope it won't come to that.' He turned towards Freda. 'Forty-one will start work tomorrow,' he declared. 'But I'd like her to spend an hour or so in the pit this afternoon. She needs to be aware of what will happen to her if she doesn't apply herself to her work.'

Barat hated the frilly pink skirt. Of all the costumes that Madame made him wear, this was the most despicable. He was proud of his masculinity, and he liked to believe that Madame valued him for his dark, muscular physique and his vigorous, ever-upright manliness. When he was dressed in nothing but the pink skirt, which was no more than a fringe of frothy lace around his hips, he felt confused and very ashamed.

His only consolation, he reflected as he stood beside Madame's dressing-table, waiting on her pleasure while she applied her make-up, was that Madame had not yet made him wear the skirt when anyone else was present. He thought that he would just about be able to bear the humiliation of wearing it while he attended on Madame during one of her sessions with a guest; he couldn't imagine, however, how he could possibly cope if Kym were to see him in it; and as for Olena – no, she must never know that he had ever worn such a demeaning, emasculating garment.

The problem was that although the skirt was the essence of femininity, it didn't prevent him responding as a man when, as now, he was within inches of his mistress's naked body. While he was wearing the skirt he was supposed to tuck his testicles and penis between his thighs, so that from the front his genital area looked like a woman's. But the proximity of Madame's perfumed breasts and her adorable face, and the friction of the hairs of his legs against the glans, ensured that his penis was long and hard, and almost impossible to contain between his thighs.

He gripped his hands together behind his back and tried to think of anything but the smooth perfection of the skin of Madame's jiggling breasts. It was useless. He could feel his erection, like a coiled spring, straining to be released. It was going to slip out. It would leap to attention in front of him, making the skirt rustle and billow. Madame would not fail to notice. And then –

'Barat,' Madame said, turning away from her mirror and granting him a radiant smile. 'Are you being a good little girl? I don't believe you are.'

Barat licked his lips. 'Sorry, Madame. I couldn't help it. I'll put it away again, Madame.'

But it was too late. Barat knew he could expect no reprieve. Madame's pretty little hands were already searching under the frilly hem of the skirt.

'What's this nasty big thing, Barat?' she said, gazing up at his blushing face. 'What a naughty girl you are. What do naughty girls deserve, Barat?' As she spoke she caressed the length of his iron-hard member.

Barat closed his eyes. 'Punishment, Madame,' he said with a sigh.

'That's right,' Madame said brightly. 'Run and fetch the cane, little girl.'

Barat didn't run. When he was wearing the pink skirt, Madame liked him to skip about the room like a child. It was particularly demeaning when he was excited: his erection held up the front of the skirt, and bounced ridiculously as he skipped.

'Madame,' he said, when he had returned with the cane, 'may I speak?'

Madame flexed the thin wooden rod. 'Yes, Barat,' she said. 'Of course, I may decide to give you a few more strokes if you're impertinent. Little girls can be so provocative.'

Barat knew he was going to be punished anyway. It was worth a little extra pain to obtain the answer to the question that haunted him. 'Thank you, Madame,' he said. He summoned his courage. 'Will you tell me, please, Madame,' he began, and then paused. 'This skirt,' he stammered. 'The things you make me do. The punishments. I find all this very difficult, Madame.'

'Of course you do, Barat. That's why I find you so enjoyable. But what do you want to know?'

She knows what I want, Barat thought. She's toying with me, as she always does. 'When, Madame? When will I be permitted to have Olena? I can wait. But I must have some hope. How many more days?'

'Days?' Madame said, with an unfeigned surprise that made Barat's insides turn cold with disappointment. 'I will grant Olena to you, Barat, only when I have finished with her. And only if you continue to serve me properly. Do not presume that she is already yours.'

A queasy panic afflicted Barat. How long would it take for Madame to tire of Olena? Barat's days of waiting, yearning and servitude seemed to stretch before him like an infinitely long road.

'Don't worry, Barat,' Madame said, still stroking his erection. 'I won't forget to pay some attention to you. Now bend over for your caning, little girl. And don't forget to tuck away this horrible, monstrous thing between your legs.'

As he leant forwards Barat pressed his member down. It was as hard as marble, but the position he was required to adopt made it just possible for him to point the shaft downwards and then to clench his thighs together to hold it in place. He was almost doubled over, his hands were locked together behind his knees, and he trembled with the effort of keeping his legs pressed together.

'Good girl,' Madame said softly. Barat felt her fold back the hem of the hated pink skirt. Madame's hand wandered lightly across his buttocks. Her fingertips crept into the cleft between them, but Barat didn't feel the sudden chill of Madame's moisturising cream: on this occasion, it seemed, Madame did not intend to plug his anus before punishing him. He cursed himself for feeling disappointed.

Madame's fingers slid lower, and caressed the hard sac of Barat's testicles and the underside of his rigid shaft. They came to rest on the head of his penis, stroking the twin bulbs of highly sensitive skin divided by the stretched frenum. 'How very vulnerable you are, Barat,' Madame whispered, 'when you are excited. I advise you to think pure thoughts, little girl, and make this big thing shrink.' Even as she spoke, however, her fingertips continued to circle, and Barat realised that if she didn't stop soon he would start to come. 'I'm minded to cane you on the backs of your thighs, my dear, and if this thing remains inflated I don't see how I can avoid striking it, at least a little.'

Madame's fingers withdrew, and Barat exhaled a sigh of relief. He had had a reprieve. He wondered, though, how he would be able to contain his excitement once Madame's cane-strokes started to sting across his balls and his cock. It would be supremely embarrassing to come while bent over and being caned, with his hot sperm pulsing out and dripping down the backs of his legs.

Still, Madame would certainly cane his buttocks a little first. Perhaps, he hoped, the pain would serve to take his mind off his arousal. He closed his eyes and waited for the first stroke to land.

He felt nothing. He opened his eyes, and found Madame kneeling in front of him and looking up at him with a mischievous glint in her dark eyes. 'Look, Barat,' she whispered. She cupped her plump breasts in her hands and held them up towards him. Her fingers teased her nipples. They were almost touching his face. 'Do you like them?'

'I worship them, Madame,' Barat murmured. 'I worship you.'

Madame released her breasts, but kept her chest lifted towards Barat. She caressed the generous curves with the cane, and pressed it against her nipples. 'What would you do to me, Barat, if our positions were reversed?' she said. 'Would you be a kind and considerate master, as I am kind and considerate to you? Or would you be cruel?' She tapped the cane against the undersides of her breasts, making them tremble. 'I promise you, Barat, you will never have the opportunity to find out.'

Barat groaned. His mistress knew exactly how to torment him.

'Don't close your eyes, Barat,' Madame said, emphasising her instruction by pinching his left nipple. When she knew she had his attention she licked her red lips lasciviously. 'If you're very good today,' she said, 'if you take your caning like a good little girl, and if you behave yourself while I'm playing with Olena, and if you lick me properly when I tell you to, then I might let you come this evening.' She cupped her breasts again, and glanced down at the creamy valley between them. 'I might even let you come here,' she whispered.

Even the prospect of having Olena was driven from Barat's mind. The thought of spilling his seed over his mistress's tits filled his head. He would do anything to please her. 'Thank you, Madame,' he said.

Two thickset, unsmiling dwarves, dressed in black leather, escorted Talia to the small cellar that contained the pit. The room, with stone walls inset with iron rings, and lit by lamps, resembled the dungeons beneath the oldest part of the Private House, and Talia felt almost at home. She knew that she was there to experience a taste of the punishment she would receive if she failed to please her new employer, and she found that she was impatient to begin. She assumed that she would be chained and whipped, and her sex and buttocks were tingling with anticipation. She had been handled so intimately by Freda and Fredric while they had measured her, and the depths of her vagina and anus had been plumbed so thoroughly, that she was dripping wet with arousal. It seemed an age since she had last had even a perfunctory spanking, and her neglected bottom was eager for a vigorous whipping.

Once she had made it clear that she intended to put up no resistance to whatever was in store for her, one of the dwarves left. The wooden door closed behind him with a heavy thud. The other stared at her thoughtfully, and his ugly face broke into a leering grin.

'Pretty,' he said, reaching up to grasp her left breast. 'Young. New. Now the fun begins.'

'Fun?' Talia said.

'Not for you,' the dwarf replied. 'Fun for me. For the audience, too,' he added, pointing upwards.

Talia looked up, and saw that halfway up one of the high walls there was a gallery. Sitting in it was Edmund Jones.

He leant forward. 'This is the viewing gallery,' he said, raising his voice a little so that she could hear. 'Customers pay well for a seat here, Forty-one. Even when you're being punished you're putting on a show. Don't forget that. The only private place is your bedroom.'

The dwarf opened a wooden chest and took from it a handful of leather bands. 'Put these on,' he instructed Talia. 'Wrists, ankles, waist, and just above the knees.'

As Talia buckled the straps about her limbs and waist she saw that all of them were provided with metal rings. It's going to be easy, she thought, to secure me in almost any position. The idea of being held motionless during the punishment only added to her excitement.

Meanwhile, the dwarf had begun to work a large handle that was set into the wall. As he turned it, Talia saw that what she had thought was a grille covering a square hole among the flagstones was in fact the top of a large cage, which was rising from the floor.

It stopped when the top was level with her waist. The hole from which it had risen was dark. This, Talia realised, was the pit. She looked up at Edmund. She realised that her expectation of a straightforward whipping was going to be disappointed. Edmund clearly had devised a punishment much more devious.

The cage had only three sides, constructed of grids of sturdy metal bars. The fourth side was open. The top of the cage, also, was a metal grid, but now Talia saw that across the centre, parallel with the open side, there was fixed a padded leather yoke that was clearly designed to support a person's neck. It was shaped to be higher at the back, to provide a rest for the back of the head, and lower at the front. Her body, she realised, would be fastened inside the cage, but her head would protrude from the top.

Part of the top of the cage, between the yoke and the open side, was hinged. The dwarf lifted it, and it fell back with an echoing crash against the cage's side. The dwarf clambered on the remaining part of the top of the cage and unfastened the front of the yoke. 'Get in,' he said, pointing into the pit.

Talia approached nervously, and sighed with relief when she saw that the pit was not deep. The wooden bottom of the cage was only as far below the floor of the cellar as the top of the cage was above it. There was even a ladder, with two rungs, to make it easy for her to descend.

It wasn't cold in the cellar, but even so Talia shivered as she stepped down into the pit. The cellar wasn't brightly lit, and the bottom of the cage was in deep shadow. Talia tried not to imagine rats. The floor was dry, however, under her bare feet, and she heard no scuttling that might indicate rodents or large insects. As her eyes became accustomed to the gloom she saw that between the cage and the walls of the pit there were hawsers, cogs, pulleys and toothed bars of metal that, she assumed, were part of the mechanism for raising and lowering the cage. There was a mysterious hole in the centre of the floor.

She turned to face the front of the cage. She was above ground only from the waist up: in the cage she was even shorter than her dwarf gaoler. It was strange to see the world from such a low viewpoint. She looked up to the gallery: Edmund was still there, staring down at her.

She had no further opportunity to survey her surroundings. The dwarf secured the padded leather yoke around her neck. She found that she could move her head from side to side, but with her hands tied behind her she was completely helpless. She had no choice but to stand upright. She realised that when the cage was lowered, only her head would be above the level of the cellar floor.

She soon discovered, however, that this was by no means the full extent of the bondage she would have to endure. The dwarf jumped from the top of the cage, went to the chest to collect a selection of ropes, and then climbed down the short ladder into the pit.

Talia could hear him moving, and she could feel him touching her, but she could not lower her head enough to catch a glimpse of what he was doing. She felt him untie her wrists, and it was clear that he was tying ropes to the metal rings on the cuffs she wore around her wrists, ankles, and waist. She also discovered that the dwarf was taking advantage of the darkness in the pit, and of her helplessness, to touch her intimately. She saw that Edmund was smiling with amusement at the expressions that crossed her face as the dwarf's hands explored her body.

Her wrists were tied to the sides of the cage, just below the level of her shoulders. Her ankles were secured so that they were apart, but not uncomfortably so, and close to the front of the cage. A rope was tied from the back of her waist to the back of the cage, and another from the front of her waist to the front of the cage, so that she could move her torso only a little. Finally the straps that were tied around her legs, just above her knees, were attached, as far as Talia could tell, by slack ropes to parts of the mechanism between the sides of the cage and the walls of the pit.

Talia was surprised, given the amount of rope that the dwarf had used, that her bonds were not more tight and stringent. She could move her arms and legs a little and, she discovered, there was even a narrow ledge at the back of the cage on which she could rest her bottom. It wasn't at all uncomfortable.

The dwarf, after giving Talia's breasts a final rough squeeze, climbed out of the cage. Talia could turn her head enough to see that he went towards the massive handle that controlled the height of the cage. She expected the cage to be lowered into the pit, but the dwarf did nothing. After a few moments, the heavy door of the cellar opened and Edmund strolled in.

'Are you comfortable, Forty-one?' he enquired.

Talia nodded cautiously.

Edmund laughed. 'You won't be for long,' he assured her. 'Are you familiar with the medieval instrument of torture known as the Little Ease? No? It was a very simple device: a room so small that the prisoner inside it could neither stand, sit, nor lie. It sounds harmless, but of course within minutes the pain from the straining, cramped muscles must have become unendurable. And there was no hope of respite.'

He saw the horrified expression on Talia's face, and laughed again. 'Don't worry, Forty-one. Did you really think that I would subject you to such an unsophisticated punishment? The pit is designed to be uncomfortable, certainly: its objective is to make you value the peace and luxury of your bedroom. And it's true that I couldn't resist adding a few modern refinements. However, there is a way to avoid the discomfort, as you will discover. Lower the cage, Pietro. Number Forty-one is about to discover why my staff prefer to meet my expectations rather than spend a night in the pit.'

The dwarf began to turn the handle. The ledge under Talia's bottom seemed to retract against the side of the cage, and she had to stand upright. As the cage, and with it Talia's head, supported by the yoke, began to sink into the floor, Talia found that standing upright was increasingly difficult. The floor, she realised, was not moving: as the cage descended, the space in which she stood was decreasing.

She tried to keep her legs straight, but with her neck held in the yoke, and her waist tied front and back, she was obliged to keep her torso upright and bend her knees. In any case, she realised that the ropes that ran from her knees towards the sides of the cage were now taut, and were pulling her knees apart with increasing force. She was obliged to adopt a squatting position – a position that opened her bottom and her sex more and more as the cage continued its inexorable descent. Talia remembered the hole she had seen in the centre of the cage's floor, and she was not at all surprised to find that, as the top of the cage came down almost to the level of the cellar floor, something smooth and cold pressed into the damp channel between her widely parted sex-lips. Nonetheless she uttered a little cry of surprise.

'The artificial phallus has found you, I see,' Edmund said. 'I advise you to adjust your position so that it fits inside you. It's fixed in place, and you have another six inches to go.'

Talia wriggled her hips, but she was already positioned correctly over the blunt-nosed cylinder. As the cage continued downwards, pressing her into an ever more uncomfortable squat, Talia felt the hard, cold object fill and stretch her.

'It's too big,' she cried out.

Edmund shook his head. 'Nonsense,' he said. 'I grant that it's almost the biggest that you can accommodate. But now you see why we took such trouble to measure you precisely. There you are,' he said, as with a clunk the top of the cage came to rest, level with the floor of the cellar. 'You're in the pit. Is it cosy and comfy in there, Forty-one? Would you like to spend the night in the pit, or would you prefer to be in your own room – the private room that you can enter only if I release the key from your collar?'

The pit was, Talia had to admit, a fiendishly inventive device. The padded yoke supported some of her weight, and she could flex her arms to provide a little support, but even so the muscles in her calves and thighs were already beginning to protest. The object in her vagina seemed to widen considerably from tip to base, so that if she tried to gain some relief by lowering her hindquarters she could feel her vulva being opened as the phallus went deeper into her.

'I couldn't stay like this for half an hour,' Talia protested. 'I'd be in agony.'

'Then an entire night in the pit,' Edmund said, 'would, I'm sure you agree, be a powerful incentive for a lazy or unco-operative worker to behave better in future. You're going to be a hard-working, obedient member of my staff, aren't you, Forty-one?'

'Yes,' Talia almost shrieked. 'Yes, I promise. Just tell me what I have to do to get out of here. Please.'

Edmund smiled indulgently. 'I don't think I'll release you yet,' he said. 'But I will tell you how to gain some relief. Pietro, your gaoler, has, like many of his kin, a prodigious carnal appetite. When he lowers the pit into the floor, it signifies that he needs to sate his desires. Look: you can see that he's ready.'

Talia turned her head. The dwarf had unlaced the front of his leather britches and was fondling a massive erection.

'He'll let you take him in your mouth,' Edmund said, 'if you ask him. And, of course, to do so he'll have to raise the cage. Ask him, Forty-one. Sucking the guard's penis must be preferable to squatting in the cage, surely?'

Talia needed no further encouragement. 'Pietro,' she called out, 'would you like to come in my mouth?'

The dwarf grinned and nodded. He rubbed his hands along the length of his erect penis, and then he began once again to turn the handle. The cage began to rise from the floor.

Talia gasped with relief as her legs straightened under her. Soon she was standing upright, her bottom was resting on the ledge, and it was already difficult to recall why squatting on the thick phallus had seemed so harrowing.

Holding his rigid member before him like a standard the gaoler strode with a rolling gait to stand in front of the cage. Now that the cage had been raised his crotch was at the same level as Talia's head. It occurred to Talia that the dwarf must have very few opportunities to look down on anyone. He was taking full advantage of the situation now, however. He put his hand to his thick lips and made an extravagant kiss. '*Bellissima!*' he shouted, and he pumped his huge erection to show his appreciation of Talia. Then he leant forward and wiped the dark, velvety head of his penis all over Talia's face, leaving thin trails of clear fluid. With her neck enclosed within the yoke, Talia could only screw up her face and shut her eyes.

Then she felt the bull-nosed hardness nudging at her lips, and she opened her mouth to receive the hot cylinder of flesh. The dwarf leant further forwards, over Talia's head, and rested his hands on the bars of the top of the cage behind her. He began to thrust rhythmically with his hips.

'I understand,' Talia heard Edmund say, 'that a guard, once he has used a prisoner's mouth to his satisfaction, will usually leave the cage raised afterwards. Until the urge takes him again, of course. I'm told that Pietro and his clan are renowned for the strength and, I fear, for the frequency of their sexual urges.'

Talia gave up trying to use her tongue to please the dwarf. He seemed oblivious to anything she did to vary the passage of his penis between her lips, and he was evidently content to use her mouth merely as an aid to masturbation. After only a short time his thrusts became quicker, and Talia heard him begin to gasp as he breathed. Her mouth and nose filled with the musky scent of semen, and then, suddenly, he was coming.

The first jet, hot and fierce, shot down Talia's throat. The dwarf pulled back, so that Talia was able to make him cry out with pleasure by licking his urethral slit, and the second spurt filled her mouth. It was apparent that Pietro, like Emilio, produced a remarkable amount of seminal fluid. Talia couldn't swallow it all, and already the third load was filling her mouth again. There was nothing she could do to stop the creamy goo spilling from between her lips and coating her chin and neck. The dwarf's penis was outside her mouth now, but it continued to produce jet after jet of hot, viscous semen. Talia saw that he was holding his member like a hose, but then she had to close her eyes as spurt after spurt rained on to her face and hair and dripped on to her shoulders, neck and breasts.

'Quite remarkable,' Edmund commented.

Talia blinked open her eyes. The lids were heavy and sticky with semen.

'You look a mess, Forty-one,' Edmund said. 'But at least you'll be able to rest now. Pietro won't lower the cage again until he feels the need for another of his prodigious orgasms. When do you think that will be, Pietro?'

The dwarf tucked his pliant but still impressively large member into his britches. 'Half an hour, boss,' he shouted, with a laugh. 'Half an hour, you bet.'

'Half an hour,' Talia repeated. She shook her head. Her hair was dripping with thick liquid. 'He's exaggerating. Isn't he?'

Edmund smiled. 'I'm afraid not, Forty-one. I think that, if you were spending the night here, you'd find that his enthusiasm would begin to wane by the early hours of the morning. Just imagine, though, what a mess you'd be in by that time. You might even begin to think that it would be preferable to let him lower the cage. But I think you'd soon find yourself begging Pietro to use your mouth again.'

He took a watch from his waistcoat pocket. 'I really must be getting along,' he said. 'You'll start work tomorrow, Forty-one. I'm going to put you on show immediately. Breakfast in the canteen at seven-thirty. Report for rehearsals, clean, bright, and eager, at eight-thirty. You'll stay in the pit for another forty-five minutes, and I hope that by the end of that time you'll know that you never want to experience it for an entire night.' He turned to the dwarf. 'Pietro, you will have Forty-one until three o'clock. Then, as long as she has behaved well, you are to release her, remove the key from her collar, and give it to her.' He turned back to Talia. 'I'm allowing you a short and easy day, as it's your first,' he told her. 'I suggest that you go to your room and clean yourself, then find someone to show you round. Dinner will be served at six-thirty – I know it's early, but the evening customers will start to arrive by seven. I suggest that you take a tour of the emporium before you retire, to get an impression of the performances we produce.'

'Very well,' Talia said. She had no better plan. She had no idea of how she could escape, and she needed to find out as much as she could about Edmund's strange palace of amusements. 'What should I wear?' she asked.

Edmund snorted a laugh. 'Your collar, Forty-one. It suits you. You won't get on well here if you're bashful about being seen naked.' A frown appeared on his face. 'I wonder if you still haven't understood why you're here,' he said. 'It's very simple. You will work for me until it has become ingrained in your nature to think of nothing but pleasing the customers. I will watch your progress, and I will work you until I am sure that your obedience and your eagerness to perform owe nothing to even the slightest glimmer of hope that you might derive any enjoyment for yourself. You are to become an automaton, Forty-one. A pleasure doll for the delight of others.'

As Olena waited for the day's test to begin it occurred to her that it would almost be preferable if Madame insisted on keeping her naked. Apart from a pair of perilously high-heeled shoes she was wearing only a flimsy dress of white voile, fastened by a single catch at the waist. She could feel the thin material clinging to her breasts and her bottom, and she had seen, in the mirror in her room, that her nipples, and the dark line of neatly trimmed hair above her sex, and even the slit of her private place, were visible.

132

Nonetheless the dress covered all of her intimate parts, and allowed her the illusion of modesty and respectability. It enabled her almost to suppress, or at least to keep in check, the lewd thoughts that swam constantly into her mind.

She knew that Madame's first instruction to her would be to take off the dress. She also knew that she would obey, and that the act of obedience, and the flood of shame that she would feel at revealing her naked body, would be enough to tip her into the dark, seductive sink of her own depravity. From that moment it would be impossible to conceal her arousal: her private place, already warm and damp and tingling, would flood with her aromatic juices. No matter how hard she tried, it was a foregone conclusion that she would fail any test of her purity, and succeed only in demonstrating that no act, however perverse, would fail to excite her.

For today's test Olena had been brought to a room on the ground floor of Madame's house. Madame had implied that this would be the venue for Olena's tests for several days to come. It was a sort of conservatory, although it contained only a few climbing plants. The sloping roof was of glass, and two sets of French windows could be opened on to the tree-ringed garden. Only the roofs of neighbouring houses could be seen over the treetops, but Olena felt particularly exposed.

There was none of the colonial-style furniture that might have been expected in such a room. There was a large armchair, in which Madame was now seated, but on which Olena imagined herself kneeling with her bottom raised, ready for the punishment she knew she would be found to deserve. There was a leather-upholstered couch, and a tall, padded box, on which Olena knew she could be arranged for inspection or spanking. The walls were lined with shelves and hooks, and among the stored paraphernalia Olena could see coiled whips, and leather straps of all sizes and lengths, and an umbrella stand full of canes and rods. And, of course, there were mirrors: tall, adjustable mirrors in wooden frames on metal castors, and large mirrors fixed on the wall opposite the windows. Olena could not fail to see her own reflection, and her watchers could see her from every angle.

Kym, dressed in her grey uniform, was standing beside Madame's chair. She gave Olena a secretive smile whenever their eyes met. Olena was used to people desiring her: it was sinful to be the object of so much admiration, but she couldn't help enjoying it. She had the impression that Kym was going to enjoy watching her being tested and punished. It was a consolation to Olena that others took pleasure in her incorrigible licentiousness.

The masked, cloaked man was there again, standing incongruously in a corner. It could only be Barat. Olena wished, for his sake, that he would reveal himself soon. The longer he concealed himself, the more difficult she would find it to feign surprise when he threw off his disguise.

Still Madame gave no instructions, but continued to gaze at Olena. Madame was wearing a corset, stockings and high shoes, all in black, and a necklace inset with red stones that matched the scarlet of her lipstick. There was nothing covering her breasts and bottom, and she was sitting with one leg resting carelessly on the arm of the chair, so that whenever Olena glanced at her she couldn't fail to see Madame's private place. A riding-crop hung from a loop around her right wrist. From time to time she reached out and touched Kym under her skirt. At her feet was a large box that, Olena was sure, contained instruments that would be used in today's session of testing.

In the garden the leaves were beginning to turn from green through a spectrum of red, orange and umber. Olena could hear the wind as it rustled through the branches.

'Let's begin,' Madame said at last. 'Olena, take off your dress.'

Olena felt for the catch at her waist. Her private place was hot, her breasts felt swollen, and she was momentarily dizzy with despicable lust. Once again, she knew, she was about to reveal the sordid iniquity of her nature. Once again she would take pleasure in the vilest of deeds. She would beg to be punished, but she knew that the pain and humiliation would only fuel the flames of her passion. In the end she would be allowed to reach a climax, and prove to herself and everyone watching her that she was utterly steeped in sin. Then, for a while, she could be at peace – until the lewd thoughts began to trouble her again.

Olena closed her eyes as she parted the front of the dress. She felt the thin material slide down her body to the floor. She took a deep breath, and guiltily realised that by doing so she was drawing attention to her breasts. When she opened her eyes she found that, as she had expected, every gaze was focused on her body. She felt her cheeks begin to burn with shame, as warm as the desire that was building in her loins.

'Olena, my dear,' Madame said, 'you are quite simply magnificent. Each time I see you undress I find myself lost in admiration. However, we must proceed with today's business. I have decided, Olena, on a particular role for you in my household. However, I intend to introduce you to the requirements of the position by increments. I want to be quite sure that each individual element is, on its own, enough to kindle in you the desires that you find so shameful.'

'Yes, Madame,' Olena said. She had no idea what Madame la Patronne had in mind, but she was pleased that the mistress of the house seemed to have abandoned the pretence of not comprehending Olena's sinful nature. Olena felt secure among people who understood, and did not condemn, her depraved soul.

'Most of us,' Madame declared, 'do not enjoy being physically restrained. No one likes to be rendered helpless, do they?'

Olena could already guess the nature of the trial she was to endure. 'Not usually, Madame,' she ventured.

Madame laughed. 'But you are not a very usual person, are you, Olena? I wonder if you are so perverse that you can actually find pleasure in being tied and fettered?'

Olena already knew the answer, but she was too ashamed to confess. She blushed more deeply. In the

Private House she was often tied up, either when someone wanted to penetrate her, or for the subsequent punishment, or both. Her lovers and trainers had commented frequently on how aroused she became as soon as she felt the ropes or chains around her limbs.

Madame opened the lid of the box in front of her chair, and took from it a pair of long, black, shiny gloves and a black garment that appeared to be a corset, but with additional parts the purpose of which Olena could not determine. Madame gave the things to Kym. 'Dress Olena in these,' she said.

Kym smiled as she approached Olena, and her pale eyes were bright. It was clear to Olena that Kym anticipated enjoying her work.

Olena pulled on the gloves, which were a very tight fit, while Kym fitted the corset around her. Despite the size of her breasts and buttocks Olena was slender, but the corset was designed to cinch her waist into a tiny circle. Kym swore under her breath as Madame urged her to pull the laces ever tighter. Olena had to stand with her legs apart and hold on to one of the mirrors to brace herself against the force of Kym's tugs.

At last the corset was tightened to Madame's satisfaction, and Kym tied the laces in the small of Olena's back. Olena panted lightly, trying to become accustomed to breathing with a band of relentless pressure around her middle. She couldn't help catching sight of herself in the mirrors, and she was mortified to see that the corset exaggerated the swelling of her breasts, hips and bottom. It had been some time since Olena had worn such a constricting garment, and she remembered now the way in which the constant compression seemed to make her unable to ignore the waves of tingling warmth in her private place.

'Well, Olena,' Madame said, 'what do you think? Is it too tight?'

Olena shyly shook her head. 'No, Madame, thank you. I rather like it.'

Madame smiled. 'We'll see,' she said, 'just how much you're enjoying the experience. You know I can always tell, don't you?'

Olena nodded. There was no point in pretending. Madame would discover, as soon as she made an intimate examination of Olena, that Olena's secret place was almost dripping. And she had no doubt that she would be examined.

'Now put your hands behind your back, Olena,' Madame said. She rose from the chair. 'I'll assist you, Kym. The arm restraints are a little complex.'

Olena made no protest and did not struggle while Madame and Kym bound her arms. It was all she could do to suppress the tremblings of desire that started unbidden through her body whenever one of the women touched her skin.

As far as she could tell, from the way her arms were positioned and from the reflections she caught sight of in the mirrors, her arms, crossed behind her back, were being fitted into a single black sleeve that was attached to the back of the corset. She was obliged to arch her back inwards as the straps holding the sleeve were tightened, and she saw her breasts jut from her chest.

When they were finished Madame and Kym stood back to admire Olena. Unable to move her arms, and with her waist constricted and her breasts thrust forward, Olena was not confident of walking in her high-heeled shoes, and Kym guided her to the nearest of the mirrors so that she could see her own reflection.

Her first thought was that her breasts looked obscenely large and prominent. With her waist narrowed and encased in black, and her arms folded behind her and also sheathed in black to her shoulders, she appeared to consist of face, breasts, bottom and legs. The sleeve that contained her arms looked seamless.

'You will have to become adept at walking while you're bound,' Madame said. 'Kym, take her on a tour of the room.'

Olena was taller than Kym, and in high-heeled shoes she towered above the blonde girl as she teetered her way around the conservatory. She was conscious that, even though she was taking small, tentative steps, in order to keep her balance she had to push out her bottom as well as her breasts, and exaggerate the sway of her hips. As she walked she caught sight of her reflection, and was fascinated and appalled by the blatant invitation of her posture. Her buttocks, always prominent, now rolled against each other with every step; her breasts, held proudly before her, bounced and trembled as she walked.

It became clear that Kym was not immune to Olena's alluring gait. Olena found that the blonde girl would look over her shoulder and, if she found that Madame could not see what she was doing, she would let the hand that was supporting Olena's waist slip down to cup a buttock, or slide upwards to caress the side of a breast.

'Please,' Olena whispered to her. 'I'm trying not to have sinful thoughts. I must at least do my best to pass the test.'

'Don't be daft,' Kym replied, and lightly pinched Olena's right nipple. 'We all know you're loving this. In your room, while you were dressing, you were already as wet as a weekend in Blackpool.'

'Yes,' Olena admitted, regretfully.

'Stop chattering, you two,' Madame called out. 'Kym, bring Olena back to the mirror.'

Trying to hide her blushing face behind the tresses of her long, dark hair, Olena retraced her steps towards Madame. She was becoming accustomed to walking in the corset and high heels, but there was nothing she could do to prevent the tips of proffered breasts jiggling with each step. When she reached the mirror beside which Madame was standing, Madame gestured for her to stand facing her reflection. The mirror was a long oval supported between two ornately carved uprights that were set into a wide, heavy base on four small wheels.

'Move closer, my dear,' Madame said, and when Olena stepped forwards, so that her feet were almost touching the base, she had to stand with her legs apart to straddle the bottom of the tilted mirror. She felt the lips of her private place open, and she felt the wetness that had been pooling inside her begin to trickle downwards.

'Kym, lock the castors,' Madame said. 'I don't want the mirror to be able to move. Move your feet further apart,

Olena. More than that, my dear. That's better. And lean forward, so that we can all see your cunt and your arsehole.'

Choking back a sob of shame, Olena did as Madame instructed. The tips of her breasts were almost touching their reflections. When she looked down, between the spheres of her breasts, she could see in the mirror the reflection of her sex gazing accusingly up at her, its naked, opened leaves glistening, its dark, inviting hole the unmistakable evidence that she was eager to be penetrated.

Olena gazed hopelessly into the reflection of her face. Others might see in the redness of her cheeks and neck only embarrassment and humiliation, but Olena saw also the damning evidence of her warm arousal; her eyes were bright with tears of shame, but Olena recognised in the dark depths the glint of her unspeakably vile desires.

Surely, Olena thought, it was not necessary to examine her. Madame must be able to see already that being bound, and paraded around the conservatory, had been enough to bring out all of Olena's wicked desires. What Olena deserved, and craved, was chastisement, and as Madame began to stroke one of Olena's outthrust, parted buttocks Olena imagined the riding-crop falling, again and again, in lines of fire across her bottom. She shivered with lust.

'Tie her ankles to the castors,' Madame said, 'and then we'll see how she likes being completely immobile.'

It had not occurred to Olena to move from the position Madame had instructed her to adopt, but as she felt Kym tightening cords around her ankles she realised that she could no longer move her legs together even if she wished to. Her private places, which she had voluntarily exposed, were now displayed at Madame's pleasure. Her traitorous body reacted to her predicament, as she had known it would, by vibrating with ever more pent-up lust.

She was not even to be allowed to hide her face. Madame gathered Olena's tumbling curls and tied them with a ribbon. Her hand stayed at the nape of Olena's neck, and turned Olena's head so that, standing on her toes, she could gaze into her troubled eyes. Olena, trained by hundreds of lovers, parted her lips as Madame kissed them. After a while Madame drew back a little and watched Olena's eyes as she licked Olena's lips with the tip of her tongue.

'Whip me,' Olena whispered. 'Please.'

'Not yet,' Madame replied. 'I haven't finished tying you up.'

The final ropes, black and fine, ran from the sleeve that contained Olena's crossed arms, over her shoulders, and to the twin spirals of wood between which the mirror was suspended. When the cords were pulled taut Olena could not stand upright. She was obliged to lean forwards, echoing the angle of the tilted mirror, with her breasts pendant towards their reflections and her bottom pushed outwards and held open.

'I think that bondage should always be at least a little uncomfortable,' Madame said. She stroked a few stray curls from Olena's forehead. 'Are you comfortable, my dear?'

Olena shook her head. Her enforced position made the corset bite around her waist, and the muscles of her legs were beginning to ache.

'A normal person,' Madame declared, 'would find it impossible to remain sexually aroused while suffering discomfort.' She cupped one of Olena's pendant globes in her hand, and laughed when she felt the nipple harden. 'But you're not a normal person, are you, Olena?'

With a farewell pinch that sent a spasm of pleasure through Olena's body, Madame's hand left Olena's breast and came to rest on her hip.

Uttering little gasps of desire Olena opened her eyes and gazed at the portrait of yearning lust she saw in the mirror. No, she wasn't in the least normal: she wasn't good, or decent, or pure, or clean, and she wasn't the slightest bit in control of her desires. The entire surface of her body felt sensitised, so that the gentlest touch set off rippling thrills; her breasts and bottom felt hot and swollen, and heavy with longing for punishment; and her private places were empty, hungry mouths that only Olena could hear crying out to be filled.

'Let's see whether you're enjoying this predicament,' Madame murmured.

Olena exclaimed, and her body went rigid, as Madame's cool fingers rested against the sticky heat of her sex.

'Very wet indeed,' Madame said. Her fingers probed the open, unguarded centre of Olena's being. 'Wetter than yesterday, I think. Look, Kym. Have you ever seen such a ready flow?'

Olena groaned with pleasure and despair.

'Hold her open, Kym,' Madame said, 'and I'll see how deeply I can insert my fingers.'

For a few moments there was silence, but for the wet sounds of Madame's hand moving in and out of Olena's sex, and Olena's pants and sighs. In a moment of clarity between waves of pleasure Olena glanced towards the masked man, and felt a spasm of sympathy for Barat.

'Look, Kym,' Madame said. 'My hand's in her up to the wrist. There can be no doubt that she finds it exciting to be kept bound and helpless.'

'So she'll have to be punished, Madame?' Kym's voice sounded eager.

'I'm afraid so. Go and fetch a selection of straps.'

Olena felt Madame's hand slipping from her, and she uttered a moan of protest. But at least she was going to be punished at last.

'Those will do,' Madame said. 'Put them on the chair. I just have to find out whether Olena's other little hole is as keen to be filled, and then I'll begin the whipping.'

Olena's head spun with delight as Madame's slick fingers slid into the tight circle of her most intimate place. 'You've failed another test, my dear,' Madame said. 'I'm very pleased with you. You even like me doing this while you're tied up, don't you?'

'Oh, yes,' Olena gasped. She ground her blushing breasts against the cool surface of the mirror and revelled in the discomfort of her bonds and of Madame's fingers filling her.

'Look, Madame,' Kym said, with awe in her voice. 'She's dripping on to the glass.'

Olena moaned with embarrassment. 'Please, Madame,' she murmured. 'Please whip me now. I need it. Please whip me hard.'

'I will,' Madame assured her. Her fingers began to withdraw from Olena's bottom. 'I'll use the straps first, while you're tied in this position, as hard as I can, until your lovely big bottom is a deep shade of red. Then we'll untie your ankles and lay the mirror flat on the floor. I'll use a thin cane, to reach the most sensitive places, while you lick the mirror clean. Will that do, Olena?'

Olena shivered. She could hardly wait for the first lash. 'It will help, Madame. Thank you. I'm sorry to be such a nuisance.'

'You can thank me later,' Madame said. She flicked the tail of a strap against Olena's right buttock. 'I'm going to rest in my room this afternoon. I want you to share my bed. I suppose you've been trained in pleasing a woman?'

'Of course, Madame,' Olena said. 'I will be pleased to serve you.'

'Good girl,' Madame said.

Olena heard the swish of leather, and then cried out in ecstasy as the strap crashed against her bottom and an explosion of pain flared and faded. The longed-for chastisement had begun at last, and Olena closed her eyes and surrendered to the waves of sensation. Each lash stoked the fire of her lust even as it appeased her emotions of guilt and sinfulness. She was already looking forward to the bitter-sweet sting of the cane.

'I have guests this evening,' Madame said, pausing between strokes. 'Kym, I want you to show Olena how to prepare the rooms and serve refreshments.' Another two lashes fell in quick succession.

'All right, Madame,' Kym said. 'You know, Olena really likes this. She looks ready to come.'

Olena, overcome with pleasure, could only groan her agreement. Her bottom was already a blaze of heat, and Madame had several more straps to try.

'I'm sure she is,' Madame said. 'The filthy slut. And she knows better than to have an orgasm until her punishment is completely finished. If she's good, and keeps her bottom well presented, I'll finish her off with my fingers before we untie her. But before then I have to make sure she suffers.'

Olena could hardly have been happier. She was yet to have a caning, and then she would be allowed an orgasm. The strap stung her again and again.

There was a pause, during which Madame caught her breath. 'The three-tongued tawse next, I think,' she said. 'Yes, that's good and heavy. Just ten on each side with this, right across the mid-point. Tomorrow,' she added, after the force of the first blow with the tawse had caused Olena's knees almost to buckle, 'I intend to subject you to another test, Olena. I fully expect you to fail it.'

Olena winced as the tawse crashed once again into the tender flesh of her left buttock, and then she smiled contentedly. Daily testing meant daily punishment. Her bottom would be continuously sore.

Five

From the first Talia was put to work in the private rooms of Edmund's palace of amusements.

All along the ground floor, facing on to the street, the doors of the row of houses owned by Edmund were thrown open in the evenings. Sprightly music spilled out along with the lamplight, and echoed from the silent façades of the buildings on the opposite side of the street. Garlands of coloured lights, that flashed messages of welcome, surrounded the gaping doorways. The strong men and the wrestlers from Edmund's menagerie of staff, with voices loud enough to be heard over the hubbub from within, stood on the pavements and encouraged all classes, types and ages of people from the city to enter and sample the entertainments, and to try their luck at the games.

Within the doors the public rooms were a riot of colour and noise. Here there was a band playing syncopated music, with professional dancers in spangled costumes who at the end of each tune bowed low and held out their hats for coins; here a juggler, a fire-eater, clowns with slapsticks and bellowing horns; here a row of ingenious, garishly illuminated machines that performed mechanical miracles – a warbling, flying bird, an automaton that answered questions on slips of paper from its mouth, a display of fizzing fireworks – whenever money was inserted into them. Crowds wandered from marvel to marvel, gasping in surprise and laughing. Games of chance, in which the visitors were tempted to gamble their money for prizes of toys and gewgaws, were everywhere: Find the Lady, Wheel of Fortune, *Vingt-et-un*.

Most of the staff who were in training, and who, like Talia, went naked and collared by day, worked in the evenings in the public rooms, dressed in costumes appropriate to their tasks. Some, who had made attempts to leave Edmund's employ, were unobtrusively tethered to their place of work. Any others who might be tempted to try to escape through the invitingly open front doors were deterred by the risk of capture by the barkers posted in the street, and by the threat of a night spent in the pit.

However popular and profitable the public rooms, the private, secret chambers of Edmund's house were the source of his prosperity. In these rooms, too, all was gaiety, and laughter, and colour, although the glittering lights were less glaring and the music was softer. The customers, though fewer in number, were just as addicted to the ingenious amusements and games that Edmund and his staff had prepared for them. The difference was that in the private rooms there was no entertainment that could be procured for only a few coins. Here the fees paid and the amounts gambled were substantial, and the customers expected to see strange, perverse performances.

On her first evening in the private rooms Talia's job was to be one of the exhibits that greeted the select and wealthy customers who knew the password that would allow them through the unremarkable door at the side of the row of properties and who could afford the price of admission.

In a sense, Talia reflected, her task was simple. She was simply on display, and there was little she could do as she was tightly bound. She was in a box, enclosed on all four sides. She was dressed in a sequinned bodice, like a circus performer's, that fitted tightly around her body and had a short, pleated skirt. The bodice supported, but did not cover, her breasts. Her legs were clad in shining stockings, and she had gloves and a headdress that matched the bodice. Her face had been expertly made up by one of the other entertainers, but she knew that in future she would be expected to apply her own powder and rouge and colours. She still had on her collar, but it was obscured by a necklace of gaudy costume jewellery. She could feel the key to her room resting against her neck. All she had to do was to perform well, and the key would be given to her and she would be allowed to rest in the sanctuary of her own private bedroom.

The box consisted of two parts. The lower half contained the motor and the machinery. Talia was kneeling in the upper half, so that her face was only a little higher than those of the customers who came to watch her. Her knees were wide apart and were pinioned in place against the sides of the box. There were padded ledges that ensured that her knees were lifted a little from the floor. She was, she supposed, half kneeling and half squatting. Her feet were held, by ropes around her ankles, a little way apart under her bottom. Her sex was concealed under the fringed skirt, but Talia could feel the slim cylinder that projected up through the floor and into her vagina. Her elbows and wrists were tied to the sides and top of the box. A contoured pad that covered the inside of the back of the box supported her back and her head, but also pushed her chest forwards so that her breasts were prominent. Screw clips around her nipples were connected by thin wires to pulleys in the top corners of the front of the box.

It was dark inside the box, but never for long. The upper half, in which Talia was secured, had three sets of double doors that opened outwards. When open, the topmost doors revealed Talia's face; the middle doors revealed her breasts; and the lowest set showed her from the waist down. The opening of each set of doors switched on lights inside the box that illuminated the part of Talia that became visible. The doors opened at random, it seemed to Talia, and each set remained open for an unpredictable length of time. Sometimes two of the sets of doors would be open together; occasionally all three. And very rarely, for a few moments of darkness and privacy, all the doors together would be closed.

'Come and see the new attraction,' called the dwarf who stood beside the cabinet. 'Put your money in and watch her go.'

Talia rarely saw the dwarf take money, but she knew when the machinery was about to be set in motion. The doors in front of her face would open, and instead of seeing chattering groups of smartly dressed customers passing the cabinet on their way to darker pleasures deeper in the house, she would find a man, or a woman, or several people, standing in front of the box and gazing intently at her with amused smiles on their faces. Then she would hear the whirr of the motor, and the show would start.

The doors would continue to open and close, but now they seemed to remain open for longer. Little by little the hem of Talia's skirt would be hitched up, until she was exposed from the waist down. The phallus in her vagina would move: up and down a little, or from side to side, or in a circular motion, or with a slow or rapid vibration, or with some combination of movements. The wires connected to her nipple clips would tighten, and pull the tips of her breasts upwards and outwards a little way, and then release them, and then pull them again.

The doors would open to show the phallus moving inside her sex, or her breasts being pulled and jiggled on wires, or her face as she reacted to the things being done to her by the machinery. When all three of the doors were open, Talia noticed, through the haze of sexual arousal that affected her senses once the machine had been working for a few moments, the customers chose to look at her face.

'Look at her,' they would say. 'Quite pretty, if a little on the skinny side. I say, she's enjoying this, isn't she? Pretty little titties – they're just asking for a whipping. And she's absolutely dripping wet, the little slut.'

Talia, adrift on an ocean of surging pleasure, was pleased that the customers found her attractive. As the evening wore on, however, she became desperate for her arousal to reach a climax – and it was clear that the machinery was not designed to bring her to an orgasm. She found herself lost in complex fantasies, all of which entailed being spanked very thoroughly by Anne. She had not had a spanking for days, and her unsatisfied arousal was making her ever more conscious of the lack. She would have settled for just a kiss and a cuddle. But the best she could hope for, she knew, was the comfort of her bed. And that was infinitely preferable to the pit.

Olena's buttocks, Barat noted, still bore faint traces of the previous day's punishment. Madame la Patronne, he knew, would not be pleased that she had slightly misjudged the severity of her strokes. Perhaps today, when this ridiculous charade of testing Olena was over, he would see Olena's perfect breasts dancing under Madame's whip.

Olena was wearing the corset and long gloves she had worn the day before, and once again her arms were sheathed behind her back, so that the superb lushness of her curves was emphasised and her breasts jutted proudly. If Barat had charge of Olena, he swore to himself, he would flog her tits as often as her arse. He would employ servants to whip her front and back while he plunged his manhood into her mouth.

Damnation! He cursed quietly. His cock had reared up again and the sensitive tip had scraped against the rough cloth of his robe. He felt a trickle of sweat on his forehead as he willed his erection to subside. He couldn't adjust his position: he had done some trivial thing to displease his mistress that morning, and although after much pleading he had persuaded Madame to let him watch the session with Olena in the conservatory, his hands were tied behind his back. He leant forward to lessen the friction of his glans against his robe.

Instead of shoes Olena was today wearing boots of black leather. They had thick soles, and heels that lifted Olena even higher. They encased Olena's legs from knees to ankles like a second skin. They must be heavy, Barat thought. Olena had had to practise walking in them.

Olena's lustrous waves of dark hair had been plaited into a single thick braid that hung down her back and was decorated with red ribbons. Kym, Barat supposed, had been appointed to plait Olena's hair. Barat's envy and dislike of Kym were keener than ever now that the blonde brat was permitted to spend time with Olena – Olena who was here only because Barat had arranged it, Olena who by rights was his.

Olena's hair had been plaited because today Madame had decreed that she was to wear a helmet, similar to the one that Barat was stifling in. The heavy braid issued from the back of the black dome that had been fitted over Olena's head. The helmet, supple but tight-fitting, included a broad collar that surrounded Olena's throat and neck and extended up to her chin. It covered her ears, so that Madame was obliged to stand close to her to give her instructions, and it had panels that extended beside her eyes to narrow her field of vision. It was held tight by a buckled strap across Olena's forehead, and the strap, like the collar, and the other straps that ran crosswise over the top of Olena's head, had metal rings set into it so that Olena could be tethered.

Wearing the helmet, however, had not been Olena's test, and it seemed that today the helmet would not be used to secure Olena in any way. Madame, it had transpired, had wanted to discover whether Olena would continue to feel lustful arousal even when wearing a gag that filled her mouth and prevented her from uttering all but the most muffled sounds. The helmet was constructed to allow for the fitting of a metal cylinder, padded with leather, in the wearer's mouth.

It had taken longer for Madame to explain to Olena what was to be done to her than it had taken to fit the gag in Olena's mouth. Now Olena was ready to be examined.

There was, of course, no doubt that Olena would fail the test. As Madame presented Olena to her own reflection in one of the tall mirrors, Barat thought that no one in the world could fail to be aroused by the spectacle. The high boots made her legs impossibly long and slender; the corset and the position of her bound arms made her breasts and buttocks even more prominent than usual; fenced in by the black panels beside them, her eyes were wide with trepidation; between them and the black bar that filled her mouth her face was scarlet with shame. She looked magnificent, and Barat knew that Olena was far from immune to the sin of pride. He could just hear the indistinct, muted noises of protest from behind the gag, and he suspected that being unable to relieve her feelings of mortification and excitement by expressing them in speech would only inflame Olena's passions.

In a loud voice, Madame explained that she would administer a short spanking, so that Olena could experience the difficulties of crying out in pain or protest while wearing the gag. If Olena was not already feverish with lust, Barat thought, then the spanking would surely reduce her to a state of quivering arousal.

It was clear, however, as soon as Olena was bent over the top of the padded box, and her legs were parted in readiness for Madame's hand, that the gag had had no effect at all on her licentious nature. Her sex-lips were open and they, and the insides of her thighs halfway to her knees, were coated in a shining film of her wetness.

Barat always revelled in the sight of Olena displaying her bottom and her cunt. He was still bent forwards, almost as far as Olena, in his attempts to prevent the delicate skin of his member chafing against his robe, and he had to crane his neck upwards to watch what Madame was doing. Despite the discomfort he could not take his eyes off the scene.

Although the spanking and the examination were blatantly unnecessary, Madame proceeded with her stated plan. Between the resounding slaps of Madame's palm against Olena's rounded buttocks Barat could hear, like a distant counterpoint, the sweet sound of Olena's muffled gasps and moans. He made a mental note that when he had Olena to himself he would keep her gagged some of the time so that he could enjoy the little sounds she made. What tiny noises would she make, he wondered, while he thrust his member into her arsehole or while he was torturing her nipples?

When Olena's buttocks were uniformly pink the spanking stopped, and the examination began. There could be no doubt about Olena's excitement: during the spanking her juices had started to leak from her sex, and there was now a small pool of liquid on the floor between her ankles and clear, viscous strands hanging from her labia. Nonetheless Madame probed Olena's vagina thoroughly, using an artificial phallus which, when it was completely coated in fluid, she used also to test the readiness of Olena's anus to accept penetration.

It came as no surprise whatsoever to Barat when Madame proclaimed that Olena had failed the test and would have to be punished. The elation he felt when Madame added that today's chastisement would be applied to Olena's breasts was immediately doused, however, as Madame went on to say that the punishment would be deferred until the afternoon and would take place in the privacy of Madame's bedroom. Olena, peering over her shoulder, appeared to be as disconsolate as Barat: he was sure that by now she was desperate for punishment.

Madame took pity on Olena's muffled pleadings, and Barat was consoled by the sight of Madame training Olena to walk with high, quick steps while still encased in the black costume. The training consisted of Madame, with a leather strap in her hand, following Olena as she tried to walk according to Madame's instructions.

Madame wielded the strap with wristy, upward flicks against Olena's reddened buttocks, each stroke emphasising Madame's orders to Olena to lift her knees higher, and to take small but increasingly rapid steps. As Madame followed Olena in circuits of the conservatory, the slaps of the strap and the reports of Olena's heels on the floor increased in tempo, and were overlaid by the sound of Olena's muffled gasps. The sight of Olena's punished bottom rolling from side to side mesmerised Barat, but he was able to tear his gaze away from time to time to glance at her stupendous breasts, which bounced with increasing vigour as she stepped higher and faster, and at the expression of mortified pleasure on her blushing face.

He hoped that Madame would remember to untie his hands. His rigid member was yearning for relief.

* * *

The next evening Talia had been allocated to another mechanical booth, but at the last minute she was reprieved from being pinioned in a box. One of the customers, a wealthy regular, had requested an impromptu game of chance on which he and his circle of friends could gamble, and Talia was one of three young women who were selected to take part.

The game, Talia was told, was a race, and so she was surprised when she was taken into a chamber, of which one half was furnished as a comfortable saloon and the other resembled a bathroom.

There were about a dozen customers lounging in groups on the red-velvet-covered sofas and armchairs. Most were youthful, but some were middle-aged; most were men, but there were women, too, and these appeared to be companions of the men rather than members of the staff. All were at ease in their expensive clothes, and were chattering excitedly as they sipped champagne from tall glasses and waited for the entertainment to begin. Talia saw that Edmund was seated among his guests, and behind him stood one of the brown-coated technicians, clipboard in hand, who was already making notes of the bets that the customers called out.

Talia was naked but for her collar and a dusting of powder that made her body glitter in the lights. As she entered the room all eyes turned towards her, and she stood in the doorway, abashed by the attention. The dwarf who was escorting her pushed her into the room. 'Get up on the stage,' he snapped.

'Oh, look,' a voice called out. 'A pretty little redhead. I'll bet fifty on her. Each way,' the voice added, provoking a gust of laughter.

Talia, blushing, mounted the three steps to the other half of the room. Here the walls and floor were entirely clad in white tiles. Sunk into the raised floor was a row of shallow trays, with drainage grilles, and running in a maze across the back wall were metal pipes and flexible tubes. Were it not for the fact that the arrangement was clearly intended for public viewing, Talia would have thought it resembled a set of communal showers.

Five women were already on the tiled stage. Two of them were, like Talia, naked and collared. They appeared as apprehensive as Talia felt. One was a short, curvaceous girl, with a pretty heart-shaped face and straight blonde hair. Her blue eyes were wide, and she looked very young. The other woman was a little older, was tall and slender, and had a classically beautiful face surrounded by dark curls. Talia realised why she had been chosen to complete the set of competitors: with one blonde, one brunette and one redhead on display before them, the customers could easily identify which of the three they wanted to bet on.

The other three women on the stage were also on the staff, and were dressed in abbreviated parodies of nurses' uniforms, with tight bodices and tiny skirts made of shimmering white material, and long gloves of thin rubber. Each of the competitors, it seemed, was to have an attendant.

The dwarf who had brought Talia to the room now clambered on the stage and released a chain that was secured to the tiled wall. As he played it out Talia noticed for the first time the arrays of pulleys, ropes and straps that were being lowered from the ceiling. Talia's nurse, wearing an expression of professional detachment under her heavy make-up, touched Talia's arm. The rubber glove was cold, and Talia shivered. The nurse positioned Talia at the front of the stage, in front of one of the harnesses that were being lowered. Talia was standing in line with the blonde and the brunette. It was clear to Talia that the competitors were to be exhibited to the customers before being tied up and hoisted above the stage. She wondered what the competition would consist of. The nurses' uniforms suggested a medical theme. Perhaps the three women were going to be given a mock examination, with medical instruments. Perhaps the winner would be the one who could take in the largest speculum, or the one who reached a climax first. Talia thought that when she was suspended from the ceiling her bottom would make an excellent target for a whipping. Surely this evening, at last, she would receive at least a spanking.

'Nurses, prepare your patients,' Edmund ordered, and the hubbub among the customers subsided. The performance was about to begin.

Talia's nurse made her stand with her hands behind her back and her legs parted. As usual when she was made to expose herself in front of an audience, Talia was becoming aroused. The clammy touch of the nurse's rubber-clad fingers and the coarse comments that rose from the seated customers seemed only to increase her excitement.

'Push your tits out,' the nurse whispered in Talia's ear. She was standing behind Talia. 'You'd better not lose this game, you little slut, or we'll both be in trouble.'

The nurse's cold fingers grasped, squeezed and kneaded Talia's breasts. They pulled and pinched her nipples until Talia tossed her head and groaned with each stab of pain. She could feel wetness gathering in her sex. She glanced to her side and saw that the blonde and the brunette were receiving similar treatment from their attendants. The laughter and shouts of the audience grew louder.

'One final squeeze,' Edmund declared, and the audience applauded wildly as the nurse cupped Talia's breasts tightly and gave her nipples a particularly vicious pinch that made her cry out.

'Good girl,' the nurse whispered. 'Give them a show. That's what they're paying for. Now bend your knees and let them see your cunt.'

Talia, and the other two competitors, adopted the ungainly position. Standing beside Talia the nurse reached between Talia's thighs to pull and open her sex-lips.

Then the three nurses came to stand in front of their patients. Talia's nurse turned her back to the audience, stepped between Talia's open thighs, and placed her lips against Talia's. Talia heard applause. The nurse smelt of make-up and scent, and Talia, deprived of affection for several days, responded to the kiss by opening her mouth and moving her lips hungrily against the nurse's.

The nurse, surprised, withdrew slightly. 'You're keen,' she murmured. 'Still, the punters like it.' She pressed her mouth against Talia's, and put a hand behind Talia's head

154

in order to adjust their position so that the audience could see the passion in their kisses. Talia heard a murmur of approval from the crowd.

It was, however, as nothing to the roars and cheers that echoed from the tiles when the three nurses slowly lowered themselves to kneel in front of the three patients. Talia knew that the nurses would be wearing nothing under their tiny skirts, and as they leant forwards to press their faces into their patient's groins their private parts were exposed and pushed towards the audience.

The crowd clapped and whistled while the nurses used their lips and tongues to excite their patients. Talia's nurse, her face wet, glanced up during the performance. 'You're already soaking,' she said. 'You're really enjoying this, aren't you?'

Talia, whose nipples were still smarting and who was being carried on increasingly frequent ripples of pleasure towards the brink of an orgasm, could only nod.

'Then show it,' the nurse hissed. 'Just be glad you don't have to fake it.'

Talia saw that the blonde and the brunette appeared to be already in the throes of multiple orgasms. They were panting, moaning, and tossing their heads from side to side as their nurses lapped at their sexes.

Talia surrendered to the sensations that were stabbing through her, and although as she uttered wordless exclamations and rotated her neck she felt her arousal begin to abate a little, she was gratified to hear applause from the audience. She found that she wanted to please them. And she didn't want to spend a night in the pit.

On Edmund's command the nurses drew back from their patients and won another round of applause when they lowered their faces to the tiles and lifted their bottoms to the audience. Talia, who by now had once again reached the point at which she could feel the imminence of a climax, sighed with frustration.

She was allowed no time to pine, however, as her nurse immediately instructed her to turn round and bend over. Now it was the turn of the patients to show their bottoms and private parts to the customers. Talia could feel that her own sex was covered in wetness, and she was sure that the other two women were in a similar condition.

As Talia had expected, the performance included an internal examination with medical instruments. Talia could hear the excited shouts of the audience, but she didn't know what was to happen until she felt the cold touch of metal between the lips of her sex. A slim cylinder slid into her vagina as the customers applauded.

The instrument was an adjustable speculum. Talia felt the nurse's fingers busy at the base of the device, which widened inside her. It was becoming uncomfortable. Talia's vagina had never felt so stretched and full. She began to moan in complaint.

'That's right,' the nurse whispered. 'Let them know how it feels. But I want this nice and tight in your slippery cunt. If it comes out you're disqualified, and we'll both suffer. So let's make sure it stays in.' The speculum stretched Talia a little more, and she groaned.

'That will do,' Edmund called out. 'Stand back, nurses, and let us admire your handiwork. What a pretty row of wide-open sluts.'

Despite the discomfort, Talia discovered that the speculum inside her did nothing to reduce her excitement. It felt wonderful to have her vagina so completely filled. The nurses held the patients bent over so that the customers could gaze at leisure at the sight of three rounded bottoms and three gaping holes.

Talia's nurse gripped Talia's wrists in a rubber-clad hand. 'Pretend you're struggling a bit,' she whispered, and Talia began to wriggle her hips as she felt the cold fingers of the nurse's other hand in the cleft between her buttocks.

The nurse's fingers were coated with thick ointment, and in spite of Talia's half-hearted struggles they slid easily into the tight ring of Talia's anus. As the nurse pressed the ointment more deeply into the little hole, Talia was so suffused with pleasure that she knew the slightest of touches in the right place would bring her to a climax. The tip of her clitoris felt so stiff and sensitive that Talia was sure that it was protruding from its hood. Sometimes, particularly when Anne had tied her up to play with her, and she had become so aroused that she was almost delirious and her clitoris was as hard as wood, she would open her lips in surrender to Anne's sweet kisses and would cry out her orgasm into her lover's mouth as Anne smacked her favourite leather strap against Talia's projecting, defenceless little pearl of sensation.

But it was clear that no one was going to smack her or allow her to come. The nurse's fingers withdrew, leaving Talia moaning with frustration.

'That concludes the first part of the performance,' Edmund announced. 'Ladies and gentlemen, you have seen the three fillies. Now, while they are being harnessed for the race, I will once again explain the nature of the competition, and ask you to place your final bets.'

The nurses, assisted by the dwarf, placed their patients in the three webs of rope and leather that had been let down from the ceiling. Each harness was a complex sling, the main component being a concave hammock of black hide that supported its occupant from her neck to the backs of her knees, but which was split into two from its mid-point and which had so much of its centre cut away that the occupant's buttocks, her sex and the backs of her thighs protruded obscenely. Talia had been tied up many times, but she had never found herself in bondage that supported her so well but left her so utterly exposed.

Her wrists were attached, together, to the topmost part of the sling, above her head. Her ankles were not bound, but she could not alter the position of her legs because each was supported, mainly behind the knee, in what was effectively a separate sling even though it formed a part of the main hammock. The leg slings could be adjusted independently, Talia soon discovered, in three dimensions, and she found herself half lying, half sitting in the hammock, with her arms tied above her, her legs pulled wide apart, and her knees at the same level as her face. Her sex, still held open by the speculum, was on display for all of the audience to see, as was her anus and her rounded bottom. The customers cheered and clapped as the dwarf pulled on the chain and the system of pulleys hoisted all three young women into the air. Talia noticed that each of the women was suspended above one of the drainage trays.

'No medical examination can be considered complete,' Edmund declared, 'until the patient has been thoroughly purged. Therefore my three nurses will shortly administer enemas to their patients.'

Talia sighed. Now she knew why her anus had been greased: it was to ease the insertion of an enema tube. She felt a little nervous, and she knew that it was going to be embarrassing to expel the enema from her bowels in front of so many people. She and Anne loved playing with each other's arseholes, and often combined thorough anal explorations with the spankings they gave each other. And they had occasionally enjoyed pissing games, too: Talia thought that Anne looked delightfully coy when she squatted to pee. So Talia thought it was quite likely that she would enjoy the enema. She was sure that she would like the feeling as the liquid went in; it was the coming out, in front of all those people, that daunted her.

Still, there was nothing for it. She was tied up, and in any case she had to put on a good performance.

'The nurses will now show you the enema containers,' Edmund went on. 'As you can see, ladies and gentlemen, all three are identical in size and contain an identical amount of the same liquid. All three tubes, too, are of exactly the same length and diameter. This will be a completely fair race. The only difference will be in the performance of the competitors.

'The taps will be turned simultaneously, and from that moment no more bets will be accepted. The winner, ladies and gentlemen, will be whichever of these wenches manages to contain the liquid for the longest time. In other words, the last to let go will win. The loser, conversely, will be the unfortunate young woman who loosens her bowels first. I call her unfortunate because, in addition to the shame of losing the race, she will also have to be punished. Nurses, insert the tubes!'

158

Talia's nurse squatted between her parted thighs. As she slid the bulbous nose of the length of tubing into Talia's anus she gently stroked Talia's stretched-open sex-lips. 'Comfortable?' she said, jiggling the tube. She placed a kiss on the inside of Talia's left thigh.

'It is, actually,' Talia replied. 'I feel very full.'

'Not half as full as you will shortly,' the nurse assured her. 'You can win this, my darling. You must. We'll both suffer if you don't.'

'Your last chance to try your luck, ladies and gentlemen,' Edmund cried. 'Place your final bets now.'

There was a flurry of last-minute betting. 'Twenty on the pretty little blonde to lose.' 'Fifty on that terrific dark girl. To win, of course. She's a thoroughbred.' 'A hundred on the redhead to lose. She's too skinny to keep all that liquid in!'

'I say!' A man's voice rang out. 'That blonde girl's got splendid titties. Seems a damned shame not to give them a bit of a whipping, seeing as she's all tied up ready for it. They're lovely and big but they're just too pale, damn it. I'll pay two hundred to see them pink with red stripes before the race starts.'

'A very generous offer,' Edmund said, 'and a capital suggestion. We can delay the off for a few minutes. Lower the blonde's legs,' he called out to the dwarf.

Talia glanced towards the blonde girl. Her blue eyes were wide with surprise and trepidation. She looked younger than ever – perhaps still in her teens, Talia thought – and her pale prettiness reminded Talia of Anne. Naked, tied up, with her sex held open, a tube issuing from her anus, and her breasts full and soft, she looked adorably perverse. Talia could understand why the young man would wanted to see her whipped.

It was, Talia reflected, completely unfair. The blonde girl probably didn't even want to have her breasts punished, particularly now when she needed to concentrate on the enema race. It crossed Talia's mind to volunteer to take the whipping instead: she was still quivering with desire, and yearned for the sting of the lash. But she realised that the young man probably had a liking for small blondes with large breasts. And the customer always gets what the customer wants, she told herself.

'Nurses,' Edmund called out. 'Two of you hold the blonde steady. Third nurse, take off your uniform and administer the whipping.'

'An extra fifty for the naked nurse!' the young man shouted exuberantly. 'Another fifty if she makes the little blonde scream!'

It was Talia's nurse who disrobed and, naked but for high-heeled shoes, stockings and her nurse's cap, crossed the tiled stage to take a short, thin whip from the dwarf. She strode back, flexing the leather-clad rod and drawing cheers from the audience. She stood next to the blonde's sling and grasped a handful of the girl's hair.

'Give her forty,' Edmund instructed her. 'Twenty on each breast. And make them good and hard.'

'Ready, slut?' the nurse said, in a voice loud enough to carry to all of the spectators. 'This is going to hurt.' Then she added, in a whisper, 'Start screaming when I get to thirty.'

There was, however, a limit to how much Talia's nurse could lessen the strength of her blows. Edmund was watching, and he would detect any lack of enthusiasm on the nurse's part. And the young man would complain if the blonde girl's breasts did not bear the vivid marks of forty lashes. And so the blonde struggled in her bonds, and cried out, and begged for mercy, as the whip swished and fell and as her breasts jiggled and reddened. Talia, feeling ever more frustrated, could only watch, and imagine that the delicious lines of fire were being drawn on her own flesh.

The blonde remembered to start screaming, and when she did the spectators broke into applause that continued until all forty strokes had been applied. The girl's voluptuous breasts were a warm shade of pink, and covered with lines of angry red. Her blushing cheeks were wet with tears.

'Turn on the taps,' Edmund called out. 'Let us fill up our competitors. Three, two, one, go!'

Talia felt the nozzle in her anus twitch. Nothing happened for a few moments, and then she felt the strange sensation of warm liquid flowing into her rectum. It was, she decided, quite wonderful: comforting at first and then, as she began to feel full, simply arousing. If only, she thought, someone would give me a good, hard spanking; my bottom, my sex and my arsehole feel so beautifully sensitive.

She relaxed in the hammock and revelled in the slow waves of pleasure that flowed over her as the liquid pulsed into her rectum. There seemed to be no end to the amount of fluid she was expected to take in. She hadn't had time for a pee before being brought to this room, and her bladder felt full. Her vagina was still being held wide open by the speculum. And now a seemingly endless stream of warm liquid was filling up any remaining space! As the discomfort grew, and became almost painful, Talia promised herself that if she ever escaped from Edmund she would introduce Anne to the delights of the enema: it was as good as a spanking, albeit rather more subtle.

At last the containers were empty: their contents were inside the three women. The nurses extracted the nozzles, and an expectant hush descended on the room.

Talia won the contest easily. The blonde girl, as Talia had expected, was the first to show signs of distress. Within moments she was panting and moaning and writhing in her bonds, and the warnings and gentle caresses of her nurse seemed to do nothing to calm her. A thin trickle of liquid bubbled from her anus and dripped, with the sound of rainfall, into the tray beneath her.

The audience, sensing that she could not retain her cargo of fluid much longer, concentrated its attention on her. 'Let it go, blondie,' yelled the spectators who had bet on her to lose. 'Hold on, you stupid little slut,' came the reply from those who had bet that she would win. The noise of the crowd increased as the trickle from the blonde's anus became a continuous stream.

Talia glanced at the blonde. Her face was bright pink with shame, and tears of humiliation and despair were flowing from her eyes. Her punished breasts rose and fell with each laboured breath. Her belly, like Talia's and the dark woman's, was swollen. Even though she knew she was going to lose the competition, she was still vainly trying to stem the escape of the enema from inside her.

Talia wished she could tell the blonde how delightfully pretty she looked. She hoped the blonde wouldn't have to suffer a whole night in the pit: she was, after all, providing plenty of entertainment for the spectators.

Even though Talia was enjoying the sensation of being so full, she understood why the blonde was having difficulties. With her legs wide apart, Talia soon realised that it was pointless to clench the muscles of her thighs and buttocks: only the tight sphincter ring of her anus prevented the liquid from escaping. The pressure was continuous, and far in excess of any normal feeling of wanting to empty her bowels. Talia wished she could relax and savour the sensation, but she couldn't afford to lose her concentration for even a second. She realised that the arduous training in muscle control that she had received at the Private House was helping her, as were the games that she and Anne had played with curiously shaped probes and strings of beads. So far, she thought, she had not allowed a single drop to seep from her.

The effort of keeping her anus closed seemed to increase the pressure on her bladder, and she knew that very soon she would have to pee. The opened speculum in her vagina felt like a massive cylinder of solid metal, and the longer she squeezed her sphincter the more uncomfortable the speculum became. She could see the tip of her clitoris, straining upwards like an arrowhead between her parted sex-lips, pushed forward by the distension of her belly. Like a baby bird craning from its nest for food it demanded attention: a caress, a kiss, a smack. But she hoped no one would touch it, as she knew she would certainly come. It would be a wonderful explosion of orgasm, pissing and shitting, but she wouldn't win the competition.

With a despairing cry the blonde suddenly gave up her attempt to retain the fluid. She hung limply in her harness, sobbing, as the enema gushed from her, at first a fierce jet, then a waterfall, then decreasing pulses. As the liquid splashed into the tray and gurgled down the drain the audience erupted into a frenzy of applause and shouting.

The crowd's attention turned now to Talia and the brunette, and both were urged with increasingly frantic calls to release the liquid or to hold on. The two remaining competitors glanced at each other. The brunette smiled and cocked her head. She had decided, it seemed, that as she could no longer lose there was no point in prolonging her discomfort. She uttered a loud sigh, and closed her eyes and turned her head aside as the liquid spurted from her anus.

Talia had won. She could let go now. She no longer had to grit her teeth, and squeeze her sphincter so tightly that it ached. But she had a perverse whim to hold everything in for as long as she could – or at least until she was sure that she had the undivided attention of everyone in the room.

'The redhead wins!' Edmund shouted, and the crowd broke into wild applause. 'Well done, Forty-one,' Edmund mouthed to Talia, and she felt a pang of pride. Everyone was staring at her. She acknowledged the applause with slight nods of her head. And then, when the applause had died down, she relaxed her urethra, and a fountain of clear pee arced into the air. The applause resumed, louder than ever, and Talia let her anus open at last. She gasped with pleasure and relief. The sensation was almost as good as an orgasm.

She knew she had done well. She had pleased Edmund, and she had pleased the customers. At the end of the evening, for certain, she would be given her key and would be allowed another night in the comfort and privacy of her little room. She had earnt it.

As Kym escorted Olena to the conservatory she silently rehearsed the lines that she had to speak. She felt nervous and excited.

This is ridiculous, she told herself. Olena's the one who's to be tested, not me.

Olena, walking beside Kym and looking like a pagan goddess of sensuality in her thin white dress, appeared entirely serene. Kym had helped Olena prepare herself, however, and she knew that Olena was already aroused by the thought of what was to come. Another day, another test; inevitable failure, certain punishment. It seemed that Olena would never tire of demonstrating her licentious nature.

The conservatory was unoccupied, except for its usual furniture and the pale rays of the autumn sun. Olena looked momentarily confused and disappointed.

'Madame will be late this morning,' Kym said. 'She has to deal with Ba– I mean, with her manservant. He has misbehaved again.'

'It's all right, Kym,' Olena said. 'I know it's Barat. I think I've known from the very first day. But don't tell him I've recognised him. I'm sure he thinks he's going to surprise me.'

Kym and Olena shared a smile that turned into a fit of girlish giggling. It always cheered Kym up when Barat was in trouble with Madame, and it was great to find that Olena had the same opinion of him.

But Kym was under instructions from Madame. Today, at least until Madame arrived, she was to be in charge of Olena's testing. The thought made her chest tighten with nerves and, she realised, also made her feel very sexy.

'Madame has entrusted you to me,' she told Olena, doing her best to keep her face and voice severe. 'Take off your dress.'

Olena looked at Kym and didn't obey immediately. Kym saw that she was blushing. 'Oh,' Olena said, and then a small smile appeared on her luscious lips. 'This will be fun, won't it?'

Kym tried to look uninterested as the thin material slid from Olena's bountiful body. Olena was right, though: both women were going to enjoy the experience of playing together in Madame's absence.

Kym walked slowly around Olena. 'Fold your arms behind your back,' she said, and she watched without expression or comment as Olena obeyed and her awesome tits seemed to grow even larger and rounder.

Kym had always thought that the grey uniform Madame made her wear was drab and dowdy. Now, though, the close-fitting blouse and the short, pleated skirt seemed almost military, and most definitely appropriate. She imagined that she was a soldier and that Olena was a prisoner of war – a captured spy whom Kym was about to interrogate. The mere fact that Kym was clothed, however skimpily, while Olena was naked, made Kym feel confident, in control – and excited.

With a nod Kym completed her cursory inspection of Olena's body, and she strolled to the umbrella stand. She felt Olena watching her as she selected a thin riding-crop. She flexed it between her hands. She swished it experimentally through the air. The sound was thrilling. She found Olena gazing at her, and the women exchanged another conspiratorial smile.

'Kneel on the armchair,' Kym said. She had to maintain her strict demeanour. As Olena ran to the chair and adopted the position, with her knees wide apart on the seat of the chair and her magnificent bottom pushed up and back, Kym wondered whether Madame would be displeased if she found that Kym had punished Olena a little. Madame's instructions had been thorough, but she hadn't been able to cover every eventuality. And even Kym hadn't expected to be seized with the desire to whip Olena's bottom.

'As usual,' Kym announced, 'you're to be tested, Olena, to discover whether you remain in a state of arousal – sexed up and panting for it, in other words – even when you're made to endure one of those kinky acts that Madame's visitors like but which normal human beings think are wicked and perverted.'

Olena murmured. She had rested her head on her arms, which were folded across the back of the chair. She looked, Kym thought, more comfortable and contented than anyone had a right to who was stark naked, showing off her rudest places, and about to be subjected to an unknown but demeaning ordeal.

'Well?' Kym asked, and she flicked the tip of the crop against the inside of Olena's left thigh, quite near the top. 'What do you think, Olena? Are you feeling sexy already?'

Olena looked over her shoulder. Her eyes were sleepy with desire. 'You know I am,' she said. 'I can't help it. I'm very wicked. You saw when you helped me dress. You touched me. And you can see now. I know I'm very wet. It's shameful.'

Kym swished the riding-crop. 'Yes, I can tell from here that you're ready,' she said. 'You really are a disgraceful young woman.' Kym fought to control her voice and her breathing. It felt wonderful to dominate Olena. The riding-crop, its handle nestling in her hand, felt entirely appropriate. She felt she radiated authority. She knew that under her skirt she was as wet as Olena.

'We'd better play safe, though,' Kym said. 'I ought to make sure you're really sexed up before I start the test. And we've already proved that nothing gets you going like a little taste of the whip.'

The riding-crop whistled again, and this time its supple, leather-bound length landed lightly across Olena's waiting bottom. Kym found herself grinning with pleasure at the sound of the crop and the sight of the thin red line it drew on Olena's right buttock.

Kym remembered that there were mirrors everywhere, and straightened her face. It wouldn't do to show Olena that she was anything other than stonily severe. Still, wielding the crop was such fun! The first line was already fading, so Kym used the crop again to make another mark.

Why, Kym wondered, had she never done this before? Looking back at her conquests of shy young women she realised that some of them, at least, would probably have been delighted if Kym had tied them up and whipped them. But the furthest Kym had gone was to administer a half-hearted spanking to one of them.

If I enjoy it this much when I'm seeing to a thoroughly womanly girl such as Olena, Kim thought, what will it be like when I take charge of someone who's really my type?

The temptation to aim the crop at the tenderest parts of Olena's proffered hindquarters was difficult to resist, and

Kym began to realise that being in command of someone was a task that required thought and subtlety. She remembered that one of Madame's skills was continually to remind her victim that he or she was vulnerable and visible. 'I think you're getting wetter, Olena,' Kym commented, and 'Lift your bottom a little more, Olena, I want to be able to see everything.' She laid the strokes of the riding-crop lightly, and in the main in horizontal lines across Olena's bottom, but every so often she would vary this regime by making the tip of the crop flick into the funnel of Olena's arsehole or against her moist sex-lips.

Kym found it difficult, too, to make herself stop, but she did so when Olena's bottom was blushing and a shade darker than usual. The lines made by her gentle crop-strokes faded almost immediately, but the colour, pleasingly, remained.

'You're a filthy little pervert, Olena,' she stated matter-of-factly. She knew how to provoke her companion's lascivious desires. 'You obviously enjoyed that. You're as wet as you were yesterday. There must be something wrong with you, you know. You like being whipped. You're abnormal.'

'I know,' Olena said. She looked over her shoulder again. Her face was flushed and her eyes were bright. She smiled sadly. 'I'm sorry I'm so horrible.'

'You're not,' Kym assured her. She wasn't sure whether Olena was playing along with the game, or if she was really upset. 'But you do need to be tested, so Madame knows exactly what makes you aroused, and then you will have to be punished.'

'I can't wait,' Olena said, with such heartfelt emotion that Kym was sure she wasn't dissembling.

'The test is straightforward,' Kym said. 'You can stay where you are for the time being.' She burrowed in one of the boxes until she found the item that Madame had told her to use. She walked round to the back of the chair so that Olena could see what she was carrying. 'You're to wear this. In your arse.'

It was a tail: a large anal plug made of black rubber, attached to which was a plume of long, shining hair. Where it was fixed to the plug the hair was plaited, and concealed in the plait was a small silver ring that could be attached to a belt around the wearer's waist, so that the tail would stand erect. After the short plaited section the thick, glossy hairs of the tail hung loose, and Kym was sure that once inserted into Olena's beautiful bottom the tail would swish and sway like a thoroughbred's.

'Look at the size of this rubber bit,' Kym said. 'All of that will be inside your arsehole. It won't be comfortable. I can't believe you'll enjoy having it up there.'

She looked at Olena's face. Olena was gazing at the tail with undisguised desire. 'Even if you do like the feeling of your arse being stuffed full,' Kym said, 'no one could possibly like being made to look like an animal. It's going to be horribly humiliating. I'll make you run around on your hands and knees, you know. And then we'll see whether you're still excited.'

'I will be,' Olena murmured. 'I know I will be. But I suppose we have to try it.' Her eyes were shining with anticipation.

'Get up,' Kym said. She had no doubt that she was going to be almost as stimulated as Olena. It gave her a shock of pleasure every time Olena obeyed one of her instructions. 'I'm going to make you put it in yourself. And I'm going to watch you very closely.'

'Where do you want me?' Olena asked.

'On the floor,' Kym said. 'You're dirty, so it's where you belong.' She thought that she might be overdoing the strict mistress act, but she found that Olena obeyed with alacrity and with a devoted look in her eyes.

'Knees up, legs apart,' Kym said. She dropped the tail on to Olena's stomach. 'Put the rubber bit up your cunt first,' she said. 'Play with it until I tell you to stop. Then I'll use the crop on you again while you smear grease on the plug. Then you'll push it into your arsehole, nice and slowly. And then you'll go for a run with it.'

I hope Madame doesn't interrupt us before I've given Olena a very thorough test, Kym thought. I haven't had this much fun for years.

* * *

Talia was on display again, bound inside one of the row of cabinets that greeted visitors to the private rooms of Edmund's domain. As a reward for her performance the previous evening she had been allocated an amusement machine that allowed her to wear some clothes and in which she was permitted to have orgasms. The mechanism would administer pain, of course, as well as pleasure, and she was tied in a revealing position from which she could not move, but she had not expected to be allowed unalloyed enjoyment. Her function was, after all, to entertain Edmund's guests.

She was dressed from neck to waist in a tight-fitting suit of thin black rubber, and she had stockings, of the same material, that reached the tops of her thighs. Her ankles, knees and wrists were fastened to the sides of the cabinet and, as the box was open-fronted, everyone who passed her could stop and admire her exposed private parts. She was completely exposed: her sex was freshly shaved, and taut silver chains ran from clips on her outer labia to the tops of her stockings. Thick straps ran under and beneath her rubber-covered breasts, and over her shoulders, to support her against the back of the seatless, frontless chair. She was also able to take some of her weight on her feet, which were resting on platforms at the sides of the cabinet, and through her arms, so that she was able to lift and lower herself slightly.

In the space below the place where the chair's seat would have been were the motor and the mechanical parts of the amusement machine. They were uncovered, so that the spectators could see them working. The parts that affected Talia were a thin metal cylinder, with a rubber base and a cord leading down to the machinery, that was embedded in her anus; a pad of soft, moist material, positioned so that it was almost touching the top of her opened sex-lips, and that rose on a slender metal stalk from the motor beneath her; and a short drum that was rotating slowly just under her open vulva. Like a hairbrush, its surface was covered with stiff bristles.

'Try your luck, ladies and gentlemen,' cried the show-man who was attending Talia's booth. 'Just a tenner starts the machine. Get a fiver back each time the lovely girl stops the mechanism. You want to see how it works, sir? It's only a tenner for the entire performance.'

There was no shortage of customers who were prepared to pay.

'Thank you, thank you, one and all,' the showman said. 'Now stand by, ladies and gentlemen, and watch the pretty redhead squirm with pleasure.' He pressed a button on the side of the cabinet and stood back. The machinery below Talia hummed into life.

Edmund had explained to Talia how the mechanism worked, so she was not surprised when the cylinder in her anus started to vibrate. She knew that coloured lights would now be flashing along the length of cord, so that the audience would know that the anal vibrator was working. Talia wanted her arousal to build as slowly as possible, but with so many people watching her, and with insistent little tremors stimulating her anus, she found that she couldn't help becoming excited. With her sex-lips pinned open she could not conceal the fact that her juices were flowing.

The metal stick rising from the motor flicked forwards, and the moist pad tapped against the top of her slit, just where the tip of her clitoris was peeking from its hood. A bell gave a silvery chime, and lights flashed along the length of the metal stalk. Talia gasped, and a shiver ran through her. She heard the comments of the spectators.

The one thing that Edmund had not told her was how long the machine would continue to work. The customer's payment had started the mechanism, but when would it stop and allow Talia to rest?

The cylinder in Talia's anus was vibrating faster. Its tip seemed to be moving independently, rotating inside her, while the base felt as though it had enlarged, and was stretching her, and was throbbing at a slower pace than the rest of the cylinder. Meanwhile the soft pad was bouncing faster and faster against her clitoris. Talia was drowning in waves of delicious sensations, and could no longer think about how much time she would have to endure the machine's attentions. She closed her eyes and surrendered.

As she drifted down through clouds from the endless blue sky of her orgasm, she became aware that the spectators were applauding. She realised, too, that the machinery was still operating. She had known that it would be. She had come too soon. Now what was she to do? Would she be able to climb to another climax without any respite?

It seemed that she would. The ripples of pleasure from her first orgasm had not yet faded, and already she could feel another building inside her. The cylinder in her anus, still moving, vibrating and throbbing, was now also administering tiny electric shocks that made her jolt and moan; the moist pad was beating a rapid tattoo on her most sensitive bud of flesh. Lights were flashing all over the booth and the mechanism it contained. In the brief moments when Talia opened her eyes she could see that people were arriving from all over the room, drawn by the lights, her cries of ecstasy, and the excited chatter of the crowd watching her.

The second climax came quickly. Talia arched her back, as much as she could in her restraints, and gave a shout of joy that was almost a scream. Her audience cheered.

But the machinery didn't stop. Panting for breath, and slowly recovering her senses, Talia knew that she would not be able to come again. Not without a rest. Not without some relief from the incessant burrowing and throbbing inside her anus and the continuous stimulation of her clitoris. The sensations were almost painful now. She would have to stop the motor.

She knew how to do it, but she hesitated for a moment. Perhaps, if she held on for just a few more minutes, the machinery would reach the end of its allotted time and stop of its own accord. But, she thought, my job is to entertain. She realised that the machinery was probably designed to continue until she had stopped it at least once. And so, biting her lower lip against the anticipated pain, she lowered her body.

She cried out in pain as the sensitive membranes of her vulva came to rest on the curved brush. It stopped rotating, but the upward pressure of the sharp bristles was continuous, and it felt to Talia as though the very core of her being was pierced with scores of needles.

The machinery, however, had stopped. The anal vibrator and the soft pad were still. And they would remain so, Talia knew, for as long as she could bear to hold the bristly drum in her opened sex.

Through eyes bleary with pleasure and pain Talia saw the showman flourish the winnings of the customer who had paid to start the machinery.

Some of the spectators remained, fascinated by the sight of Talia's suffering as she sat impaled on the most excruciating of seats, or waiting to see when she would lift herself off so that the machinery could restart and begin to stimulate her again.

The showman, however, wanted to maximise his takings from the booth, and he announced that the show was over. He turned off the motor, and Talia felt the relaxation of the pressure of the spines against the inside of her sex. The brush retracted downwards. Talia could at last collect her thoughts and gather breath.

'Roll up, roll up, ladies and gentlemen,' the showman started to call. Talia prepared herself for another performance.

Olena had known that the tests she had undergone during the previous days had all been leading towards a final trial, or sequence of trials, by which Madame intended to plumb the depths of Olena's addiction to perversity.

Today Olena was dressed in all the elements of the costume in which she had already been tested piecemeal. She had on the corset, the high-heeled boots, and the long gloves, all in black. The helmet, complete with the cylindrical gag and the blinkers, restricted her hearing, her sight and her speech. Her hair, issuing from the helmet and held in a loose bunch with a red bow, was matched by the tail that protruded from her anus. From the clips attached to her nipples and labia hung little silver bells that tinkled at her slightest movement.

She was on her hands and knees. Mirrors had been placed in front of her and behind her so that, despite the blinkers, she could see her reflection. Madame, walking around her, kept taut the reins that were clipped to the gag, so that Olena was obliged to keep her head up.

'What a pretty little pony,' Madame exclaimed. Olena could hear her, despite the helmet, so she must have been keeping her voice raised for Olena's benefit.

Olena saw in the mirrors that Madame was standing behind her. She felt Madame's hold on the reins relax, and saw Madame's hand begin a swift descent. Even before the smack landed, Olena began to arch her back further inwards and lift her bottom. She had been trained how to present herself for punishment, and in any case she knew that she deserved every smack that Madame cared to give her.

Madame delivered six hard slaps to each of Olena's buttocks. This did nothing to assuage Olena's feelings of shame, but added substantially to the turmoil of lustful urges that she was experiencing. 'Magnificent haunches,' Madame declared. 'And a pretty tail, too. I can't wait to whip you up to speed, little pony. But first I had better find out whether being turned into an animal has been enough to quell those naughty symptoms of excitement that I discovered earlier.'

In truth, since Olena had arrived in the conservatory and disrobed, Madame's fingers had not stayed long away from Olena's private places. It was therefore not surprising that once again Olena was so wet that she was dripping from her sex. The short spanking, which had served only to inflame her passion and to remind her that she was the kind of wicked girl who took pleasure in being punished as well as in being made into an animal, had summoned forth more lubrication, which Madame's questing fingers could not fail to find.

The test was, she knew, unnecessary. At the Private House she had been subjected to a course of pet training, and she was already only too well aware of how much she had enjoyed the humiliation of being made to perform like

173

a young bitch on heat. Being dressed as a pony was as nothing compared with the obscene and demeaning acts she had performed, and enjoyed, as a dog.

She felt Madame's fingers brush against her sticky sex, and she lifted her bottom again to assist Madame's examination. In the mirror she saw her face redden and her eyes cloud with desire as Madame's fingers parted her sex-lips and once again probed into her private place.

'Naughty, naughty, naughty,' Madame said, and played with Olena's tail. Olena gasped with pleasure. 'You do like being a pony, don't you?' Madame went on. 'I'm very pleased with you, my dear. It seems there is nothing too degrading for you to enjoy. I can't even say that I'm surprised any more. You've failed every test. I don't believe there's a trace of decency in you.'

As Madame spoke she continued to stroke Olena's tail, making the plug move deep inside Olena's anus, while the fingers of her other hand made embarrassing squelching noises as they probed into Olena's sex. Olena's whole body was trembling with pleasure, and she lowered her head and felt tears of shame prickling in her eyes. Madame was right: Olena knew that she was despicably depraved.

Madame stood up, and pulled on the reins. 'Come along, pony,' she said. 'I want to see you walk around the conservatory. Kym, fetch me a whip. This little pony seems happy to show off her hindquarters, but I want to make sure she swishes her tail from side to side as she walks.'

Olena swung her hips from side to side as she walked on her hands and knees. Madame, holding the reins and following, kept up a lewd commentary about her appearance and encouraged her progress with occasional stinging lashes of the whip.

'Good little pony,' Madame said. 'We'll do another circuit of the room, and then we'll see how prettily you can prance and trot on your hind legs. Oh, look, Kym, she's getting wetter and wetter. Look at the insides of her thighs.'

Olena's consolation, as she progressed around the conservatory in a dizzying confusion of shame and arousal, urged on by the stimulating stings of Madame's whip on her bottom, was that she was sure that Madame now understood the perverse and unalterably wicked nature of her personality. Madame would no longer even feign reluctance when Olena begged her for punishment, nor would she demur when Olena pleaded with her to wield the rod harder and faster. And she would allow Olena to reach an orgasm, either during or after the chastisement. And, for a while, Olena would be content.

Talia had rehearsed her performance in the morning, she had rested and watched some of the other rehearsals during the afternoon, and now she was once again about to be unveiled before an audience.

She could hear the restless crowd on the other side of the curtains. She was tense with excitement. Anxiously she tried to remember everything she had learnt that morning. She was naked, but for her collar, and kneeling with her knees apart. Her sex was hot and moist. Her long titian hair was plaited and coiled on her head, so that it would not interfere with her performance. Around her on the small, low, semicircular stage were large rectangles of white card, propped upright against sturdy supports. Between the cards were tins of paint: black, blue, yellow, green and red, opened and ready for her to use. In between her knees was the brush.

'Quiet, please, ladies and gentlemen,' said a voice from beyond the curtain. 'The painting class is about to begin. Please allow me to present today's guest artist, number Forty-one.'

The curtains parted, and Talia blinked in the spotlights before remembering to smile and bow. The spectators, each of whom had paid to watch her, applauded. Talia felt a glow of pride, as well as the weight of the responsibility she had to give a memorable performance.

Talia held up the brush for the audience to see. She flicked her fingers through the fine hairs of its tip, and then she caressed the shaped cylinder, already slick with ointment, that was the brush's flanged base. Still kneeling, she turned her back on the audience and leant forward, pushing her bottom out. The spectators applauded again, and cheered.

In her few days in Edmund's employ Talia had learnt the importance of putting on a good show. Therefore she didn't immediately insert the brush, but instead she placed it on the stage between her legs as she parted them slowly, revealing more and more of her private parts to the audience. She slid her hands up the backs of her thighs, and toyed with the lips of her sex. She dipped two fingers into her vagina, and then withdrew them. She used the fingers of one hand to hold open her labia, and then explored her splayed vulva with the fingers of the other hand. She closed her eyes and couldn't help moving her hips: she was becoming very aroused.

Encouraged by the cheers of the spectators she kept one hand in her sex, and with the other she began to play with her anus. At first she merely caressed the silky funnel of darker skin, and then she began to press inwards with one finger, and then two. Through a haze of pleasure she heard the delighted cries of the audience, and smiled.

She continued to play with herself, and found herself rising towards a climax. She forced herself to concentrate on the performance. She was there for the customers' enjoyment, not her own. She pulled her fingers from her anus and picked up the brush. Looking over her shoulder and smiling brightly at the spectators she pressed the base of the brush against the ring of her anus and pushed it slowly in.

When the whole of the base was inside her, so that only the thick flange and the slender stalk of the brush protruding from it were visible, Talia crawled on hands and knees, back and forth across the stage, while the audience applauded.

'Thank you, ladies and gentlemen,' said the showman who was standing at the edge of the stage. 'Forty-one will first demonstrate that she can write. She will then go on to paint a landscape. Is there anyone who would like her to write a name? Yes, you, sir. What is your name, please?'

'Algernon!' shouted the young man whom the showman had selected. He was red-faced and laughing, and Talia assumed that he had said the longest name he could think of, to try to make things difficult for her.

'Algernon it is!' the showman declared. 'Off you go, Forty-one.'

Talia had found, in rehearsal, that it was almost impossible to write even the shortest name using paint and a brush in your backside. But legibility was not the point of the performance. The audience, she knew, would be happy to watch her struggling with the brush and the paint, and would convulse with laughter if she knocked over an easel or, even better, a full pot of paint. They wanted to watch the revealing and demeaning positions she would have to adopt as she tried to direct the brush's tip into a pot of paint and then on to the card.

It was easier, Talia found, to accomplish the tasks in front of a cheering, noisy audience than it had been in the quiet of the rehearsal room. Determined to put on a good show, Talia made sure that her breasts jiggled whenever she bobbed up to dip the brush into the pot. She lowered her breasts to the stage when she lifted her bottom, and she exaggerated the wiggle of her hips as she tried to make the brush form letters on the card.

There was no point, in any case, in trying to keep her breasts clean. Once the audience had begun to tire of watching her trying to write, the showman would set her to paint a landscape – and for this she would use not only the brush but also her breasts, dipped into the paint-pots and rubbed against one of the cards and, finally, her buttocks, over which the showman would pour paint so that she could create large colourful effects by wiping them on to the card.

The result would look nothing like a landscape, but the audience wouldn't care. Talia would end the performance with her naked body smeared and dripping with coloured paints, and as she bowed in response to the applause the brush in her bottom would rise to greet the cheers.

'I can't read a single letter,' shouted a voice from the crowd, and Talia lifted her head from the floor to grin at the audience. She shook her bottom, and the crowd cheered. She knew that she was going to entertain them successfully. The showman would tell Edmund that her work had been satisfactory, and she would avoid punishment for another night.

She was, she supposed, as happy as she could be, in the circumstances. But nothing assuaged the yearning of her heart and her body for someone to hold her, kiss her, cuddle her, spank her, and take her to bed.

Barat stood, shivering, in the centre of the lawn. It was, in his opinion, far too late in the year for outdoor exercise, particularly without suitable clothing. And as he was wearing nothing but a pair of boots, a leather harness that held in place the rigid box over his genitalia, and the helmet that he wore to conceal his identity whenever Olena was being tested, he considered his attire entirely unsuitable.

It was all right for Madame and Olena, he thought. Olena was cantering in circles around him, followed by Madame holding the reins, and both women were flushed, glowing, and obviously quite warm. Olena's buttocks, marked with fiery stripes made by Madame's whip, looked particularly heated. But even the sight of Olena in her pony costume could not inflame Barat's ardour. The pale autumn sunlight fell on him but had little warmth. His task was to stand in the middle of the garden, holding a long rope tied to Olena's helmet, so that she could run only in a circle around the perimeter of the lawn. He felt cold, miserable, and very exposed.

Why, he wondered for the thousandth time, did Madame delight in tormenting him? He was wearing less than Olena. It was unfair. And he was standing right in the middle of the lawn. It was true that the garden was surrounded by tall trees, but they had lost most of their leaves now, and he was sure that he could be seen from the upper windows of the neighbouring houses.

He had been looking forward to watching Madame put her new pony through her paces in the garden. He had expected to be concealed somewhere in the house, so that he could enjoy some privacy while he stood at a window and gazed out at the stimulating sight of Olena running and prancing in the open air. But Madame always found a way to ruin his pleasure. And now, even though he found himself staring at Olena's magnificent breasts as they bounced in the corset's quarter cups; and at her blushing, excited face as she tossed her head; and at her reddened arse with its luxuriant tail, it was never long before he became aware of the cold and of his exposed nakedness. His manhood wasn't even erect enough to strain against the inside of the box covering it.

'That's enough!' Madame cried. 'Whoah, pony. Stop now.' Madame was panting from the exertion of her run. 'You've exhausted me, little pony. That's enough exercise for today. We'll get you into the stable and Kym will take off your bridle and bit. You can have a drink and a rub down. Then you're to give me lots of pony kisses, and once I'm satisfied I'll watch you pleasure yourself. You're such an adorable pet.'

Barat cursed and shivered. Once again there was to be no role for him as Madame enjoyed her new toy. Madame had become besotted with Olena, who was hardly to be seen these days other than in her pony costume. The conservatory had been converted into sleeping-quarters for Olena. Madame called it Olena's stable. Kym seemed to spend all her time bathing Olena, and brushing and plaiting Olena's hair, and massaging soothing ointments into Olena's muscles, and her chastised buttocks and breasts, and her arsehole. It was also Kym's job to ensure that, in Madame's absence, Olena was kept in a state of wet readiness. Kym seemed entirely happy in her duties. Meanwhile Barat was left to polish Olena's corsets and boots and helmets, as well as to perform all the household chores that he had once shared with Kym.

Madame was treating him badly. And there was nothing he could do about it. If he were to complain, Madame would never allow him to have Olena.

'I'm going to shower and change,' Madame announced. 'Kym, would you please hose down the pony before you stable her? You might as well play the hose over our stable boy, too. He looks as though he could do with a cold shower to douse his lusts.'

This was too much. Olena, he was sure, would enjoy the humiliation of being sprayed and soaked with cold water. But surely Madame did not intend to let that common slut Kym subject him to the same treatment? He would protest. But then he glanced at Olena, at her breasts rising and falling as she recovered her breath, at her face wearing an expression of secretive anticipation, and once again he knew that he would surrender to anything Madame required just to have an hour alone with her.

Kym was standing at the wall of the house. With one hand she aimed the nozzle of the hose towards Olena; the other was on the tap.

'Ready, Olena?' she called out. 'Here comes your wash-down, little pony.'

In the darkness of the enclosed cubicle, Talia waited for the show to begin. Her booth was at the end of the gallery of amusements, set on a platform at a distance from the row of boxes in which she had been displayed on previous evenings. Now they were occupied by other trainees; young men and women who were learning how to please Edmund's customers. Talia had a separate cubicle of her own.

The machine into which she was bound had been designed especially for her. It had taken a long time to fit her into it, and she was still not sure what all the components would do when the motors started. But Edmund seemed very pleased with the device, and with Talia's appearance, and he had decreed that the box was to be given pride of place, and that he would personally present the entertainment to a chosen group of his most illustrious clients.

Talia's mouth was dry with excitement and anticipation, but she knew that it would not remain so for long. She had drunk several bottles of water before being arranged in the cubicle, and her bladder was already feeling full. She hoped the performance would begin soon. She could hear voices, among them Edmund's, outside the cabinet. There seemed to be a large crowd gathering.

Then she heard Edmund's voice again, louder than previously. He was making an announcement. The door of the cabinet was closed, but Edmund had come to stand beside it and she was able to hear what he was saying.

'Ladies and gentlemen, honoured guests,' he declared. 'Thank you for your patience. You will not be disappointed, I assure you. This evening I have something very special. A brand new entertainment. A masterpiece of the toymaker's art, if I say so myself. To perform the piece, please allow me introduce a new star in the firmament of amusements, the lovely Lucietta.'

The door of the cabinet swung open, lights flickered into life inside the box, and Talia blinked, and gasped at the throng craning their necks to see her and applauding thunderously.

She remembered to incline her head to acknowledge the cheers. It was almost the only movement she could make. But her mind was racing. Edmund had called her a star. He had given her a name. She was no longer an anonymous, numbered trainee. She was Lucietta. The number on her room would be removed, and her new name would be set there instead. Few of Edmund's staff were so privileged.

Talia's appearance was attracting a buzz of comment from the crowd. She was not surprised. She was clad entirely in black rubber, from her head to her toes. She knew that the outfit was sewn together down her back, but from the viewpoint of the spectators it appeared entirely seamless, like a second, black, shiny skin. The smooth surface was broken in only four places: the front covering of the headpiece had been removed, to reveal her face; there were two tight holes through which her breasts, distended by the constraint, protruded; and there was nothing covering her private parts.

She was secured in a half-kneeling, half-squatting position, with her knees tied wide apart. As before, her sex and her anus were on display, and the spectators could easily see that both were penetrated by artificial phalluses that

181

rose through the floor of the box. Their function was relatively straightforward: like Talia, the spectators expected the phalluses to rise and fall, thrusting in and out of her, when the machinery began to operate. The thin transparent tubes that ran into Talia's mouth and from between her sex-lips, however, were less easy to explain, and Talia could hear many puzzled comments.

'All will be revealed,' Edmund declared. 'I will turn the machine on, bit by bit, and I will explain as I go along.'

Talia saw him turn to the side of the cabinet, where she knew the control buttons were set. Then she heard the faint, brief hum of a motor, and she felt a gush of fresh water enter her mouth through the tube. Her mouth was sealed shut by the surgical tape that held the tube in place between her lips, so she had no alternative but to swallow. The water flowed in a steady stream, and Talia had to let it all trickle down her throat.

'As you can see,' Edmund said, 'water is now flowing into Lucietta's mouth at a constant rate. As you can imagine, this makes her want to relieve herself. But I'm afraid she can't.'

Talia hoped that Edmund was about to reveal how she could pee. The pressure in her bladder was becoming very uncomfortable.

Edmund leant into the cabinet and with delicate fingers parted the top of Talia's sex-lips. 'You see?' he said. 'Lucietta has been fitted with a catheter, so that her urine can flow directly from her bladder by means of this tube. It is held in place by this inflatable collar, which as you can see, has been expanded so that she cannot possibly expel the tube. The muscles that normally control the opening and closing of her urethra are, of course, quite useless now: she can do nothing to prevent the flow of urine.'

Several of the spectators pointed out that they could see nothing at all flowing along the tube.

'You're quite correct,' Edmund said. 'That is because the catheter has been fitted, here, with a valve. The valve is closed: no urine can escape. Poor Lucietta must be feeling very much in need of a pee, I suspect.'

Talia nodded her head and looked imploringly at Edmund.

Edmund laughed. 'Of course,' he said, 'we must allow Lucietta to relieve herself. It's very simple: all she has to do is to lean forward and press against this lever.'

At last Talia understood the function of the thin metal rod, considerately padded with a cylinder of cloth, that crossed the cubicle in front of her chest and just below her breasts.

'When Lucietta presses against the lever,' Edmund said, 'and maintains the pressure, the valve in the catheter opens, and her urine will flow down the tube and into this holding tank.'

Edmund nodded to Talia, and she needed no further incentive to relieve the pressure in her bladder. She leant forwards until her rubber-clad ribcage was touching the horizontal rod, and then she pressed against it. It moved easily, and Talia heard the clicks and whirrs of switches and motors.

For a moment nothing seemed to happen, and Talia was suddenly aware that holding open the lever obliged her to adopt a position in which she was thrusting forward her breasts for the appreciation of the crowd.

Still there seemed to be no release of the tension in her belly. However, the machinery was clearly working. The cylinders in her vagina and anus were moving, slowly, up and down. It was irritating to be stimulated when she was so desperate to pee. Then she saw two small drums on metal stalks swing inwards from the sides of the cabinet. They stopped in front of her chest. Talia saw that attached to the drums were short flaps of leather. She realised that as long as she pressed her chest against the lever her breasts were very close to the drums. If the drums were to start rotating at speed, the leather flaps could not fail to smack against her breasts.

Still the valve in the catheter did not seem to have opened. But the drums in front of her started to spin. The crowd watched in awed silence as the leather flaps swung upwards and slapped against the undersides of Talia's outthrust breasts.

Talia smiled. She knew that she was putting on a good show. The spectators, she thought, probably expected her to recoil from the smacking, but she had no intention of doing any such thing. This was the first spanking of any kind she had received since arriving at Edmund's house, and she was determined not to miss a moment. The phalluses in her sex and anus were moving faster now, and even the pressure in her bladder seemed to add to her excitement. She suspected that she would not reach an orgasm, no matter how long she pressed against the lever, but that was not the point of the performance. She would nevertheless remain on a plateau of sexual arousal while she entertained the spectators. They wanted to see her breasts suffer a severe punishment, and she was determined not to disappoint them.

At some point, as she gasped and moaned with pleasure and pain, Talia realised that her bladder no longer felt as full as it had.

'You see, ladies and gentlemen?' Edmund said. 'The valve has opened, and you can see Lucietta's urine flowing along the tube. It collects here, in this tank, and once it reaches a certain level it triggers a switch, here, that turns on the motor that works the pump, here. The pump then drives the liquid up this tube. Look: it's beginning to work.'

The little drums in front of Talia's chest stopped turning but, to Talia's relief, only for a moment. They restarted, rotating in the opposite direction, and the tops of Talia's breasts, and her nipples, received the regular slaps of the leather flaps. Although she could tell that the pressure was lessening, she still felt that she wanted to pee and she was aware that the tube fixed between her lips was feeding her a continuous stream of water that would refill her bladder almost as quickly as the catheter emptied it. She would, she thought, be able to take short rests from pressing against the lever, but for the time being she was happy to feel the phalluses filling her and moving inside her, and the leather straps making her breasts wonderfully sore and sensitive.

'The urine now flows up this tube,' Edmund went on, 'under pressure from the pump. The tube disappears behind Lucietta's back, but I can tell you that it runs up the back of her costume, right to the top of her head, and it emerges – well, *voilà*! There is the pretty fountain.'

Talia, biting her lower lip as she endured the throbbing pain of her breasts and enjoyed the waves of pleasure that swept through her body, became aware of a sound like falling rain. She felt a drizzle of moisture fall on her face and cool her heated breasts, and she saw droplets glinting on the smooth surface of her rubber costume. She understood at last the function of the nozzle she had seen pointing skywards at the very top of her helmet. By pressing against the lever she had set off a fountain of her own pee which would shower down on her whenever she filled the tank.

The spectators shouted and cheered when they saw the fountain rise from the top of Talia's head. Talia acknowledged the applause in the only way she could, with a nod of her head that sent a cataract of urine down her face and splashing on to her breasts. She was glad that her mouth was covered with tape.

The drums stopped rotating again, and the stalks that supported them moved at an angle. When the drums restarted the leather flaps now struck the outer sides of Talia's breasts, and they made a louder report with each smack now that Talia's breasts were wet.

I'll let the machine do the sides of my breasts, Talia thought, and then I'll lean back and take a rest. This is a wonderful machine. I'm going to be spanked and penetrated all evening, under a shower of my own pee. Edmund is so inventive. The customers are enthralled. And I'm a star. I'm Lucietta.

'Good little pony,' Madame said. She lay languorously on her bed with her thighs wantonly parted. She was naked, but the riding-crop was still hanging from its loop around her right wrist. 'What an affectionate pet you are. Come here and cuddle me.'

Olena moved up the bed and into her mistress's embrace. Madame's body was soft and warm, and smelt of spicy perfume.

'Your face is sticky,' Madame said with a giggle as Olena responded to her kisses. 'You make me so wet when you lick me.'

'I'm sorry, Madame,' Olena murmured. 'I like licking you,' she added, and felt her face redden with shame as she confessed. 'You taste lovely.'

'I do, don't I?' Madame said, and giggled again as she lapped with her tongue at her juices on Olena's lips and chin. She turned on her side. 'Keep still, pony,' she said, and she applied herself to the task of cleaning Olena's face.

As she licked, she began to caress and squeeze Olena's breasts. The fingers of her other hand traced the raised welts on Olena's bottom and stroked the tail that was the only part of the pony costume that Olena was still wearing. Olena shivered with pleasure and breathed out a sigh.

'Such a delightful pet,' Madame whispered. 'I can't keep my hands off you. You're thoroughly wicked.'

Olena was only too well aware of her wickedness. It was sinful to enjoy the caresses of a woman, and utterly depraved to enjoy the taste of a woman's private place. It was sinful to find pleasure in the humiliation of being made to wear a tail, and in the warm, full feeling of the tail's plug in her bottom. It was sinful to take pride in the size and firmness of her breasts, and to engender lustful thoughts in others by displaying them. 'I know, Madame,' Olena replied. 'I'm incorrigible.' She could feel the cool length of the riding-crop against the backs of her thighs as Madame stroked her sore bottom. 'But even so, please –'

'Hush.' Madame stopped her mouth with a kiss. 'There will be plenty more punishment today. You know I like to keep you well marked.'

It was true: since Olena had become Madame's pet pony, Madame had become more severe, and she no longer waited until the marks of one chastisement had faded before administering another. Olena, who was in a constant state of shame and excitement because she couldn't help enjoying the degradation of being an animal, was reassured to find that whenever she looked in a mirror there were stripes on her breasts and buttocks.

'Thank you, Madame,' Olena said.

'You're a good pony,' Madame said, 'and a very special pet. I'll whip your breasts in just a moment, and then I'll penetrate you and let you have an orgasm. Would you like that?'

Olena nodded. She felt tears of gratitude in her eyes. Madame was so kind to her.

Madame drew back from the embrace and pulled herself upright against the pillows at the head of the bed. She patted her thighs. 'Across my lap, pony,' she said. 'I want to fuck your arsehole today, so I'll have to remove your tail. Would you like a spanking as well?'

Olena knelt on the bed beside her mistress. 'Yes, please, Madame,' she said. 'I'm afraid I'll need it.' There could be no doubt that Olena would find pleasurable the extraction of the anal plug, and she was sure that such pleasure could not be anything but perverse, and merited a very thorough spanking.

Olena had known for months, if not years, that there was no hope for her. She was an incurably depraved slut. However, she still found herself surprised and ashamed at the thrill she derived from the simple act of displaying herself for punishment. Every element of the little ritual – the firmness of Madame's thighs beneath her hips, the bowing of her head, the inward arching of her back when Madame touched her there – gave a small, exquisite sensation of joyful anticipation. No matter how often she parted her thighs, pushed out her bottom, and put on show her most private places, she always felt wonderfully dirty, wanton and aroused.

Madame played with the tail, sending jolts of sensation into the depths of Olena's body. 'Such a shame this has to come out,' Madame said. 'It suits you so well. And a pony ought always to have a tail.'

Olena silently agreed. She loved the feeling of wearing the tail in her anus, and she found that she felt empty without it. These days, when she was alone in her bed she would slide a finger or two into her anus before settling down to sleep.

Madame began to slap Olena's bottom, lightly at first, and then with increasing vigour. Olena pressed her face into the bedclothes and surrendered to the stinging warmth. Maintaining the spanking with one hand, Madame began to tug gently at the tail. Olena relaxed her sphincter muscle and groaned with pleasure as she felt it expand to allow the flanged base of the plug to emerge. Madame drew the plug out slowly and carefully. Olena, trembling with pleasure, thought that if she gave herself over to the wonderful sensations she would reach a climax, but she knew that she should not give way until she had been punished enough.

'It's out,' Madame announced, and gave Olena's left buttock a final slap. 'Get up, pony, and take your tail to the bathroom for a wash. Then you can help me dress. I've got something new for you.'

When Olena returned from the bathroom, with her tail shampooed and dried and its plug washed and newly lubricated, she found Madame standing in the centre of the bedroom holding a harness of leather straps.

'Come along, pony,' Madame said impatiently. 'Help me into this thing.'

Olena was so accustomed to wearing her pony costume that she didn't understand at first that the harness was for Madame. It consisted of a sturdy belt; a triangle of leather, with a round hole, that fitted over Madame's pubic mound; and two straps that ran from the triangle, on either side of Madame's sex, and across her buttocks to the back of the belt. Olena had seen and experienced similar harnesses at the Private House, and she was not at all surprised to see an artificial phallus lying on the bed. She was, however, a little taken aback by its size. She picked it up, and was relieved to find that its surface was soft and that despite its rigidity and massive girth it was a little flexible. It was black, and looked sinister, which to Olena seemed appropriate.

'I chose a big one for you,' Madame said. 'I want the first time I fuck you to be memorable.'

'Thank you, Madame,' Olena said. She was already imagining, with unmistakable thrills of excitement, what it would feel like to be penetrated by the black monster. It had been a long time since she had accommodated anything quite so large. She tightened the buckles of Madame's belt. The harness was in place, and the black phallus projected from the centre of the triangle, from precisely the point where Olena's tongue had recently been teasing the tip of Madame's clitoris.

Madame was no longer holding the riding-crop, but instead she had placed on the bed a thin dowel of wood. It appeared innocuous, but Olena knew that it would whistle through the air like an angry gnat and sting like a wasp. Olena realised that Madame had been watching her as she gazed at the rod. 'Fetch it to me,' Madame said, 'and then kneel here, in front of me.'

Olena brought the thin cane to her mistress and knelt. She folded her arms behind her back and pushed out her chest, as if she was wearing her pony costume. Her breasts had not received any punishment since the previous day, and although they were now virtually unmarked, Olena's anticipation made them feel hot and sensitive.

'Good pony,' Madame said. 'Keep quite still. I don't want to have to do this twice. My arm's already aching from whipping your hindquarters.'

'I'm sorry, Madame,' Olena said. 'I don't mean to be so much trouble to you.'

Madame stroked Olena's hair and cheek. 'It's no trouble, my dear,' she said. 'It's a delight to punish you. Your body is perfectly formed to take the whip. You endure pain beautifully. And you respond so readily and so abundantly to the stimulation. I don't think I'll ever tire of punishing you.' Still stroking Olena's hair, she lifted the slender rod and directed it in a wristy, singing arc on to her left breast.

Olena started and cried out. The pain was even more intense than she had expected. As Madame stood back a little and began the caning in earnest, Olena pushed out her breasts and suppressed her gasps and cries. She didn't want Madame to reduce the power and pace of the cane-strokes. The pain was almost unendurable, and Olena was in heaven. She wished there was a mirror in which she could watch herself being caned. She would have liked to see her breasts pinkening, and the pattern of dark-red lines spreading and deepening across them. She gave a heavy sigh of satisfaction: as always happened during a sustained punishment, it felt suddenly as though a deep shaft had opened within her, and an electric charge began to vibrate through the core of her being, from the surface and interior of her breasts to the aching voids of her sex and anus, and to the very tip of her clitoris.

Kym, later, would be scornful of Olena for letting Madame punish her so severely. But Olena was sure that Kym, too, would do the same in Madame's place. And Kym would smooth soothing oils into Olena's breasts, and into the soft skin around her anus, and the two young women would play with each other until they both reached orgasms, and slept.

'Almost enough,' Madame said. Her breath was short. 'Your breasts look like red balloons, pony. Now stay there and suck this. I want you to make it all shiny before it goes into you.'

Olena opened her mouth and engulfed the upper half of the phallus.

Madame seemed content to let Olena hold the phallus in her mouth. When Olena glanced up she found Madame gazing down at Olena's generous lips, stretched taut around the circumference of the shaft. With her left hand Madame reached down to caress Olena's hair, while with the other she aimed light blows of the cane at the undersides of Olena's breasts.

Olena was grateful that Madame did not thrust the massive cylinder in and out of her mouth, like most men did. The phallus, although shaped like an erect penis, was larger than any man's that Olena had taken into her mouth. Olena was able to remain in the state of blissful reverie into which she always drifted during a long chastisement. Her breasts felt wonderfully sore and swollen. She found herself wondering why she couldn't help but enjoy being penetrated. No matter how it was done, it was shameful that she took such pleasure in it.

Her sex was always so open and ready to be penetrated, especially after she had been punished. She could feel the wetness seeping from between her sex-lips now. If she had been even the slightest bit pure, she was sure that sometimes it would have been difficult for her lovers to enter her sex. But there was never the slightest difficulty. Even the largest penis or phallus slid into her easily, to an accompaniment of embarrassing wet sounds. It was as if her sex was hungry to be penetrated.

But then, she thought, allowing her mouth to be penetrated was perhaps even more indicative of her sinfulness. Did she ever keep her lips closed or turn her head away? No: whenever a penis, limp or erect, or even an artificial phallus, was presented to her face she always voluntarily parted her lips, inclined her head, and took it in. She could not pretend that she was ever taken by surprise, or tricked into performing oral sex: even when she was blindfolded there would be the soft nudge of warm flesh against her lips, and she would instantly surrender. The reason, she had to conclude, was that she liked to have her mouth filled. And what could be more shaming than that?

The answer was, of course, that it was more shaming – utterly degrading, in fact – to welcome the penetration of her most intimate, secret little hole. She knew that even to think about it was wrong and wicked. And she didn't merely think about it. She enjoyed it. Unlike her mouth, her little hole would always put up some resistance, even when Olena herself had abandoned any idea of protest. It was as if her body, even though it usually seemed to inflame her desires, wanted to restrain this darkest impulse of her perverted mind. But Olena knew that she had become almost addicted to this most sinful of all acts. There was always the pressure, gentle or insistent, and then the delicious moment of surrender, and then the pang of pain as the penis or phallus sank into her. It was never entirely comfortable, but what had Olena done to deserve comfort? It was as if she was enjoying the forbidden pleasure and suffering the punishment for it simultaneously.

Madame at last interrupted her thoughts. She pulled the glistening black shaft from Olena's mouth. 'That's enough, pony,' she said. 'I'm ready now. Get on the bed. It's time you were fucked.'

Olena rose unsteadily to her feet and went to the bed. Her private place was sticky and hot between her thighs. She was ready and eager to be penetrated. As she was arranging herself on knees and elbows, with her bottom raised and ready, she remembered something.

'Madame,' she said, looking over her shoulder, 'may I ask a question?'

'Inquisitive little pony,' Madame said, climbing on to the bed behind Olena. 'What is it?'

'You said you'd never tire of punishing me, Madame,' Olena said. 'Did you mean it? I'm sorry, that sounds impolite. I mean, are you going to keep me? I thought you were going to give me to Barat. Or maybe return me to the Private House, when you have secured something you want from the Supreme Mistress.'

'So you've recognised my manservant, have you?' Madame said with a chuckle. 'I can't say I'm surprised. He thinks he's going to surprise you. But he's going to have to wait. I'm very pleased with my new pony, and I'm not going to share you with Barat. As for the Private House: I will shortly take delivery of another bargaining counter. So perhaps I will keep you for my own. Now push those hindquarters right up, little pony.'

Edmund had led Lucietta, naked, on a leash clipped to her collar, to the party at which she was to be welcomed into the elite corps of Edmund's entertainers. It was late at night, and most of the customers had left. The lights outside the building were off, and the corridors and rooms were dark and silent.

But here, in the suite of opulent rooms adjacent to Edmund's private quarters – a part of the establishment Lucietta had never previously visited – all was colour, light and gaiety. Nearly every one of Edmund's star entertainers was present, each still in his or her gaudy, outlandish costume, and Edmund had also invited some of his most valued customers to attend.

Lucietta stood behind Edmund and felt overwhelmed by the crowd and the noise. She had become so accustomed to performing for anonymous audiences that she was nervous at the thought of meeting individuals. She felt that she had never been a very social person. But these days she found it difficult to remember her life before she joined Edmund's company of troupers. Her home had been in a forest, she thought. But that seemed so unlikely that she dismissed it as a fantasy. The face of a pretty, young, impish blonde woman kept appearing in her thoughts, and at such times Lucietta would feel a pang of emotion – loss, perhaps, or merely nostalgia.

She felt a pull on the leash, and stumbled forwards. 'Don't be shy,' Edmund told her. 'Just think of this as another show. Look at them: they're all performing.'

'Thanks, Edmund,' Lucietta said. 'I'll be fine.' She flashed a wide smile. On with the show.

'Ladies and gentlemen,' Edmund said, and then waited for the hubbub to subside. 'Charge your glasses, please. There is plenty of champagne for all, with the compliments of the management. Now join me in drinking a toast to our guest of honour tonight. Here she is, ladies and gentlemen, a new star performer, the lovely Lucietta.'

Lucietta bowed and blew kisses as everyone in the room clapped and cheered.

'For one night only,' Edmund announced, 'Lucietta is yours. Enjoy her in any way that you choose. I am sure she will not disappoint you.' He turned to Lucietta. 'Off you go, angel. Give them the performance of a lifetime.'

'OK, boss,' Lucietta said. 'Thank you for making me a star.'

'My pleasure,' Edmund said. 'You're a natural. And you've been good for business.'

Lucietta strolled into the centre of the room, and was soon surrounded. She revelled in being the centre of attention.

'I must have her first,' a sonorous voice exclaimed. It was Reynaldo, a burly gymnast. 'I've wanted her since she first arrived here. Lucietta, come here. Undo my trousers, sweet girl, and suck me dry.'

Lucietta soon lost count of how many men and women had her, and she could not remember all the acts that she was required to perform. She felt tired but elated. Lick this, she was told, over and over again; put this into this hole, put that into the other hole; hold yourself open while I do this; keep still until I've finished whipping you just there.

She recalled some of the more unusual and uncomfortable requests. A slim, elegant lady in a shimmering gown had produced a box of pins and had told Lucietta to decorate her breasts with them: the lady herself had taken the last half-dozen and had pressed them carefully into Lucietta's nipples. Lucietta had been tied up for a while, and at one point had been used by three men together.

No one, it seemed, wanted simply to kiss her, or to put her over their knees for a gentle spanking. But Lucietta didn't really mind: she was in a state of almost semiconscious arousal as she drifted from one group of guests to another, offering herself for their amusement.

The only slight worry, that nagged at the back of her mind, was that the party seemed to be going on for ever, and she knew that she should get some sleep. There would be a show to put on tomorrow, as there was every day.

She was lying on her back on a couch, concentrating on breathing and making a good job of licking the anus of the woman sitting on her face, when she heard Edmund's voice.

'Here's my new starlet,' he cried. He sounded jovial. 'Is she keeping you entertained, my dear?'

'Rather,' said the woman. 'She's got a strong tongue.'

'She's a pretty little thing,' said the man who was kneeling between Lucietta's thighs and writing his name many times in very small letters on her sex-lips. 'Very obliging.'

'She is, she is,' Edmund replied. 'Such talent. But I fear we won't enjoy her for much longer. I can see that she's ready. And I have signed a contract for her, so there's no way out. A deal is a deal. Tomorrow, or the next day at the latest, I'll have to deliver her to her new owner.'

Lucietta, with her tongue embedded in the woman's anus and her thoughts awash with arousal and the sound of applause, heard Edmund's words and found that she was neither surprised nor concerned. Wherever she went, she would remember to put on a good show.

Six

Kym couldn't hide her annoyance. She didn't care if Madame heard the stamping of her feet as she climbed the stairs, and she didn't care if she woke up the new member of staff.

Madame had relieved her of the task of helping Olena to bathe and dress each morning. From now on Madame would attend herself to the morning rituals of her little pony, as she insisted on calling Olena. Kym hoped that she would at least be permitted to continue to look after Olena in the evenings. She enjoyed the quiet hour that she and Olena spent together every day in Olena's stable, after Madame had exhausted herself and her pony, and before dinner and the arrival of guests. By the evening Olena, who had usually been in her pony costume all day, would have been made to perpetrate several very degrading acts and would have been well whipped. She would have given Madame at least one orgasm, and would have been permitted to have a climax of her own. She was usually tired and docile by the time Kym arrived to remove her costume. Then Kym would take her, naked, out into the garden to hose her down, and then wrap her in a large, coarse towel that she would use, back in the stable, to rub warmth back into Olena's limbs. She would use the towel to dry Olena's breasts, bottom and sex, too, rubbing the reddened, welted skin harder than was necessary. This always excited Olena, and after several vigorous attempts Kym would have to stop trying to dry Olena's ever-moistening sex. Kym would point out that Olena was a naughty girl, and Olena would ask politely for a spanking. Kym was becoming adept at warming Olena's rotund buttocks.

Then Kym would instruct Olena to display her tits, and then her cunt, and lastly her arse and her arsehole, and Kym would massage oils and perfumed ointments into Olena's sore flesh. It seemed that Kym's use of obscene words made Olena even more aroused. Then there would usually be at least a quarter of an hour before dinner, and rather than help Barat in the kitchen Kym would take Olena into the pony-stall, and the two women would lie together on Olena's bedding. Kym had found that Olena, who by this time was tired and languid but very aroused, would do anything that Kym ordered her to. Although the conservatory was now known as Olena's stable its shelves were still stacked with boxes containing every sort of toy and implement of punishment, and Kym usually selected a few to use on Olena. Since she had become Madame's pony Olena seemed more eager than ever to accept every sort of indignity. Kym took great pleasure in every one of Olena's willing surrenders, and she found herself during the working day daydreaming about ever more inventive ways to give Olena the torments and humiliations she craved. It worried Kym, occasionally, that she seemed to be turning into a complete and utter pervert, but she always concluded that, as she liked women, most people regarded her as a deviant anyway.

Even if she were allowed to keep her evenings with Olena, she would have no more mornings. Instead she was supposed to look after a new person whom Madame had taken on. Kym supposed that she ought to be grateful that there would be another pair of hands to help with the housework. But still, she couldn't help feeling thoroughly put out.

She knocked on the door and without waiting for a response walked into the new person's room.

The curtains were still drawn and the room was gloomy. Kym could see only that in the bed a human shape was stirring. She knew that the new employee had arrived late the previous night, but she saw no reason to allow the fact to interfere with her timetable of duties. She marched across the room and pulled back the curtains.

'Rise and shine,' she said loudly. 'Madame doesn't appreciate malingering.'

Light spilled into the room. Kym turned and saw a pretty, slender young woman with masses of tousled dark-red hair, struggling sleepily to sit up in the bed.

'Good morning,' Kym said. Suddenly her new task seemed much less onerous. 'Sorry, but I've got to get you up. It's late.'

'Hello,' the newcomer said. She seemed shy and, disoriented in her unfamiliar surroundings, very vulnerable. She was absolutely delicious. 'Are you my new owner?' the young woman asked.

Kym laughed. 'I wish I was,' she said. 'I mean, I wouldn't mind being the boss around here. But no, I'm just on the staff. The place is owned by Madame la Patronne. We're both working for her. I'm Kym. What's your name?'

The young woman looked uncertain. 'I'm called Lucietta,' she said.

'Pretty name,' Kym said. 'Well, Lucietta, you can't lie in bed all day. Let's get you dressed.'

'Of course,' Lucietta said, and she folded aside the sheet that she had pulled up to her shoulders.

Kym was disappointed to find that Lucietta was wearing a nightshirt. Still, Kym could see that she had long, slender legs, and that her skin was pale and freckled. She was without doubt, in Kym's opinion, utterly adorable.

'Would you like me to help you?' Kym asked hopefully. 'I'll run a bath, if you like. Do you have any clothes?'

'Clothes?' Lucietta said, as if she didn't understand the word. 'Am I supposed to wear clothes?'

'I'd better ask Madame,' Kym said. It seemed as though she wasn't going to have the opportunity to get more closely acquainted with the newcomer. Not yet, anyway. It would be just my luck, she thought, if Lucietta's the sort who doesn't go for girls.

'What is this place?' Lucietta said. 'Am I allowed to ask?'

'You can ask,' Kym replied. 'But I don't know what to say, really. Madame owns the house. Most evenings she has guests, sometimes alone, sometimes two or three at a time. She entertains them in her special rooms. I do most of the housework, it seems to me. More than that lazy sod Barat, anyway. I'll go and find out what you're to wear.'

With Madame's lingering help it had taken a long time for Olena to be ready that morning, but now she was standing proudly beside her mistress, and happy to be encased in her pony costume. She had become so accustomed to the tightness of her corset, the weight of her boots, and the full feeling of her tail in her bottom, that she felt almost more ashamed when she was completely naked than when she was reduced to being a pony.

She wished that poor Barat could feel more at ease in his bondage. Increasingly often Madame made him attend her while she was washing and dressing her pet. Olena was sure Madame had him watch the proceedings only to increase his frustration. Now he was kneeling in front of his mistress, naked but for the helmet and mask that he still wore whenever Olena was present because he was still under the misapprehension that Olena had not recognised him. Drops of clear liquid still sparkled on the helmet's black surface: this morning, as she did from time to time, Madame had made Barat lie in the bath while she squatted over him and relieved herself over his head. Today she had untied him temporarily so that he could touch himself while she peed on him, and as he gazed up at his mistress, who was still wearing only a transparent peignoir, his erection was still thick and upright.

It had been a long time since Olena had been penetrated by a man, and she found herself gazing at Barat's penis and hoping that Madame would not postpone much longer the day when she was to be lent to Barat for his use. She realised that once again, as happened so often, her thoughts had turned to sinful things. In Madame's house,

199

as at the Private House, it was almost impossible for Olena to think of anything else.

Barat's expression as he looked up at Madame was of devotion and desire, but also anguish. It was as if he hated to admit the longing he felt for his mistress and the pleasure he took in being her servant. Olena could well understand the conflict of emotions he felt, but she wished she could tell him that he would feel much better if he accepted the contradictions of his nature, as she had learnt to accept her wickedness and her need for chastisement.

'Look, pony,' Madame said. 'My manservant is having inappropriate thoughts. See how big and red his cock is.' She reached down and gripped the shaft. 'Put it down,' she said sternly to Barat. 'Make it nice and soft, or I'll be angry with you.'

She retained her hold on Barat's member, which remained resolutely stiff.

'I'm warning you,' Madame said. 'Obey me or suffer the consequences.'

Barat groaned. It was clear that with his mistress's hand sliding up and down his member there was no prospect of it diminishing in size.

'You're a disobedient wretch,' Madame declared, releasing Barat from her grip. 'Turn round and present your bottom. Pony, fetch me a cane.'

Olena heard Barat muttering curses as he turned on hands and knees. Madame, swishing the cane that Olena had brought to her, waited with a gleeful smile as he reluctantly lifted his bottom towards her.

'I don't want to hear your petty complaints,' Madame said to him. 'Pony, kneel in front of him and hold his hands together between your knees. Hold his head between your breasts. That should keep him still and quiet while I deal with his fat backside.'

Olena heard Barat whimper with pleasure as she enveloped his head between her breasts. The leather helmet and mask were cool, and still damp with Madame's urine, but Barat's panting breaths were hot against her skin.

After only two strokes with the cane Madame stooped next to her manservant and felt for his manhood. 'It's bigger and stiffer than ever,' she told Olena. 'He's almost as wilful and wicked as you, pony. Don't you dare come, little man,' she said to Barat. 'If you do you'll lick up the mess and then spend the rest of the day tied up in your room.'

Madame continued to fondle Barat's genitalia while she flicked the cane against his buttocks. Olena felt his body trembling with the effort of suppressing an orgasm. Olena knew how he felt, and sympathised with him, but only a little: every day she had to endure hours of chastisements and stimulating examinations before she was permitted to reach a climax.

With a gay laugh Madame released her hold on Barat, stood upright, and began to cane him in earnest. Olena watched in fascination as the cane rose and fell. She hoped that Madame would not exhaust her whipping arm on Barat. The sight and sound of the cane made her desperately aware of her own need for punishment.

'Release him,' Madame told Olena when she stopped the caning. 'Come and stand by me, pony. Turn around, wretched little man. You may kiss my feet to show your gratitude.'

Barat kept his striped and glowing bottom raised as he lowered his head to Madame's feet. The mask prevented his lips from touching her, but he pressed the leather against her toes.

'Kiss the pony's hooves, too,' Madame said. 'She let you press your ugly face into her lovely big breasts.'

Barat rubbed the front of the mask fervently against Olena's boots.

'That's enough,' Madame said angrily.

Barat knelt upright. His manhood jutted almost vertically from his groin. 'Please, Madame,' he said. He was attempting to disguise his voice, and the mask distorted his speech.

'What?' Madame said. 'What are you saying? What do you want now, you miserable creature?'

Barat's eyes, visible through the slits in the mask and glittering with tears, were fixed on Olena. 'You know, Madame. You know what I want.'

'Oh, I see,' Madame said. 'And what would you do, little man, to achieve your heart's desire?'

'Anything, Madame. I've told you again and again. Anything.'

'Anything?' Madame seemed torn between amusement and anger. 'Very well, then. We'll see. Immediately.'

She wasn't Lucietta. She was Talia. She remembered everything.

It was the name Barat that had troubled her. It was almost the last thing that Kym had mentioned before she had left the room. Talia hadn't been able to stop thinking about it. The name had seemed familiar, and important. How did she know the name Barat, the name of one of the servants in the house of her new owner?

Then the memories had returned, in a swirling flood of images that overwhelmed her. She had sat on the end of the bed until everything was organised in her mind.

She was Talia. She was the leader of the foresters, the people who lived in the wide woodlands on the Private House estate. She was a subject of Jem Darke, the Supreme Mistress of the Private House. And she was in love with Anne.

How could she have forgotten her darling Anne? They had spent the summer in each other's arms. They had parted only weeks previously. It seemed like years had passed.

Now she remembered why she had set off from the House. She remembered her visit to Barat's home village; her arrival in the city; her drive in the taxi; and everything that had happened to her at Edmund's emporium of amusements. She exhaled a deep breath. She had endured a great deal. And, she reflected with a smile, she had learnt some interesting techniques that she would delight in trying again, with Anne, when her blonde lover returned to the House at the end of her college term.

Above all, she had succeeded in finding Barat. He was here, in this house. And Barat would lead her to the kidnapped Olena. Talia shrugged off the persona of the showgirl Lucietta. She was once again Talia, strong and fearless, the leader of her people – but still, she had to admit to herself, yearning for the affectionate spankings that she had come to revel in with Anne.

She stood up and made for the bathroom. She would wash, dress in whatever clothes she could find, and then set off on her quest. The first step, she said to herself as she adjusted the temperature of the water in the shower, will be to find that young woman Kym again, and to discover everything she knows.

As Barat followed Madame to her bedchamber he wondered what further indignity she would find to inflict on him. She had already pissed on him, caned him, and made him kiss her feet. He kept his gaze fixed on her swaying buttocks, clearly visible through the voile of her peignoir, and consoled himself with thoughts of what he would do to Olena once he had passed his mistress's final test of obedience.

It was, in any case, too late for him to protest now. He dared not speak much, in case Olena recognised his voice, and he had allowed Madame to tie his hands behind his back. He cursed and stumbled forwards as Madame tugged on the leash she had secured around his cock and balls.

He could still hear the clop of Olena's boots behind him. He realised that Madame did not intend to dismiss her pony while she played with him. Olena would be there, in Madame's room, watching him as he endured whatever torments Madame devised for him.

He took a deep breath and resolved that he would withstand even the humiliation of Olena's presence. Whatever the cost, he was more determined than ever to possess, and use for his pleasure, the beautiful, perverse, divinely curvaceous nymph who should have been his, and his alone, years previously. He would whip her and toy with her until she was delirious with excitement; he would plunge his manhood into her mouth, her cunt, her arse, and then, as his seed filled her, he would unmask his face and reveal to her she had been vanquished by Barat, whom she had scorned and ignored.

'You're still big and hard, you incorrigible man,' Madame said to him, almost indulgently, as she led him into her bedroom. She pulled him towards the bed. 'Lie face down,' she told him, and she pulled the pillows into a mound at the centre of the bed. 'I want to see your bottom open and your little hole looking up at the ceiling.'

Barat squirmed and struggled into the required position on the heap of pillows. It was difficult with his hands tied. No doubt Madame intended to make him look ridiculous. She shrugged off the thin garment she had been wearing, and Barat craned his neck to look at her naked body. Although he was often required to gaze at his mistress's private parts, usually when ordered to lick them, he was rarely allowed to see Madame entirely unclothed. Olena, the object of his obsessive lust, was so much in his thoughts that sometimes he forgot how pretty, shapely and desirable his mistress was.

Barat supposed that he had been placed on the bed, with his arse up, for a whipping. His buttocks were already sore from the cane, but he vowed that he would stoically endure another chastisement. His erection was pressed into the mound of soft pillows, and he hoped that a little pain might help to take the edge off his arousal. However, as Olena, looking spectacularly submissive in her pony costume, was within his sight, he feared that punishment might have the opposite effect. He knew that he would not be permitted to have Olena today if he were to soil Madame's bed with his emissions.

'Now then, pony,' Madame said, 'run and fetch me your spare tail.'

It was a moment before Barat understood the import of Madame's instruction. As Olena trotted towards Madame he realised that he had not been positioned for a whipping, but so that a plug could be inserted into his arsehole.

He began to struggle, trying to protest, but then he slumped once again over the pile of pillows. He would have to submit. It was not, after all, the first time that Madame had pushed things up his arse to humiliate him. When he was alone with his mistress he often found the experience strangely stimulating. It was just very annoying to have to put up with it in Olena's presence. At least Kym wasn't there to witness his ordeal.

'Very good, my dear,' Madame said to Olena. 'I think you should do it, pony. Remember to use plenty of ointment. This naughty man isn't used to wearing a tail every day.'

By the gods of the elders, Barat cursed, this was even worse: Olena herself was going to fuck his arse. It was all the wrong way round. He started as he felt the cold nudge of the anointed plug in the crease between his parted buttocks.

'It won't go in, Madame,' Olena said, pressing the nose of the tail's plug against Barat's ring of muscle.

'Of course it will,' Madame replied. 'The wicked man won't get any reward at all unless he co-operates. Put your hand underneath and touch his nasty big penis. I think you'll find you'll be able to push it in soon enough.'

Barat hardly remembered to breathe. Olena's gloved hand was burrowing through the bedclothes. She was going to touch his cock. There: she was touching it. This was a moment he had dreamt of for years. He had to concentrate on retaining the seed in his balls – and he felt his arsehole open, and something enormous slid into it.

He groaned with the dull pain. He couldn't bear it: he was being stretched too wide, he was too full. But the ache receded, and he realised that all of the tail's plug was inside him.

'Now I have two little pets,' Madame exclaimed. 'But you're much the prettier, pony. Play with the man's tail, my dear. Let him know what it feels like.'

'It's making him harder than ever, Madame,' Olena said. Her hand was still resting under Barat's pulsing erection as she did things to the tail that sent tremors into the centre of Barat's body.

'He must like it,' Madame said. 'That's as well, considering what he's going to get next. Leave him, pony, and come here. Help me into my harness.'

Barat, dazed with arousal and the effort of suppressing his orgasm, was hardly aware that Olena had left his side. When at last he looked over his shoulder, he saw Olena kneeling beside Madame and helping to buckle black straps around Madame's hips. With a sinking feeling in his stomach he realised that Madame was being fitted with a strap-on phallus: a massive black cylinder shaped like an erect penis.

Madame noticed him looking at her. 'After I've spent a few hours training and testing my pony each day,' she said, 'I like nothing better than to bring her here to give her a final ride. You like it when I ride you hard, don't you, pony?'

Olena, blushing hotly, nodded. Barat thought he had never seen her look simultaneously so innocent and so lewd.

'And now I've got another animal to attend to,' Madame said. The phallus projecting from her crotch looked both menacing and ludicrous as she advanced towards the bed. 'Olena, take the tail out of him and get him ready to be ridden. You'd better use lots of ointment again.'

Barat closed his eyes. He wasn't afraid of the pain, although he knew that the experience he was about to undergo would not be in the least comfortable. It was the humiliation he couldn't bear. I'm a man, he wanted to shout. I am the only man in this room. I have a cock, and it's hard and ready and hot and about to burst with thick seed. I should be the one to do the fucking. I will fuck both of you.

But instead, Olena, his Olena, would see him being forced open by Madame, by a woman with an artificial cock. His body was limp with despair, and he put up no resistance as Olena, with gentle fingers, eased the tail from his anus and massaged cream into the empty hole.

He felt the bed move as Madame knelt between his legs. She leant over him. The tip of the phallus nudged his testicles and Madame's nipples brushed his back. He felt her breath on his neck.

'Barat,' she whispered. 'I know you're going to enjoy this. If you can manage not to come, you will have Olena. Today. Very soon.'

When the new girl, Lucietta, appeared in the kitchen doorway Kym's first thought was an obscene expletive. She had forgotten to lock the door of Lucietta's room, and if Madame found out there would be hell to pay.

Then she realised that Madame could not possibly know, and that she could make sure Madame never did find out. In which case, she thought, Lucietta's intrusion was just the pretext she needed to abandon her tedious kitchen chores.

Then she noticed how very attractive Lucietta looked, with her long russet hair tousled about her pretty, serious face, and her slender limbs not covered by the sheet she had wrapped around her body and beneath which she was obviously naked.

'Lucietta,' Kym said. 'What are you doing here?'

'I'm not Lucietta,' the girl said with a smile. 'That was my stage name. I'm Talia. And I'm looking for you.'

'Good,' Kym said. This was getting better and better. 'I'm glad of the company. You can help me with these dishes. Or we can just talk. Come in and sit down.'

Lucietta, or Talia, or whatever her name was – Kym found herself distracted by the sight of her long, freckled legs as she failed to conceal them under the sheet – sat down at the kitchen table. Kym pulled out another chair and sat next to her, as close as she dared, so that her stockinged knees were almost touching Talia's bare thigh.

'I'll try to explain,' Talia said. 'You mentioned the name Barat. You said he was here. I'm trying to find him.'

Kym's heart sank with disappointment. Talia was looking for a man. 'You want Barat?' she said. She couldn't conceal her surprise that anyone would bother to seek out her lazy colleague.

Talia laughed. 'Not exactly,' she said. 'But I think he can lead me to the person I'm trying to find. Have you ever heard him mention the name Olena?'

Kym's spirits lifted. Talia was interested in women, after all. But then, she thought, if she's looking for Olena perhaps she wouldn't be bothered with anyone less supremely desirable. 'Olena's here,' Kym said. There seemed no reason to conceal the fact: Talia would have found out soon enough.

'She's here,' Talia exclaimed. Her face brightened with excitement.

Oh God, Kym thought, Talia seems to get more attractive by the minute. She resolved to seduce her.

Kym put a hand on Talia's knee. Talia didn't flinch – in fact she smiled. 'Why do you want Olena?' Kym asked, leaning forwards and trying to maintain eye contact. 'You're not just another member of staff, are you? You're special.'

Kym recalled the part she had played in luring Olena away from the country mansion where she apparently lived. It seemed likely that Talia had come from the same place. None of that, however, seemed as important as getting close to Talia. She lifted her hand and smoothed stray locks of Talia's hair from her face.

'You're right,' Talia said. She didn't seem to mind being touched. 'But I really can't tell you any more. I'm sorry, but I have to keep some things secret until I know more about what's going on in this house.'

'That's all right,' Kym said. 'We all have secrets.' She hardly knew what she was saying. She wanted only to keep Talia in conversation, and to keep her gaze locked on Talia's big dark eyes, and to let her fingers linger on Talia's pale, freckled, vanilla-scented skin. Talia must know by now, Kym thought, that I want her. Things have already gone beyond the friendly stage. We've hardly met, and yet she's letting me stroke her arm. Her face is slightly flushed, and her lovely pink lips are a little bit parted. I think she'd let me kiss her. And I want to kiss her. It would be wonderful to take her to bed. But I must find out whether she will take instructions. I can't wait to know.

Kym took a deep breath. 'Talia,' she said, 'take off that sheet. Let me see you.'

Talia smiled, and Kym's heart expanded in her chest. 'What if I refuse?' Talia said mischievously. 'What would you do to make me?' She allowed the sheet to slip from her shoulders, revealing her throat and the tops of her breasts.

Kym tried to steady her breathing. This was it: the moment of truth. How would Talia react? 'I'd put you over my knee,' she said, 'and give you a spanking.'

There could be no misunderstanding the excitement on Talia's face. 'Would you?' she whispered. 'Then perhaps I ought to be a little bit naughty. Sometimes I'm very naughty indeed.'

The two women looked at each other in silence. No words were needed: they understood each other.

Kym began to speak, but Talia interrupted her. 'Kym,' she said. 'Before I start being naughty with you, I will tell you a bit more about myself. I think you ought to know that there is a place where people like us can lead a better life. Better than here,' she said, looking around at the functional kitchen.

'The place Olena came from,' Kym said. 'The big house?'

'Yes,' Talia said. 'But it's much more than just a big house. It's bigger than anyone outside imagines. There are branches all over the world. And the whole thing is for people like us to enjoy.'

'What do you mean, like us?' Kym said. She wondered whether Talia was a member of an organisation of lesbians.

'You know what I mean,' Talia said, and she stood up, letting the sheet fall to the floor. She put her hands to her breasts and cupped them.

Kym stared. Talia was beautiful: skinny, pale, young, freckled – just the sort Kym went for. Her breasts were small but firm and round. And they were marked with fading lines.

Talia turned round, and Kym saw that her slim buttocks were also criss-crossed with fading lines and welts.

'You see?' Talia said, turning again to face Kym.

Kym found her voice. 'Sod the dishes,' she said. 'And sod Madame. I'm taking you to my room.' The sight of Talia's whipped body had made her frantic with desire.

I think I'm in love, she said to herself as she led Talia by the hand from the kitchen.

Olena stood, awaiting instructions, while Madame checked that the furniture in the stable was arranged to her liking. Olena had noticed that Barat was walking a little stiffly since Madame had penetrated him, but his ardour was undimmed: he was naked, but for his helmet and mask, and his erection stood as stiffly as ever, and now it was quivering with his barely suppressed excitement.

'I'm going to take off your blinkers, pony,' Madame said, 'and tie this blindfold over your eyes.'

Olena lowered her head so that Madame could carry out her intentions. She closed her eyes as the soft cloth tightened over them. Now, instead of the limited view allowed by her blinkers, she was able to see nothing.

'Now then, pony,' Madame said, raising her voice so that it penetrated the helmet and, Olena assumed, for Barat's benefit. 'I am about to put you at the disposal of my manservant. As you know, he has admired you since you arrived in my house, and he has been importuning me day after day. He has hardly been a good servant, it must be said, but I am minded to grant his request. Therefore you are his, little pony. Do whatever he tells you. Obey his instructions as if they were mine. Do everything you can to please him. Do you understand?'

Olena nodded. Her mouth was dry with anticipation; her private place was very much in the opposite state. Wetness had seeped from her and moistened the insides of her thighs. It had been a long time since she had been penetrated by a man. She realised, with a horrified awareness of her wickedness, that her sex was almost aching to be filled and, even worse, she was imagining the taste of his seed. She wondered whether Barat would use her mouth, her private place or her little hole. She wanted him to put his penis in all three places. She was, she realised, a disgustingly filthy slut. She hoped that Barat would be able to restrain the urgency of his lust long enough to give her a thorough punishment. It would only make her more aroused, she knew, but it might help to reduce the guilt she felt at taking pleasure from being penetrated.

Madame was talking to Barat. Olena strained to hear. 'You can take off that mask,' Madame said. 'She can't see you now. My, you are very excited, aren't you? I do believe it's grown even bigger. My advice is not to rush things. You know how well the little pony responds to being humiliated and tormented. You'll enjoy her all the more if you take the trouble to make her feel thoroughly dirty. But it's entirely up to you. Do whatever you like with her. You can mark her as much as you wish, but try not to break her skin. If you want to flog her breasts, I should remove her corset: if you leave it on it will prevent you whipping below the nipples. She's very good about keeping still, but feel free to tie her up. She looks utterly lovely in ropes or chains, and it excites her to know that she's helpless. I'll return shortly to see how you're getting on. I think I'll enjoy watching someone else putting my pony through her paces.'

Olena knew that any decent, respectable woman in her position would hope that her ordeal would be over as quickly as possible. But she couldn't help hoping that Barat would heed Madame's advice.

Olena heard the door close as Madame left. She heard Barat's soft footsteps. Her body was alive with sinful, lustful desire.

For several long moments there was silence. She could not tell where Barat was, or what he was doing. Then she started: his hand had clasped her left breast. She heard him utter a sigh that was so profound it sounded like a groan of pain.

He explored her body, clutching at her flesh as a starving man might clutch at food. His hands and lips returned again and again to her breasts and bottom, his fingers plunged again and again into the yielding moistness of her private place. Olena was becoming as frantic with desire as Barat seemed to be, but she did her best to assist him by pushing out her breasts and parting her legs.

He began to remove parts of the pony costume from her body. Impatiently he tore at the straps that held her arms behind her back. He swore under his breath as he struggled with the laces of her corset. When her breasts tumbled from the quarter-cups on which they had been resting he smacked them, this way and that, with the palm of his hand, until they were smarting and throbbing. He unstrapped the helmet from her head, tugged roughly at the braid of her hair as he untied it, and plunged his face into her thick, dark tresses. Olena was left wearing only her boots, her gloves and her tail.

Panting with lust and exertion, Barat at last ceased his assault. Olena caught her breath and wondered what he would do next.

His fingers closed on her nipples, and tugged her forwards. She leant forward as far as she could, but the pressure did not relent. She took a step, and then another, and in this way Barat led her to the place he wanted her to stand.

He released her nipples, and next she felt his hands grasp her wrists. He tied her hands together, and then she felt the rope tightening more and pulling her wrists upwards. Eventually, when only the toes of her boots were touching the floor and her arms were stretched vertically above her head, the pulling on her wrists stopped. She hung, waiting for whatever Barat wished to do to her.

She cried out in surprise and relief when she felt the first line of fire burst across her breasts. She recognised the unique sting of Madame's thin, leather-clad whip. Barat, she realised through the haze of pain and arousal, had been a careful witness of the many punishments he had seen and experienced. He had chosen the implement that was the most searing when used on a woman's breasts. Its thin, very flexible tail sank deep into the soft flesh, so that the pain of each lash seemed to fill the breasts from the inside, and it left definite, angry lines of red.

The whipping went on for a long time. Olena gave up her attempts to remain still and tried to writhe away from the lashes. She kept her legs slightly parted, as whenever

212

her thighs touched the pressure seemed to trigger a response in her loins that she feared would make her reach a climax. Her private place, she knew, was wide open, and the insides of her thighs were wet.

'Good work.' It was Madame's voice. She must have returned after Barat started the whipping. 'Discipline is so very beneficial for ponies. I must say you both seem to be enjoying yourselves.'

The whip-strokes slowed, and then ceased. Olena tossed her head. She was glad that her mistress had come to watch her, but peeved that the whipping had stopped. Her breasts were blazing and throbbing with pain, and she wished that she could see them. She pushed them forwards so that Madame and Barat could inspect the punishment they had received.

She gasped as a hand touched one of the burning orbs of flesh. It was her mistress's gentle touch. 'Excellent,' Madame said. 'I think I've never seen my pony's breasts as red as this. And some of these marks will last for days.' The hand caressed the sore skin, and Olena couldn't stop herself moaning with pleasure. She squeezed her thighs together. She was perilously close to a climax.

'Good little pony,' Madame said. She lightly pinched Olena's nipples. 'I don't think I've ever encountered anyone with such a passion for the whip. You've rejuvenated the disciplinary instincts of a jaded dominatrix, pony. Would you like some more, my dear?'

Olena nodded. Her arms were aching, but it was worth suffering the discomfort to feel more glorious, fiery lashes on her sensitised breasts. 'Yes, please,' she said.

'On you go, then,' Madame said, addressing Barat. 'But remember to keep some of the strength of your arm if you want to whip her bottom as well.'

Olena reflected, as she cried out and sobbed under the whip, that Barat had probably desired her since they had been children in the village. His arm might tire, but she suspected that his passion would sustain his energy.

And so it proved. When Barat at last tired of whipping Olena's breasts he left her hanging from the ceiling by her arms and turned his attention to her bottom. Eventually he apparently decided that Olena was not in the perfect position, and half swooning with pleasure and pain Olena felt her wrists being lowered.

Barat manhandled her into the position he required: kneeling on her bedding in the pony-stall with her knees wide apart, her bottom lifted, and her face and sore breasts pressed into the blankets. Barat had seen her on display in this manner many times, as Madame often examined her pony in the same position.

Olena was used to being punished, too, while kneeling on her bedding, and she would have remained still without restraints. Nonetheless it was reassuring to feel the ropes around her insteps, attaching them to the ends of the metal bar that prevented her from moving her ankles together, and to know that her wrists were tied to her boots, so that she had no option but to remain with her bottom raised into the air.

It took Barat some time to complete Olena's bondage, and she was trembling with anticipation of the next part of her punishment. Madame was a skilled disciplinarian, but Barat was stronger and was driven by an overwhelming lust. She hadn't received a whipping as hard as Barat's since being taken from the Private House, and she was revelling in every agonising stroke.

'Are you going to take her tail out?' Olena heard Madame ask Barat. 'She likes the sensation of being punished with it in, but it tends to get in the way if you're using anything longer than a strap.'

'Out,' Barat grunted. It was clear that he still thought that Olena had no idea who was punishing her, and that he therefore had to speak as little as possible.

'I'll do it,' Madame volunteered. 'I can't resist playing with my little pony's tail.'

Olena felt Madame kneel beside her on the raised platform that served as Olena's bed when she was in her pony role. Madame stroked her tail, and her bottom felt full and sensitive. 'You dirty little pony,' Madame said. 'You're dripping your nasty sticky juice on to your bedding. See how wet you are.'

Olena shivered with pleasure as she felt Madame's fingers paddling in her private place. Then the fingers, sticky and smelling of Olena, were nudging at Olena's mouth.

'Open up, little pony,' Madame said, and she slid her fingers between Olena's lips. Madame slid her fingers in and out of Olena's mouth, and with her other hand she gave Olena's bottom six swift slaps and then began to ease the tail's plug from Olena's little hole.

As Olena felt the delicious sensation of the plug being drawn slowly out, she sucked on Madame's fingers. She was ready to have a climax – she would have a climax if anyone would just touch the right place – but she knew that she did not deserve it until she had been thoroughly punished.

'It's out,' Madame announced, and stood up. 'Carry on,' she said to Barat. 'It's delightful to see my pony being chastised in bondage. But her bottom does look naked without its tail.'

Barat was still using the thin, whippy, leather-clad rod. It stung ferociously, and soon Olena was once again crying out and sobbing. Barat thrashed her bottom mercilessly, without pauses between the vigorous, whistling strokes. He covered all of both buttocks in stripes, but he concentrated on the most sensitive area, from halfway down the lush curves of Olena's buttocks to the tops of her thighs. Many of the strokes landed across Olena's vulnerable sex. When he needed to rest his arm Barat relaxed by aiming upward, vertical strokes between Olena's thighs. It seemed to Olena that her private place was receiving as many lashes as her bottom – not that she minded. She was drifting through clouds of sensation, and her entire body was suffused with electricity that sparked and crackled with each stroke of the whip.

Dimly she heard the sound of something falling to the floor. Barat had dropped the whip, and before Olena could work out what was happening she realised that she was airborne. Barat, given added strength by his desire to possess her, had picked her up, still bound, and was carrying her.

He placed her, kneeling, on the seat of the sofa. He tore at the ropes tying her wrists to her ankles when he realised that they were preventing her from adopting the position he required. As soon as she was arranged to his satisfaction, with her legs still held apart and with her arms and head resting on the back of the sofa, he stood behind her and pushed his erection into her private place.

Olena gasped, and then uttered a long sigh of satisfaction. Barat's member was long, thick, hard and hot inside her. It felt wonderful. Each time he thrust into her his thighs struck the swollen, smarting flesh of her bottom. She hoped he intended to smack her while he penetrated her.

'Look!' he shouted, and Olena felt his hands untying the blindfold. 'See who has mastered you, Olena.'

Olena shook her head, and found herself looking into one of the mirrors. She saw her face, red with shame and excitement; over her shoulder, grimacing with triumph, was the face of her erstwhile guardian, Barat.

'It is I, Barat!' he declared unnecessarily, and Olena was at such a pitch of arousal, and found Barat's pronouncements so irrelevant to her feverish desires, that she couldn't help giggling. She caught sight of Madame, who was also trying to keep a straight face, and she found herself shaking with laughter.

'What's this?' Barat said. 'You dare to laugh?'

'I can't help it,' Olena spluttered. 'Just get on with it, Barat, please. Everything was lovely until a moment ago.'

'You knew, Olena.' Barat's voice was tremulous. 'You knew it was me. How long have you known? Madame, did you tell her? How could you do this to me? I have been a loyal servant. I have waited so patiently.'

Olena felt Barat's erection begin to shrink inside her. She mewed with frustration. 'I recognised you, Barat. I couldn't help it. I'm sorry you're disappointed, but I really do need you to concentrate on what you're doing.' She could hardly believe how badly she was behaving. She was asking a man from her home village to use her for his pleasure. She was virtually telling him how to do it. She was a vile and sinful creature. 'Look at my bottom, Barat.

See how red and sore you've made it. Please spank it hard, until your manhood is big and stiff again. Then you can penetrate me. Use my little hole,' she added, blushing furiously. 'It will give you more pleasure.'

Barat looked down at the two incandescent, striped hemispheres of Olena's bottom. She felt his erection move and grow. He withdrew it until only the bulbous head was resting inside the neck of her private place, and he moved slightly to the side. He began to smack his hand down on to the raw skin of Olena's right buttock.

More punishment! Olena closed her eyes contentedly and rested her head on the back of the sofa. Barat's smacks were not hard, but because her bottom was already very sore each slap was searing. She had been well whipped on her breasts and her bottom, and at last she felt able to relax and enjoy all the exquisite sensations that her sensitised body was experiencing. She knew that there was no limit to the amount of punishment she deserved: if she were to be whipped for every minute of every day for the rest of her life, she suspected that it would not be enough to drive the perverse thoughts from her mind. But she also knew that there was a point, when she had been chastised thoroughly, at which the flashes of pain ceased to be merely enjoyable and merged with the thrilling pulsing of her private place and her nipples in one overwhelming, glorious feeling of heightened pleasure. Once she had reached that plateau of sensation it seemed as though reaching a little higher, to an explosive, exhausting climax, was almost inevitable. At the Private House they had told her that this feeling indicated that she had received enough punishment, and that she could without shame accept the reward of a climax. Olena knew that she would never be without shame, but she had allowed herself to be persuaded that it was permissible to have an orgasm.

She was ready now; so was Barat. She could feel that his manhood had grown again to its fullest size. He pulled it out of her.

'Where's the whip?' he muttered. 'I'll make your arsehole smart before I use it.'

But Barat had dropped the whip beside Olena's bed, and he was too impatient to retrieve it. Olena felt the hot, blunt nose of his manhood pressing into the cleft between her buttocks, and she tightened her grip on the back of the sofa.

Still distended from holding her tail, Olena's little hole offered little resistance to Barat's powerful push. His thick, hard staff slid into her narrow passage. He cried out with triumphant pleasure while Olena gasped as she enjoyed the familiar feelings of intrusion, pain and fullness.

Barat began to thrust back and forth. The fronts of his thighs brushed against Olena's tender bottom. Olena gasped and moaned with every thrust. It was too much: it was almost unbearably good. She didn't deserve this much pleasure. No one did. It was divine. She wondered whether Barat would think to touch her private place. Of course not: he was using her for his pleasure, and she had no right to expect him to please her. She didn't mind. She often found that she preferred to touch herself. She knew exactly how to tease the folds of skin around the little stiff bud of pleasure; she knew precisely when to start pressing harder, and then to caress, and then rub.

She lowered her right hand from the back of the sofa and placed it between her legs. As her fingers met the hot, wet, delicate membranes a shock ran through her body and she called out. Barat, breathing harshly as he pushed deeply into her, seemed oblivious to her actions. Madame, Olena noticed, was watching her closely, with a smile on her lips and an intent brilliance in her eyes.

Olena pressed her fingers against her private place. It would take only a few seconds to soar to the giddying heights of a spectacular climax. Olena could feel it gathering inside her, like a violent storm about to unleash thunder and lightning.

But Barat, too, would come quickly. Olena could hear that his breathing and his thrusts into her little hole had become irregular. 'How do you like this, then?' Barat cried out. He went rigid, and Olena felt the spurts of his seed as they pulsed along the stem of his manhood.

218

'It's wonderful,' Olena managed to say, before the storm broke and she was racked with electric jolts of pleasure so intense that she almost lost consciousness.

When she opened her eyes she saw in the mirror her own dishevelled, contented face. Barat was looking over her shoulder: outraged, red-faced, and almost incoherent with anger.

'This was supposed to be for me,' he shouted. He pulled his shrinking manhood from inside her. 'I've waited years for this moment, and now it's ruined.'

Olena didn't understand what he was complaining about. Even if his climax had been only half as wonderful as hers, he should have been delighted.

'Oh, be quiet, Barat, for goodness' sake,' Madame said. She stared at him, and her expression altered from irritation to distaste. 'Come here,' she ordered him. When he was standing in front of her, she spoke to him in a level tone. 'I am tired, Barat, of your constant complaints and demands. You have been a useful employee, it's true, in that you enabled me to procure Olena. And you have provided me with a certain amount of entertainment. Other than that, however, your behaviour has not been good, and you have been consistently lazy about the house. Now that I have taken delivery of another young woman I can afford to make reductions elsewhere in the staffing level. Barat, you are dismissed. Clear your belongings from your room and go.'

Olena knelt upright on the sofa. She had not expected this. Neither, it was clear, had Barat. He was speechless with surprise. 'But Madame,' he managed to say at last. 'This is unfair. I was to have Olena.'

'And you have had her,' Madame said. 'Now go.'

Talia lay naked in the comfort of Kym's bed, her face turned upwards and her lips parted to receive Kym's passionate kisses. There was nothing Talia enjoyed more than being played with by a bossy blonde, and she had been denied affection for so long in Edmund's establishment that Kym's attentions were like fresh water after a drought.

Apart from being blonde and pretty, Kym bore little resemblance to Talia's darling Anne. Her hair was short while Anne's was long, and she was more curvaceous than Anne. While Anne was flirtatious, mischievous, sweetly gentle and inventively cruel, Kym was serious and blunt. But there was no doubt that when she looked down into Talia's face there was both desire and devotion in her grey eyes.

'And you'll do anything I tell you,' Kym said. 'Anything at all?'

Talia giggled. 'I've told you,' she said. She pulled her knees up to her chest. 'Would you like to spank me again? You can spank me here,' she added, drawing Kym's hand to her warm, soft sex.

'You've got a pretty cunt,' Kym said as she began to pat her hand against Talia's sex. 'I like women who keep themselves shaved. Does this hurt?'

'A little,' Talia replied dreamily. 'But I like it. Do it a bit harder.'

For a while the room was silent but for the smacking of Kym's hand and Talia's murmurs of pleasure.

'You're fantastic,' Kym said softly. 'You're getting very wet.' She leant over Talia. 'Suck my tits,' she said, and she unbuttoned the flaps of her tunic and lowered her un-covered nipples on to Talia's face.

'Yes, Kym,' Talia said, and her lips encircled the hard walnut of Kym's left nipple.

Once again silence descended. As Talia licked and sucked she slid a hand under the hem of Kym's short skirt and along her thigh, and began to caress the silky skin of Kym's shaven mound. Kym too, she found, was very aroused, and her fingers met no resistance as they pushed between her sex-lips and into the hot, yielding wetness. Kym's hand was still smacking Talia's sex, but now it paused between slaps and Kym's fingers explored the folds of punished skin.

Soon the bodies of both women were trembling with excitement. Regretfully Talia forced herself to descend from the soft clouds of desire. She took her hand from beneath Kym's skirt and pulled her mouth from Kym's delicious nipple.

'Kym,' she said, 'there's something I have to tell you.'

Kym knelt upright. 'I knew it,' she said. 'Don't tell me, let me guess. You're not really into girls. You've realised you like men after all.'

'Don't be silly,' Talia said. 'I do like men, it's true. But I prefer women. And I like you very much. The trouble is, I already have a lover. Her name's Anne.'

'Oh.' The look of disappointment on Kym's face was almost comical.

Talia sat up and kissed Kym. 'But it's all right,' she said, and she began to tickle one of Kym's nipples. 'I just thought I ought to tell you that I can't be yours indefinitely. But Anne's away at college for the next few months, and I have absolutely no doubt that she's seducing and perverting all of the fresh new students. And most of the staff, I expect. But I'll be yours until the end of term. As long as you promise to give me lots of kisses and spankings.'

'You can bet on it,' Kym said, and she pressed her mouth against Talia's. Then she pulled away and stared into Talia's face. 'But we're both employed by Madame,' she said. 'I suppose she might not even let us spend any time together.'

'Then we'll have to enjoy what time we have,' Talia said, and she pulled Kym towards her.

Both women started when they heard a knock at the door.

'Bloody hell,' Kym said. 'You're not supposed to be here. And I'm supposed to be in the kitchen. Quick, hide.'

Talia had already wrapped herself in a sheet, and she ran into Kym's bathroom. She left the door open a crack, so that she could see and hear everything that happened in the bedroom.

Kym rebuttoned her tunic and stood beside the bed. 'Yes?' she called out.

The door flew open and a naked man strode in. He was tall and heavily built, with skin the colour of milky coffee.

His penis was flaccid but still, Talia thought, of a good size. His face was contorted with anger. Talia assumed that this was Barat, and Kym's words confirmed her supposition.

'Barat,' Kym said. 'What the hell are you doing? You can't just walk in here stark naked. What do you want?'

Barat ignored everything she had said. 'I've been kicked out,' he raged. 'That bitch has sacked me. After everything I've done for her. Everything she's put me through. I'm out. Just like that. On the street.'

Kym, and Talia in the bathroom, had no choice but to listen as Barat poured out his grievances, his bitterness, his disappointment, his humiliation, and his fury.

'Barat, what will you do?' Kym said, when the stream of his invective finally dried.

'All I want is revenge,' he growled. 'Revenge on Madame la Patronne. And I want Olena.'

'Barat, be reasonable,' Kym said. 'You can't possibly –'

'Actually,' Talia said, emerging from the bathroom, 'I think I have the solution to all our problems. Listen to this.'

Olena, her gloved hands roped together and tied to a hook in the stable wall, waited patiently. Madame had dressed her again in all of her pony costume except for the tail, and despite its absence Olena felt the familiar sense of comfort and sensual security that she had come to associate with the corset, the helmet, the blinkers, the bit and the boots.

She was still feeling slightly dizzy from her climax, and she was warm and contented inside. She knew the emotion would not last. By the next morning, at the very latest, her body would start to crave attention again; her mutinous, treacherous private place would begin to warm up, and tingle, and produce the wetness that always betrayed her; she would become aware of her breasts and their nipples; she would be brought face to face, yet again, with the depraved, lustful spirit that lived within her; and she would need to be punished.

But for the moment she was content. Her breasts and bottom throbbed with soft pain, and she was at peace.

'Well, little pony,' Madame said, arriving at Olena's side, 'you need a gentle rub-down after all that exertion. I've brought some scented lotion to soothe you. I'll start on your hindquarters. I know you'd like to have your tail in place as soon as possible.'

With the bit in her mouth, Olena couldn't reply, but she nodded gratefully. She faced the wall, parted her legs and pushed out her bottom. But before Madame could apply any cream to Olena's buttocks and anus, there was a commotion in the doorway. Olena turned her head and saw Kym and Barat in the stable.

'What is it?' Madame said. 'I don't wish to be disturbed. And why are you still here?' she added, to Barat.

'Madame, I'm sorry,' Kym said, 'but please come with us. It's urgent. One of your guests is here, and he has a complaint. He's talking about reporting you to the authorities.'

'I know how to deal with the likes of him,' Madame said grimly. She put down the tub of lotion. 'Very well, I'll deal with the problem.' She patted Olena's bottom. 'I'll be back soon, little pony.'

Madame strode from the room, followed by Kym and Barat. Olena was alone. She closed her eyes and summoned her memories of the day. She had had a thoroughly satisfying series of punishments and a glorious climax, and she could still experience echoes of those intense sensations.

'Olena?'

Olena opened her eyes. Had she imagined a voice? A woman's voice, saying her name? She turned, and scanned the room with the narrow band of sight allowed by the blinkers.

At first she didn't recognise the slender, naked, titian-haired woman who was looking at her with an inquisitive smile on her pretty, freckled face.

Of course. It was the woman from the forest. Talia. They had met seldom in the Private House, but they knew each other. Talia, like most of the people in the Private House, had whipped her, and she had licked Talia to a climax, but only once.

Olena, with her lips open around the cylindrical bit, could only nod in recognition. She wanted to ask Talia why she was there, in Madame's house.

But Olena realised that she already knew. The Supreme Mistress had sent Talia to rescue her and take her home.

'Olena,' Talia said, 'you look wonderful. You're the most provocative pony I've ever seen. Do you like being a pony?'

Olena blushed and nodded.

'Then I'll leave you in your costume,' Talia said. She picked up the lotion that Madame had abandoned. 'Would you like some of this?' she asked. 'And I expect you're missing your tail. You've had a terrific whipping,' she said as she stepped closer. 'I'll bet that stung. And I'll bet you enjoyed it, you shameless hussy. I'll put some of this cream on the sore places, I'll put your tail in, and then I'll untie you. I'm going to take you back to the Private House.'

Talia knew Madame's house hardly at all, and so she had to rely on Olena to guide her.

'I'm sorry, Olena,' she said as she unfastened the bit from Olena's helmet, 'but I'll never find the others unless you tell me which way to go.'

Talia soon discovered that although Olena knew her way around the corridors and outbuildings of Madame's gloomy house, she didn't know where Kym and Barat had taken Madame.

Then, as Olena and Talia were climbing the stairs to the second floor they heard noises from one of the rooms ahead of them.

'It's Madame's room,' Olena said.

Talia opened the door to find Kym sitting astride Madame on the bed. Madame was still struggling, but Barat had already tied three of her limbs to the corner-posts, and Madame had realised that she was not going to escape from her bondage.

Talia and Olena watched in silence while Barat and Kym completed the task of tying up Madame. Talia glanced from time to time at Olena: it was clear that Olena had enjoyed being Madame's pet pony, and Talia wondered whether she would be upset to see her mistress vanquished.

'There's no alternative,' Talia whispered to Olena. 'We have to keep her secure until you and I are well on the way to the Private House.'

Olena smiled. 'I know,' she said. 'It's all right, Talia. I want to go home. And I do feel sorry for Barat. He wanted me so badly, and Madame mistreated him cruelly. But he can't possess me. I need to live with people who realise how truly wicked I am and who understand my needs. At least he can have his revenge on Madame.'

It was clear that Barat intended to wreak a thorough revenge. Now that Madame was immobilised he turned his attention to her wardrobe and dressing-table, scattering their contents on the carpets in his search for implements of correction and unusual devices. Each time he found a whip, a riding-crop, a phallus, a mechanical instrument, he would flourish it before Madame's eyes and place it on the bed. 'Then you'll get this, you heartless bitch,' he would announce, 'on your breasts, I think. And this, up your arse. And then I'll make you beg for some more of this.'

It seemed to Talia that he and Madame would be busy for several days, at least. She beckoned to Kym, who followed her and Olena on tiptoe from the room.

'Barat seems rather preoccupied,' Talia said. 'I think we can assume he won't let Madame escape. It's time to slip quietly away. Kym, where can we find coats? We can't go outside dressed like this. We'll need money too.'

'Are we going to the Private House?' Kym asked. 'Is it far?'

'It's never very far away,' Talia replied. 'The House has agents everywhere.'

Talia was dozing on the bed, with her hands still tied together, but Kym was too excited to be sleepy. She gazed down at her pretty, freckled lover. Talia was more devoted and obedient than any sex-toy Kym had dreamt of. But Talia was only a part of the miraculous life into which Kym had escaped.

Kym gazed around her room. She could still hardly believe its size; every room in the House seemed at least as splendid as this. It was a palace – a palace inhabited by graceful, confident, outrageously costumed people who lived only to indulge their passion for obedience and sensuality. The imposing country house that had so impressed her when she had taken part in Olena's kidnapping was, indeed, insignificant by comparison.

The House itself was only the start: the grounds stretched away on all sides, as far as the eye could see, and contained farms, and hamlets, and workshops, and mansions – all of which belonged to the House.

For the first time in her life, Kym felt completely safe and happy.

'What time is it?' Talia said sleepily.

'If you're awake, then it's time for some more fun and games,' Kym said. She held Talia's bound wrists above her head and lay alongside her, kissing her lips.

'You're insatiable,' Talia said, but she pressed her slim body against Kym's.

'I know you have to return to your people in the forest,' Kym said, 'so I'm determined to make the most of you.'

'And you have to start your training,' Talia replied. 'Those Mentors can be very strict. You shouldn't tire yourself out.'

'You're the one who's sleepy,' Kym pointed out.

'You keep making me come,' Talia said. 'Untie me and I'll see what I can do to you.'

'Not yet,' Kym said. 'I think you deserve another spanking first. Can you take a little bit more? I want to try the cane this time.'

'Sounds lovely,' Talia murmured. 'In a minute. I want to kiss your nipples first. And we must be quick. The Supreme Mistress has been training Olena to pull a pony-cart, and today they're going out for a run in the park. Everyone's going to watch. We mustn't miss it.'

'I know,' Kym said. Talia was licking her breasts and it was difficult for her to concentrate, 'but I want to spend every possible moment in bed with you.'

'As soon as you've finished your first course of training,' Talia said, 'you can visit me in the forest.'

It seemed to Kym that whenever Talia mentioned her home in the forest she became just a little less subservient. Kym didn't really mind: after all, Talia was the leader of the foresters, and it was clear from the attitude of other people in the House that she was an important person in the complex hierarchy that the Supreme Mistress ruled over.

But Kym was determined to be the mistress in her own bedroom.

'That's enough,' she said sharply, and Talia stopped licking her, and pouted.

'Turn over,' Kym said. 'Bottom up. Legs apart. That's right. You're going to get a caning, my pretty little forest girl, and then I'm going to make you come again. So there. And then I'll let you dress in the special costume I ordered for you.'

Talia's slender, pale buttocks were already red from two spankings and a strapping, but she displayed her bottom eagerly and it was obvious that she was aroused. Kym plunged her fingers into the wet warmth. Talia groaned.

'What's this?' Kym demanded.

'My cunt,' Talia murmured. Kym loved to make her say crude words.

'It's sopping wet,' Kym said. 'I thought you said you didn't want any more?'

'I'm sorry, mistress,' Talia said. 'I was wrong.'

Kym touched herself between her thighs. She was as wet as Talia. She couldn't get enough of lording it over her lovely freckled girl. Maybe she should turn Talia over again and squat over her face, so that Talia could lick her? But Olena would be performing soon, and Kym wanted to parade Talia in her new costume in front of everyone who turned out to watch the pony-race. Kym had ordered the dress from the House's outfitters. It was based on the accounts that Talia had given of her time in Edmund's employment. Made entirely of black rubber, it would cling tightly to Talia's body from her neck to her knees. Circular holes in the rubber would ensure that Talia's tits and arse would not merely be exposed but would protrude from the costume. And everyone would be able to see that Kym kept her lover well punished.

'What do you want?' Kym said.

'A caning on my arse, please,' Talia replied.

'Then keep still,' Kym said, and her heart sang as sweetly as the cane as she whipped it through the air and inscribed blazing lines on her lover's bottom.

Nexus

NEXUS BACKLIST

This information is correct at time of printing. For up-to-date information, please visit our website at www.nexus-books.co.uk

All books are priced at £5.99 unless another price is given.

Nexus books with a contemporary setting

ACCIDENTS WILL HAPPEN	Lucy Golden ISBN 0 352 33596 3	☐
ANGEL	Lindsay Gordon ISBN 0 352 33590 4	☐
BARE BEHIND £6.99	Penny Birch ISBN 0 352 33721 4	☐
BEAST	Wendy Swanscombe ISBN 0 352 33649 8	☐
THE BLACK FLAME	Lisette Ashton ISBN 0 352 33668 4	☐
BROUGHT TO HEEL	Arabella Knight ISBN 0 352 33508 4	☐
CAGED!	Yolanda Celbridge ISBN 0 352 33650 1	☐
CANDY IN CAPTIVITY	Arabella Knight ISBN 0 352 33495 9	☐
CAPTIVES OF THE PRIVATE HOUSE	Esme Ombreux ISBN 0 352 33619 6	☐
CHERI CHASTISED £6.99	Yolanda Celbridge ISBN 0 352 33707 9	☐
DANCE OF SUBMISSION	Lisette Ashton ISBN 0 352 33450 9	☐
DIRTY LAUNDRY £6.99	Penny Birch ISBN 0 352 33680 3	☐
DISCIPLINED SKIN	Wendy Swanscombe ISBN 0 352 33541 6	☐

Samplers and collections

NEW EROTICA 5	Various	☐
	ISBN 0 352 33540 8	
EROTICON 1	Various	☐
	ISBN 0 352 33593 9	
EROTICON 2	Various	☐
	ISBN 0 352 33594 7	
EROTICON 3	Various	☐
	ISBN 0 352 33597 1	
EROTICON 4	Various	☐
	ISBN 0 352 33602 1	
THE NEXUS LETTERS	Various	☐
	ISBN 0 352 33621 8	
SATURNALIA	ed. Paul Scott	☐
£7.99	ISBN 0 352 33717 6	
MY SECRET GARDEN SHED	ed. Paul Scott	☐
£7.99	ISBN 0 352 33725 7	

Nexus Classics

A new imprint dedicated to putting the finest works of erotic fiction back in print.

AMANDA IN THE PRIVATE HOUSE	Esme Ombreux	☐
£6.99	ISBN 0 352 33705 2	
BAD PENNY	Penny Birch	☐
	ISBN 0 352 33661 7	
BRAT	Penny Birch	☐
£6.99	ISBN 0 352 33674 9	
DARK DELIGHTS	Maria del Rey	☐
£6.99	ISBN 0 352 33667 6	
DARK DESIRES	Maria del Rey	☐
	ISBN 0 352 33648 X	
DISPLAYS OF INNOCENTS	Lucy Golden	☐
£6.99	ISBN 0 352 33679 X	
DISCIPLINE OF THE PRIVATE HOUSE	Esme Ombreux	☐
£6.99	ISBN 0 352 33459 2	
EDEN UNVEILED	Maria del Rey	☐
	ISBN 0 352 33542 4	

- - - - - - ✂ -

Please send me the books I have ticked above.

Name ....

Address ....

....

....

.... Post code.....................

Send to: **Cash Sales, Nexus Books, Thames Wharf Studios, Rainville Road, London W6 9HA**

US customers: for prices and details of how to order books for delivery by mail, call 1-800-343-4499.

Please enclose a cheque or postal order, made payable to **Nexus Books Ltd**, to the value of the books you have ordered plus postage and packing costs as follows:

UK and BFPO – £1.00 for the first book, 50p for each subsequent book.

Overseas (including Republic of Ireland) – £2.00 for the first book, £1.00 for each subsequent book.

If you would prefer to pay by VISA, ACCESS/MASTERCARD, AMEX, DINERS CLUB or SWITCH, please write your card number and expiry date here:

....

Please allow up to 28 days for delivery.

Signature ....

Our privacy policy.

We will not disclose information you supply us to any other parties. We will not disclose any information which identifies you personally to any person without your express consent.

From time to time we may send out information about Nexus books and special offers. Please tick here if you do *not* wish to receive Nexus information. ☐

- - - - - - ✂ -